Amarillo Rose

JOSS TALLMAN

Amarillo Rose

This book is a work of fiction. Names, characters, places, and other incidents either are the product of the author's imagination or are used fictitiously, and any resemblance to actual persons, living or dead, business establishments, events or locales is entirely coincidental.

The errors: historical, typos, grammar, and all mistakes otherwise are mine alone.

Author's Bridge Publishing
A CyberDiamond, LLC Company
320 Mamie Cook Road
Boone, NC 28607-7784

ISBN-13: 978-0-9882872-0-4
ISBN-10: 0 9882872-0-X

Cover created by Laurel L. Galvan, Author's Bridge Publishing
Author's website: www.josstallman.com

Amarillo Rose

JOSS TALLMAN

Author's Bridge
PUBLISHERS
A CYBERDIAMOND, LLC COMPANY

JOSS TALLMAN

DEDICATION

To: A special someone who is out there somewhere.
You know who you are.
I never stopped loving you—
JT

A special thanks to my little dog Toby whose constant
vigilance and unyielding loyalty stayed at my feet during the
long hours.

PROLOGUE

Dying wasn't so bad really, but the timing was lousy. Christmas Eve is not the best time to die, if indeed, there is a best time to die. Unfortunately, we have no option. We don't choose death it chooses us.

My name is Vernon Baxter. I am dead. I died a few minutes ago in the ambulance bringing me to the emergency room at Tri-County Regional Hospital here in Dallas. I had just mixed a drink at the bar in my home and was reaching for a cigar when I felt like I had been hit in the chest with a sledgehammer. I fell to the floor. I saw a flash of light then everything went completely blank. I was still conscious for what seemed like several seconds. I could hear my wife, Elizabeth, screaming my name and telling our housekeeper, Miss Annie, to call nine-one-one. I felt my body release fluids and I lost control of everything.

I watched the ambulance crew as they frantically tried to resuscitate me. Where I was when I watched them, I don't know.

Now, I am standing in the emergency room alone looking at myself. The place is very quiet and very bright. My shirt has been cut away, I have I.V. tubes in the back of both my hands, there is a breathing tube in my throat and I can see the burn marks left on my chest by the defibrillators. The puncture hole in my left rib cage is still oozing my blood, which was made by the huge needle the doctor jammed between my ribs and directly into my heart shooting me with an injection of epinephrine. My eyes are vacant and void staring blankly into nothing. The doctors and nurses made a valiant effort to save me but they have all gone now. There is no one here but me and me.

I seem to be ubiquitous. Apparently, I have the ability to be several places at the same time. This is new to me. Time and space do not seem to have any limits or values.

My life was a good one. I accomplished many things from the time I started out as a teenage wildcatter working on the oil rigs in west Texas, until my death a few moments ago. I made billions of dollars. I built an empire of oil wells, refineries, shopping malls, banks and many other things. I did a lot of good during my lifetime and employed thousands of people.

I discovered long ago that with a generous amount of money placed in the right hands, I could make almost anything happen and I made a lot of things happen. I was always right about this except once. During my lifetime, I found only one man, just one, whose unquenchable love for a woman could not be begged, bartered, borrowed or bought.

My only regret is that I was never able to get possession of the box owned by Ted Barrett. That box held the secret and the key to everything. It is not the box that is important, but what it has in it. If only I had been able to get to the contents of that box, I could have changed many things. I could have changed the destiny of my family, the country and maybe even the world. I can see the box now. I know where it is and I know what lies inside.

It's strange, how something can be such a priceless treasure to one person and so completely worthless to another.

If I had only been able to get my hands on what's in that box I could have made a lot of things happen. And I knew how to make things happen….

CHAPTER ONE

It was unseasonably cool for south Florida, but the burst of cold set a perfect atmosphere for Christmas Eve. Ted Barrett was mingling with guests in his spacious Palm Beach home. He was fit for a man of sixtyish but did have a slight limp. He carried a little more around his waist than he wanted to, but still he was a notable figure dressed in tan slacks and a navy blue pullover. He was a handsome man and his full head of brown hair was mostly streaked with silver these days. Ted leaned against the mantel above the wide fireplace and listened as the hardwood logs crackled and popped below.

Through the glass in his back door, he could see the sun setting across the Inland Waterway showing itself as a round orange ball. Just beyond the large sliding glass doors leading out to the patio and pool area, Ted watched the palm trees swaying lazily in the soft Florida breeze. His mind clearly somewhere else.

"Hey Ted, nice party. Looks like everyone turned out this year, but it's so dern cold. It must be in the 40's outside," came the voice of one of Ted's law partners.

"Oh hi-ya Bob, yeah looks like everyone stopped by this year. It's good to see all the people from the office," replied Ted, referring to a rather extensive law firm of which he was the founder and senior partner. "It's nice to see their families and so many friends."

"Say where's that gorgeous missus of yours?" asked Bob.

"She's in there somewhere making sure everyone has plenty to eat and something to drink," answered Ted, nodding toward the living room.

Ted's wife, a natural beauty was mingling with friends, making sure everyone was pleased and having a good time. Her salt and pepper hair and hearty laugh coupled with a magnetic personality made her irresistible. Although she was busy with friends and guests her attentions were never far from Ted. She couldn't pass by him without giving him a wink, a pat on the rear, a touch, a butterfly kiss, always touching him, always something. She was forever checking to make sure Ted had something to eat and ice in his glass, smoothing his hair. A litany of little attentions, most often Ted would pretend he didn't notice. It was a poor act. He noticed, and so did everyone else.

Laurel, one of the firm's attorneys, was with her husband, Jack and wondered: *How could two people be so loving and caring with each other every time I see them?*

"Oh Ted, I noticed that you have that box out again this year," said Bob reaching toward a small box on top of the mantle. "What ya got in there?"

"Bob no! Don't touch that box," Ted shouted. "I'm sorry Bob, I didn't mean to raise my voice to you, but please, what is inside is priceless and could never be replaced."

Bob shrugged like a scolded schoolboy and said, "I'm really sorry boss. I didn't mean to…."

"It's okay Bob, I didn't mean to yell. It's just that we are very sensitive about what's in here," said Ted picking up the box.

It was hardly a box. It was a beautiful creation made of the finest polished mahogany and inlaid with rare mother-of-pearl. Anyone could see the box must have been very valuable and extremely well cared for. Whatever treasure lay inside must also be priceless.

"Are you ever going let us know what's in there, Ted?" said Bob. "You have our curiosity on boil."

"Well, Bob, since you asked, I'm going to tell you a story. I have never told it before, but I am going to share it with all of you tonight as soon as I get everyone in the den. It's a true story and one that clings to my heart every hour of every day."

By this time Ted's wife had gathered most of the guests and shepherded them into the den and they were sitting around the fire, anxiously waiting on his words. Some of the guests had seen the box before on previous holidays but no one knew what was inside. Tonight everyone's interest was piqued, because tonight, Ted was going to reveal the mystery of the box.

Ted began: "Many years ago, back in the early 70's, I was not too far out of law school, I had just gotten off active duty as a JAG officer in the Navy. I hired on with the District Attorney's Office in Dallas, Texas. I was a young, ambitious prosecutor, looking to make a name for myself and establish a reputation as a pretty decent trial lawyer. I had a good track record and won most of my cases.

"I was trying an embezzlement case and things were going pretty well—"

CHAPTER TWO

"Mister Barrett, do you want to cross-examine this witness, or would you like to call your own expert to the stand?" asked Judge Michael Mahoney peering through a pair of thick glasses.

"Yes, Your Honor, I do have a couple questions for this witness, thank you."

Ted Barrett rose to his full six feet two inches. He was slim and fit a nice looking young man with thick light brown hair and an infectious smile. He moved about the courtroom with the grace of a panther and the attack mode of the same. Ted was a gifted orator and could talk to migrant workers or college professors with equal ease.

Ted approached the witness slowly and stared at him through a pair of almond brown eyes. The stare seemed like hours, drinking in the witness before him, watching for movement, the fidgeting, nervousness, body language, all communicating to him how to handle the witness.

"Mister Weinour," said Ted, with a trace of a southern accent. "Allow me to invite your attention to August 30th of this year. Did you observe in the ledgers of Pecos, Inc., where deposits had been made to a secret account at Republic National Bank of Texas, and said deposits were taken from the trust accounts of Creative Marketing, Inc?"

"No, I never saw that," Weinour obliquely replied.

By now, Ted had moved his position from in front of the witness to near the jury box, a well-known tactic used by experienced attorneys. Ted knew the jury would get a clear view of the witness and since he was at a distance, he would have to speak louder.

"Mister Weinour, do I understand you to say, under oath, and I remind you, sir, you are under oath, that you never made such an observation? Do I understand you to say, under oath, that you never saw a deposit slip from said trust account to a clandestine account at Republic National Bank of Texas?"

"That's what I said," returned the witness.

Ted's voice was noticeably louder, "Well, I have in my hand your deposition of September the 8th of last year, where you clearly state, under oath, that you did observe these afore spoken of deposits in Republic National Bank of Texas, and you did, in fact, make some of these deposits yourself."

Ted went on his voice even louder, "So Mister Weinour, my question is: were you lying then or are you lying now?"

"I'm not a liar," Weinour muttered.

"Mister Weinour, we have already established the fact that you are a liar. What we are trying to get straight for this jury and this judge is when you are lying!" Ted thundered. "As a matter of fact Mister Weinour, perhaps it would be easier for us to determine when you are telling the truth since you are a constant and consummate liar!"

AMARILLO ROSE

"Okay Mister Barrett," said Judge Mahoney. "I think you've made your point. I'm not going to allow any of your theatrics in my courtroom. The Oscars have already been given out this year."

"Your Honor, I move Mister Weinour's testimony be stricken from the record and that the court will dismiss him from this case."

Judge Mahoney peered through his glasses at the defense table. "Gentlemen, it appears I have no other choice than to dismiss Mister Weinour's testimony and have it stricken unless you can show me a rule of law that is germane to our situation."

The defense table was silent.

Ted had difficultly hiding the smirk on his face, but pursuant to courtroom protocol, he did.

Man, what a piece of cake, this case is mine—I could have done that from the shower this morning.

"Well, said the judge, "it appears that I have no choice but to grant the State's motion. Mister Weinour you may stand down; you are excused. Your testimony will be stricken from the record in its entirety."

"Mister Barrett," said Judge Mahoney, "would you like to call your expert witness or would you like to wait until after the lunch recess?"

"If it pleases the court, Judge, we have another hour before lunch; I'd like to get started."

"Very well, Mister Barrett, have the bailiff call your expert."

"Thank you, Judge," said Ted. "The State would like to call Ms. Lili Perez."

"Ms. Lili Perez please take the stand," echoed the bailiff.

The rear door of the courtroom opened. Ted could not believe his eyes. His insides turned to mush. His mouth was dry and his eyes stung like he had been swimming in a river of vinegar. His knees had never buckled but he sat down quickly just in case. He couldn't speak. He couldn't think.

Maybe I should have taken the judge up on that lunch recess, he thought.

He couldn't focus. Everything seemed like a movie was being shown in slow motion.

Into the courtroom walked the most beautiful creature he had ever seen. Her raven hair was a little below shoulder length and her pouting lips would be the envy of any movie star. She walked by Ted's table with the grace of a ballet dancer. She was a tiny little thing five feet, maybe five-one or two in a stretch, and the most compact, perfect figure as perfect can get. Her light blue suit was neatly trimmed in a darker blue accentuating her breasts.

Not too big, not too small, "Whew," Ted said under his breath. "Good job genes."

Lili was sworn by the bailiff and Judge Mahoney said, "Thank you for coming Ms. Perez."

Lili smiled through a row of perfect white teeth. "I am pleased to be here, Your Honor." She turned and stared directly at Ted. Her chocolate brown eyes were enormous and she seemed to be looking through him like a laser beam. Their eyes locked and held each other's gaze. Ted could not make himself look away. It seemed like an eternity.

"Mister Barrett.

"Mister Barrett.

"Oh Mister Barrett!" the judge fairly shouted, "your witness."

10

"Um, thank you, Judge," Ted stammered. "May I approach the witness?"

"Yes, of course you may approach Mister Barrett, after all she's your witness," replied the judge.

Ted rose and started toward the witness box. His knees were like Jell-O. He was not sure his legs were going to hold him. He neared Lili but could not keep his eyes from hers. It was as if he was looking into the face of a Greek Goddess.

He stared.

She stared back.

"Mister Barrett, I was hoping to get on with this trial before I go on Social Security," sighed Judge Mahoney.

"Yes, of course Your Honor. Yes, of course. I was just trying to collect a few thoughts."

"Well collect them Mister Barrett and get on with it," said the judge.

"Ms. Perez would you state your name and address, for the court's record please?"

"Yes," she replied, "My name is Lili Perez and I live here in Dallas, Texas."

"Thank you, Ms. Perez, may I call you Lili?" asked Ted.

"No you may not." Lili's retort was quick and to the point. "You may call me Ms. Perez."

Ted was shocked, but went on, "Very well then, 'Mizz' Perez would you state your occupation for the court and why you are here?"

"Yes, I am an accountant and an independent contractor. I was hired by the State of Texas, to review the books of Creative Marketing and their financial records. Also, to examine Mister Weinour's ledgers with the Republic National Bank of Texas," replied Lili.

Ted asked. "And you were hired by the District Attorney's Office as an expert witness in this case?"

"You should know Mister Barrett, you hired me," Lili replied.

Again, in a matter of minutes, Ted was dumb-founded for the second time. He was used to being in control, at the helm of his work, now this little accountant had upset his entire arena. The courtroom was chuckling.

"Yes, I did indeed hire you, 'Mizz' Perez. Have we ever met?" Ted asked trying to establish a non-prejudicial atmosphere.

"No," she said.

"'Mizz' Perez," Ted went on, "have you ever heard the term, 'cook the books'?"

"Yes, many times. That is a slang term we use in accounting. It's when intentional false entries, or deposits are made, or omitted, in the ledgers of company books," said Lili.

"Mizz Perez, have you ever cooked any books?" asked Ted.

Lili's reply was curt. "No, but I have roasted a few lawyers."

Ted was speechless. Never, had he been so tactfully censored. He felt his entire courtroom demeanor draining from him. Not being in control was definitely a new experience for him. Even Judge Mahoney had difficulty stifling his laughter. The courtroom was roaring.

Ted thought, *if I was small as a bug, I could crawl under this table.*

"Your Honor," Ted mumbled, "would you instruct the witness to answer the question?"

"I believe she said no Counselor," said the amused Judge Mahoney.

Ted recovered a bit and said, "Then Your Honor, I would like to make a motion to treat 'Mizz' Perez as a hostile witness."

Judge Mahoney leaned forward. "Do I understand it is your intention to impeach your own witness, Counselor?"

"Oh no, absolutely not, Your Honor," Ted replied. "I am just trying to gather my thoughts on the rules of Civil Procedure."

"Mister Barrett," said the judge, "all that is well and good, and in a civil trial apropos as we use the Rules of Civil Procedure in civil trials. But this happens to be a criminal trial, in case it has slipped your mind, and we use the rules of Criminal Procedure."

Good grief! I can't even remember what kind of trial I'm in, and I said that right in front of the entire courtroom, the jury, reporters, and the judge, everybody—Holy Moses— what's happened to me? It's all because of that little accountant—I'm going get that little shit if it's the last thing I do. Beautiful or not… but how do I get her? She's my freaking witness!

"Uh Judge, would the court entertain a motion to recess for lunch? It's twenty to twelve and I would like to re-arrange some of my thoughts, that is, if you and the defense have no objection."

"We're fine with that, Judge," spoke up the defense.

"Fine with me too," said the judge. Looking at Ted, Judge Mahoney took off his glasses and pinched the bridge of his nose. He steepled his fingers and said, "Counselor, I think re-arranging some of your thoughts or all of them, might be a wise investment on your part. Okay we'll break for lunch. Let's be back here at two p.m."

His gavel sounded.

Ted didn't go to lunch. He went straight to the attorney's lounge in the courthouse and found an available phone. He dialed his secretary in the District Attorney's Complex.

"Susan get Scottie down here now!" He half shouted to his secretary.

Ted listened.

"Susan I don't give a damn if he's having lunch with Santa Claus on Waikiki, find him and get his butt down here—now!"

Ted had just poured his third cup of coffee and was pacing about the attorney's lounge when a very anxious and perspiring Ray Scott burst in. "What's up Mister Barrett? Sounds important," queried Ray Scott.

Ray Scott was a nice looking young man from west Texas, with dark brown hair and a pair of deeply set hazel eyes. Ray Scott was working in the DA's office as an intern and waiting on his results from the state bar exam. He was always well-groomed and seemed to have a propensity for loud clothes. Today, he was decked out in dark blue slacks and a snappy yellow shirt accented with a pink tie. He was very bright; Ted liked that and he liked Ray Scott. Ted thought he might be Hispanic, but he never asked. He didn't care. He did know that Ray Scott didn't speak a word of Spanish and with a name like "Ray Scott?" Hispanic? Hardly, but he was always willing to pitch in and help whenever needed and Ted needed him now. Ted made a mental note to speak to the boss about hiring him as an apprentice attorney once he was admitted to the bar.

"Scottie, I've got a problem. I've got this lady accountant who we hired as an expert witness and she is hostile as hell to me."

"Mister Barrett, you don't need me, why don't you just impeach her?"

"I can't impeach her Scottie, she's my freaking witness!" Ted said in a voice that could be heard in the next county. "If I did something like that I would look like a bigger idiot than I already am. Right now, I have to figure out a way to get her ass off the stand before the defense gets a chance to cross-examine her."

"Now here's what I need you to do, Scottie. Her name is Lili Perez...."

Ray Scott interrupted. "Is she that wailing siren I just walked by in the witness room?"

"Oh you saw her?"

"Saw her? How could anyone miss her? She is flawless. All Miss Americas rolled into one," said an excited Ray Scott. "I walked by her a minute ago and my watch melted."

"Okay Scottie, put a cap on that hyper-active libido of yours. What I need to know is everything, and when I say everything, I mean everything you can find on Miss Perez. What she likes, what she doesn't like, find out her favorite color, what she does, where she does it and whom she does it with. I want to know when and where she takes a pee. Everything, I even want to know what kind of toothpaste she uses. In other words, I need anything I can use to get rid of her. Now, get going. If you have to pull somebody out of the Sheriff's Office to help you, it's okay. If anyone gives you any static tell them it's for me.

"Now get going Scottie. I'm going in there and try to get this damn thing continued. Maybe if I get down on my knees and beg, Mahoney might give us a few days. Okay go."

Ray Scott was off to find out about 'Mizz' Lili Perez.

CHAPTER THREE

Lili Perez was tired. It had been a long and unusual day for her. Instead of being in her quiet little cubicle at work she was subjected to crowds, reporters, and the hustle and bustle of the courthouse. She loathed crowds and the noise that went with them. But most of all she had to tolerate that pompous ass, Ted Barrett.

Lili unlocked the front door of her north Dallas apartment and closed it behind her. Home at last, alone and free to be herself. She kicked off her pumps, unzipped the blue suit and neatly hung it back in her closet. Lili gave little, if any, thought to who was wearing what in Hollywood or New York. Contemporary dress fads and what was in vogue, and what was out, were of no consequence to her. She kept her wardrobe neat and clean with mostly conservative, unostentatious apparel. Her little apartment was modest but tastefully her. Lili loved it here.

Slipping out of her bra and panties Lili gazed at herself in the full length mirror. Her breasts stood straight out, her belly was as flat as an Arizona mesa. Her eyes travelled down to the dark patch just below her navel.

Maybe someday—maybe someday the right man will come along. Maybe someday....

Lili was completely unaware of her natural beauty or at least she seemed to be. She was not taken with herself at all. She had heard the compliments, and the guys whistling, and the endless flirting with the colorful innuendos. Innuendos that appeared on the surface innocent enough but deep down carried their true sexual messages. William Shakespeare had it right in his play, *King Lear*. Just after Regan was poisoned by her sister, Goneril, she cried, "Jesters do oft prove to be prophets." In modern day words: "Many serious things are said in jest." Lili was used to turning heads, but she was totally unaffected by it. Perhaps she didn't notice.

Lili walked up to the mirror almost touching her nose and said in her highest falsetto voice.

"Thank you, Ms. Perez, may I call you Lili?" No you may not call me Lili.... You may call me, "Ms. Perez," and by the way Mister Superstar, self-confident, attorney for the whole world, I caught your snotty "Mizz" Perez remarks.... You, Mister Barrett, are a womanizer—the exact kind of man my mother warned me to stay away from. So, don't bother coming after me with that ruffled blond hair, and the way you cock your eyebrow, and you can keep that mischievous little

boy grin to yourself as well. It won't work on me—besides, I put you in your place today. I put you in your place but good. I have read about you in the papers, and heard about you all over town and never with the same blond or redhead—I could never be one of the women in your seemingly endless harem. I put you in your place today. I sure did.

Lili slipped on a long night shirt and went into the kitchen to make a salad.

Why is that man constantly on my mind? I've memorized his walk, I can hear his voice.... His hands are huge.... He's standing right here towering above me—I can smell him. I feel his hands on my shoulders—they are warm and gentle. I can feel his breath on the back of my neck. I am shivering....

The salad was never touched.

Lili snapped back to the present wondering what on earth was happening to her.

How can I be so taken with him? Why is he with me everywhere I go? Is it possible that I could love him? Of course not—I can't stand that man. Could he be the one who would really love me? He would never notice me. I don't fit the profile of his usual licentious bimbos. Could he be the strong gentle man I could love forever? Could he...?

Lili made a futile attempt at watching television but could not keep her mind on what was what was showing. Finally she went to bed. But sleep was not to find her. Lili lay in bed, her eyes fixed on the fan above. She allowed her mind to roam. Ted Barrett was beside her. She could hear his breathing and feel his warm skin was against her body.

She felt safe and secure with him beside her even if it was a fantasy.

Lili allowed her hands to brush across her breasts and gently ease down to her flat belly. Circling there for a moment her hands drifted down. Farther down Lili felt herself. Something was different, something was very different. She was moist.

CHAPTER FOUR

Ted Barrett sat in his north Dallas apartment his eyes fixed on the stereo. The ice in his scotch had long since melted. He still held it. The record on the stereo had ended an hour ago and continued a "blip, blip." Ted didn't hear it. His mind was focused on a little accountant named Lili Perez.

The doorbell and rapping on his door brought Ted back to the present with a start. "Who would be out there at this hour?" he said aloud. Ted opened the door and there stood a still perspiring and very tired looking Ray Scott.

"Scottie don't you know it's one o'clock in the morning?" Ted said in amazement.

"Yeah boss, but you said there was some urgency to this, so here it is," said Ray Scott, handing Ted a thick legal size envelope. "It's all there, a complete bio on 'Mizz' Lili Perez."

"Jeez Scottie good work," said Ted. "Help yourself to a cold beer. There's some Bud and Coors in there."

A cold beer was just what the doctor ordered for Ray Scott. From the kitchen came his voice. "Hey Mister

Barrett, do you always keep your salt and pepper in the fridge?"

"What…? I've been looking for them all night," sighed Ted.

"Uh no Scottie, the cleaning lady must have put them in there by mistake," he lied.

Gad, I'm losing my freaking mind… After my shower tonight I found my socks in the trash can! It's all because of that little accountant. I'm gonna get her—she won't leave my mind—do I love her? Impossible. I despise her—do I really? No….

"Come over here Scottie, let's have a look at 'Mizz' Perez," said Ted.

"You bet," came the reply, "but I can brief you. 'Mizz' Perez as you call her, is from a little town not far out of San Antone, second generation Mexican-American, the oldest of two brothers and one sister, parents both living. Her dad is a building contractor, average middle class family, fluent in English and Spanish. She graduated from the University of Texas, down in Austin. She was an accounting major, with a three point eight GPA, worked her way through college along with grants and scholarships. Likes most things women do. No real boyfriends or serious relationships past or present. Not egotistical at all about her brains or looks. She's been a knock-out since she was a child and I don't need to tell you, she's built like a brick shit-house when bricks were scarce."

"Yeah Scottie, no need to tell me how she is built and from this," Ted said, holding up a handful of papers, "she looks pretty clean."

"Clean, she is boss, but you've got one big problem," offered Ray Scott.

"Tell me Scottie, that's why we are here."

"Well, this time you've met your match, if you don't mind me saying so."

"No Scottie, spill it."

"Well boss, behind that toothy smile of hers and behind those doe-size brown eyes is a hundred and sixty plus IQ clicking in there. I don't need to tell you that one hundred is average. So if you get into a battle of wits with her do your homework and make sure your guns are loaded."

Ted shrugged, "Well Scottie, I guess we learned that in court today. She tore me a new ass."

"Like I said boss, if you get into a battle of wits, make sure you're armed. She is." Scott quietly said, finishing his beer. "Okay it's late, but I just wanted to make sure you had that info. Oh, one more thing, boss...."

"What Scottie?"

"She's an insomniac. Has trouble sleeping, takes a mild script for it."

"How did you find out something like that?"

"You don't want to know boss. I got a buddy I went to undergrad with who's a pharmacist; he works over at the mall. He looked her up on one of those new computers. Okay Mister Barrett, I gotta go. See you in the morning."

"Yeah thanks Scottie, you did a fine job. Come in late or take tomorrow off if you like."

Ted said goodnight to Ray Scott and he knew that he would be on the job first thing in the morning. Maybe he should take the day off instead and get his mind straight. Get his mind free and back to business, far away from the accountant, 'Mizz' Lili Perez.

Ted finally gave into exhaustion and went to bed. But sleep did not come.

CHAPTER FIVE

U p to the time of the embezzlement trial and prior to meeting "Mizz" Lili Perez, Ted was well-known as a man-about-town and as a man-on-the-move. With his captivating good looks and charming personality, he was quite in demand in social circles and civic organizations especially by the ladies. He enjoyed a healthy inventory of friends so Ted kept a full itinerary and seemed to be Dallas' rising star and quite possibly a future political figure even with his questionable reputation as a lothario.

The days dragged into weeks and the weeks dragged into months. Ted had won the embezzlement trial and put the embarrassment and humiliation of "Mizz" Lili Perez testimony behind him. But as time wore on so did his yearning for Lili. In the stillness of the night, when all is very quiet she visited him. He could see the huge brown eyes, and he could never forget the smile and that body. Oh sweet dreams that perfect body. How he longed to touch her. Just to hold her hand, just one small kiss on those pouting lips.

A fair amount of Ted's time was taken up by the United States Navy where he served as a Reserve Officer making the one weekend per month meetings at Navy Dallas, a local Naval Air Station. Upon graduating from law school at Florida State University, Ted was commissioned a full lieutenant in the U.S. Navy. He left Tallahassee and was inducted into the Navy's Officer Training School in Virginia. Upon graduation and being sworn in as an officer he was assigned to the Judge Advocate General (JAG) Corps in Washington D.C.

Ted cut his legal teeth trying cases as a government prosecutor, cases brought about by the misconduct of Naval and Marine personnel. Although a military court is very different than civilian courts and operates under very different rules, Ted gained invaluable experience as a trial lawyer and earned a respectable reputation as a fair but aggressive legal combatant.

Ted liked Washington. It was so different from where he had grown up in south Florida. Ted's father had been a federal agent for the Seminole and Miccosukee Native American Tribes and his mother had taught English in the Indian schools. He had grown up on a Seminole reservation in the middle of the Florida Everglades. Ted had learned how to stalk animals, to walk in the swamps and wade in water without making the slightest sound. He knew how to hunt and fish and live off the land with only the weapons or tools you made yourself from the swamp. He knew how to freeze when spotted by a panther or a bear and often by a curious alligator. Ted learned thousands of things from his Miccosukee and Seminole playmates. Things they had learned from their fathers and handed down for generations.

Things that could only be a dream to young people brought up in the cities.

Ted had chosen Florida State for a couple of reasons: they were called "The Seminoles," he liked that, and his mother had graduated from the same university some years before. When Ted first told his father that he planned to go to FSU his father's reaction was, "That's a damn girl's school!"

True enough, Florida State University, was originally founded as Florida State College for Women over a century ago and still enrolls a student body of women far outnumbering the men. Ted's response to his father's rather denigrating paroxysm was simple. "A girl's school. You got that right Dad, you got that exactly right!" Ted headed for the door. "My Mama didn't raise any dumb kids," he laughed.

Ted's college years seemed to go by in a blur. He played wide receiver on the football team, thanks to his lanky frame and blazing speed. He was in perfect shape, tall and muscle-toned from his years rough-housing and playing with the Indian kids. Some of their games were not only extremely rough but often brutal. Ted excelled and was well liked and admired by his Indian comrades because of his competitiveness and physical stamina.

Even with an active social life he was able to keep his grades above average, majoring in both Native American Culture and in Criminology. When Ted applied to law school at Florida State he was readily accepted.

Law School, like his college years, also seemed to go by in a flurry but he found the curriculum a lot more challenging than college. The work-load was much more demanding and a lot less time was available to spend for socializing with the "fairer sex."

To Ted, Tallahassee was a city. In truth, Florida's capital was no more than a sleepy little southern town with no industry or any further economic boosts other than being the seat of government for the state of Florida and two universities, Florida State University and Florida A&M University. Ted found the huge oak trees draped in their Spanish moss, the magnolias and many other things so beautiful and so completely different than anything he had ever seen in the swampy Everglades. Tallahassee had seasons and hills, a new experience for him. Ted liked most everything about Tallahassee. The seasons, the beautiful trees and foliage, the hills, the university, but most of all he liked the coeds.

When Ted found out he was going to be permanently stationed in Washington D.C., he welcomed the opportunity. The nation's capital city was just about as far from the Everglades and Tallahassee as one could get and was a whirlwind of activity.

When his four year enlistment with the Navy was nearly up he began applying for positions as an assistant United States Attorney. The bad news with the U.S. Attorney's Office, he could be domiciled anywhere in any of the fifty states. Ted could not see himself spending his career in the Dakotas or somewhere in rural Alaska. Most likely he would be assigned to one of the nation's large northeast cities. He didn't find that very appealing either. He was hoping to at least stay in the south; then fate stepped in.

Ted was busy at his desk in the JAG office when Admiral Cyrus Burnside, the JAG Commanding Officer, appeared at his door. Ted was immediately on his feet at ridged attention.

"Relax son, stand easy," said the admiral.

"Yes sir." Ted relaxed but remained standing and alert.

"Barrett," the admiral went on, "Senator Powell from Texas is having a reception Friday evening, the 16th, in the Senate Reception Area and I was hoping you might like to attend."

When the admiral said that he was hoping, he could attend sure as hell didn't mean that he was hoping. He wasn't "hoping. Admirals don't hope for anything. Admirals don't hope for a damn thing. Hoping was not a request. Hoping was not a suggestion. Hoping from a two star admiral was a freaking command to have your butt there. No excuses.

"Yes, of course sir, I would be honored to attend," Ted lied, smiling his best and you can kiss my ass smile. "Thank you, sir."

"Good." The admiral said, "good. Oh, by the way Barrett, here's your invitation, looks like they engraved them this year. Uniform of the deck will be dress whites. Since you have been promoted it will give you a chance to show off that new lieutenant commander uniform."

"Yes sir."

The admiral turned to leave and said, "One more thing, Barrett."

"Yes sir?"

"I want you to escort Lieutenant Baxter, her first name is Elaine. She's the new-hire down at the end of the hall and she just signed on with us. Ordinarily, I wouldn't ask but her father is some big muckety-muck in Texas and owns more oil wells than Orville Redenbacher has popcorn. He is a very good friend of the senator and as you know we need to keep Powell happy. He has been a big supporter for us in the budget hearings. Besides Lieutenant Commander, she's not all that hard to look at. She will be expecting you to pick her up at this address at 1900 hours," said the admiral, handing him a slip of paper with Lieutenant Baxter's address.

"Aye, aye sir," replied Ted.

Now isn't that just dandy? Not only has the old man got me going to some frigging dinner party in dress whites, which are impossible to keep clean, but now I've got to babysit some harridan from Texas—Texas? What's in Texas besides tumbleweeds and rattlesnakes? She's probably six foot four and got through college as a shot-putter on the track team, has freckles that glow in the dark, and has more hair on her butt than I do. Only reason she got in the JAG corps because her father is a home-run hitter in Texas and plays golf with the senator.

"Everything starts at 1930 hours," continued Admiral Burnside. "You know how I feel about tardiness."

"Yes sir. Aye, aye sir," Ted repeated.

The admiral was right. Lieutenant Elaine Baxter was indeed not hard to look at which happily surprised Ted. When he arrived at her condo she looked quite striking in her crisp white uniform trimmed in Navy Blue and gold.

He thought, *there's no way she can afford this place on an O-3, lieutenant's salary.*

Her dishwater blond hair was trimmed in a ducktail style conforming in perfect harmony with Navy regulations. Ted guessed her at about five-five. She was slim and shapely and greeted him with a pair of ocean green eyes.

"Why *Loo-tennant Commanda* Barrett," she drawled in a very distinct Texas accent, "how nice to fin'ally meet you."

"The pleasure is mine Lieutenant," said Ted truthfully, as his eyes quickly raced over the pretty lawyer assessing every inch of her.

Gee thanks, Admiral, I owe you one.

Ted's mind was no longer on the senator's party, or the admiral, or anything else. He was clearly focused on whatever tactical procedure he would need to get into the lieutenant's panties.

Are they pink? Maybe blue? Could be black? No can't be—she's in dress whites. They gotta be white! Maybe beige—we'll soon find out….

"Well, guess we better get going," said Elaine. "You know how Uncle Cy…. Ah, I mean the admiral is about being late. Oh Commanda, my daddy sent a car for us, so we don't have to worry about parking valets and stuff."

"Uncle" Cy? Oh dear God, what have I gotten myself into? Let's see, her name is Baxter, and "Uncle Cy," is Burnside. Her mother must be the admiral's sister. Oh lordly, lordly—so much for what color panties she's wearing—I don't care if she's not wearing any at all. This gal is "off limits." Period!

Ted looked toward the street at his aging Volvo. What met his eyes was a gleaming black Cadillac Limousine with the rear door open and a very neat uniformed chauffeur standing at attention beside it.

"Well, I wouldn't want to disappoint your daddy," said Ted, as her ushered her into the back seat. The limo had everything imaginable in it, a stereo, closed circuit television, a full bar. *Man, I could get real used to this,* he thought as he settled into the soft leather seat.

By Texas standards the event might have been just a reception, but to Ted it looked like a political super-bowl. There were tables of turkey, ham, Angus beef flown in from Fort Worth, Maine lobsters, with trimmings of every kind, four bars going furiously, with liquor flowing like a Niagara cascade. The orchestra was absent; instead there was an eight piece Country & Western group playing western swing and, of course, punctuated with Texas tunes.

Lieutenant Baxter seemed right at home as she mixed with senators, house members, and other big-wigs from the Lone Star State as they congregated around in their boots and Stetsons seeing who could out-loud the other. Many she addressed by their first name. She was very conscious of Ted and seemed to enjoy introducing him around. They were a striking couple in their dress whites, and in spite of his initial thoughts, Ted was having a good time.

Elaine disappeared in the crowd for a few moments then reappeared holding the hand of an attractive woman on her left. Ted guessed the woman about mid-fifties and noticed instantly from where the lieutenant must have gotten her aqua-green eyes. A rather short portly man was on her right, also mid-fifties, maybe early sixties. He was balding and wiping his forehead where his hair used to be with a handkerchief. He smiled at Ted.

"Loo-tennant Commanda Barrett, I would like for you to meet my mama, Mrs. Elizabeth Baxter and my daddy, Mister Vernon Baxter. Mama, Daddy, this is Loo-tentant Commanda Ted Barrett, my escort for this eve'nin."

I am so pleased to meet you, Mister Barrett," said a smiling Elizabeth Baxter extending her hand.

"Yes ma'am, thank you. It is a pleasure to meet you both. Thank you," Ted managed.

"Commanda Barrett," drawled Mrs. Baxter, "do you happen to know my big brother, Cyrie Burnside? He's supposed to have a real good job over there in the JAG Corps."

"Ah yes, ma'am, I know the admiral," replied Ted. "And yes indeed, he does have a very good job with the JAG Office."

Dear me! She called him, "Cyrie?" Her big brother! Stars in Heaven, what am I doing here? "Uncle Cy"? The admiral? The freaking two star admiral? My commanding officer? The commanding officer of every JAG officer in the whole freaking world. And here I am with his niece. Oh crap!

"Come on, honey," said Mrs. Baxter to Elaine. "Let's get a glass of wine and let these men folk talk."

Elaine nodded her acquiescence and winked at Ted. "You're on your own tiger," she whispered, as she and her mother departed for the nearest bar.

"Well young man," Baxter began, allowing the ash from his cigar to drop on his shirt, "Lanie there tells me you are one of them JAG lawyers over at Quantico like she is."

"Yes sir," Ted replied. "I've been there a little over three years."

"Whatcha gonna do when you get out of the Navy or do you plan to stay in?" asked Baxter.

"I really haven't made up my mind for sure yet. I've got a few months left to think it over. I have looked into going with a U.S. Attorney's Office somewhere, but there are a few drawbacks."

"Such as?"

"Well," Ted patiently replied, "where I'd have to live for one. But the other side of that coin is my military time will count toward my retirement if I stay in government service, so that's in the plus column. I really have to think it over. What about you, Mister Baxter?" asked Ted, desperately trying to steer the conversation away from himself.

"Me? Aw, hell son, there ain't much interesting about me. I always wanted to be a lawyer like you and Lanie there," he said lifting his chin toward the bar where the two women were standing, as if he were pointing with it. "And I woulda been a good one too. But...."

Ted wrinkled his forehead, "But?"

Baxter went on, "I've been in the awl bidness most all my life. Back then, World War Two was blazing like a wild bull at the rodeo. I was wildcattin' and drilling all over west Texas, getting that black gold out of the ground for the military. The need for crude was so demanding we had to work night and day for years. Bout that time, just after the war, Lanie came along, kinda caught us by surprise, if you know what I mean."

Ted nodded.

"So young feller, tell me more about you."

Ted gave him a brief bio making a very cognizant effort to leave out the women in his life.

"Florida?" Baxter bellowed apologetically. "You mean you ain't from Texas?"

"Fraid not," said Ted.

"You know, I been thinking about something," said Baxter. Turning to a young man standing a few feet away but within easy earshot, "Andy, run over yonder and fetch Hendry for me; he's right over there talking to the governor," he ordered, swinging his drink and indicating a tall, graying man with a group of Texas dignitaries, again pointing with his chin.

Ted had been wondering why Andy was standing so close to them. Now it dawned on him, Andy was Baxter's gofer and was standing by to carry out any whim or wish he may have at any moment.

What a pukey job, thought Ted. *Baxter must pay him a hellava lot of money to put up with all his bullshit....*

Andy quickly returned with the tall graying man in tow. "Wayne," said Baxter, "here's a young feller I want you to meet. This here is Commander Ted Barrett of the U.S. Navy's JAG Corps, same as Lanie. Ted, Wayne Hendry, the District Attorney in Dallas."

"It's nice to meet you, Commander," said Hendry, offering his hand.

Ted shook it and quietly said, "Nice to meet you as well. I appreciate the promotion Mister Hendry, but it's lieutenant commander."

"I noticed," smiled Hendry winking at Ted.

"Say Wayne, weren't you in the JAG Corps yourself right here in Washington a few years back?" asked Baxter.

"Sure was," Hendry replied, "just a few short years ago. I think Lincoln was president at the time."

Everyone was laughing when Elaine and Mrs. Baxter returned. "Ever think about going with the District Attorney's Office somewhere, Ted?" asked Baxter.

"No, not really. I haven't given it much thought," Ted answered. "Depends a lot on where it is, career opportunities, that kind of thing."

"When's your four years up, Ted?" Baxter asked.

"If I don't re-up and stay in the Navy, I'll be out of here January first. My last day with the JAG Corps will be the 31st of December, New Year's Eve."

"Well, you have a few months to think things over Ted. You will do the right thing," said Baxter. "You might even want to stay here in Washington. I think my daughter has her eyes on you."

"Dad-dee!" Elaine fairly squealed in a loud whisper. "Come on, Commander, I believe it's our dance," she said.

"It's Lieutenant Commander," mumbled Ted.

He shook hands all around and said a few parting pleasantries. He led Elaine to the dance floor and were soon swaying to Bob Will's western classic, *Faded Love.*

His daughter has her eyes on him? Her father is a Texas billionaire who calls governors and United States Senators by their first names? The admiral is "Uncle Cy?" Holy Molie, Molie Holy—what have I gotten into this time?

Out of sight from the dancing couple Vernon Baxter tugged on Wayne Hendry's sleeve. "Wayne, I want that boy in Dallas. How many new lawyers you gonna hire after the first of the year?"

"You know as well as I do, Vern, everything depends on the new budget and that's figured out by the legislature down in Austin, but I will be adding a few souls. We always do."

"Screw Austin, Wayne, I want that boy hired. We got everybody down there in our pocket one way or another don't we? I don't give a shit how you do it or what strings you have to pull with the Navy or anybody else."

"Vernon, you heard him. We don't even know if he wants to move to Texas."

"Wayne," Baxter sighed. "Maybe you didn't hear me, or maybe I wasn't clear enough. I don't care what you have to do, who you have to bribe, or who you have to shoot, have his ass working in your office January first. I want that boy hired."

"Okay Vern, I'll do my best," said Hendry.

"Good, then it's a done deal. Thanks, Wayne."

They turned to go back to the gala. Baxter stopped and turned around, "Oh, Wayne."

"Yes?"

"Who in their right mind wouldn't wanna live in Texas?"

CHAPTER SIX

Wayne Hendry was nobody's fool. He knew perfectly well what Baxter was up to. Hendry had known Vernon Baxter for a long time. Baxter never did anything for anyone unless there was something in it for himself. He also knew that he would be retiring after this term, or maybe he would stay for one more election but that was it. It was simple: Baxter wanted to hone Ted to become the District Attorney after he retired. This way Baxter would still have a button to push at city hall and keep the DA's Office off his tail and its nose out of some of his shady business deals. It's an old story of the golden rule, he who has the gold—*rules*.

Vernon Baxter was nobody's fool either. He had been keeping a file on Theodore Barrett for several months. He had come highly recommended by "Uncle Cy." As the admiral had put it: "Lieutenant Commander Barrett? He's top shelf." Lieutenant Commander Barrett was perfect. He was tall, good looking and had enough charisma for ten people.

To Vernon's way of thinking, Wayne Hendry had seen his best days. Hendry would finish out his term and Vernon had the money and the political clout to put new blood in the DA's Office. Who better than Ted Barrett? He could make that happen. Now, he might have gained a little unexpected bonus. His daughter, Lanie, was clearly making goo-goo eyes at the lieutenant commander. Maybe she wanted to marry him?

He could make that happen too.

As the evening wore on Ted found himself happily enjoying Lieutenant Baxter's company. She was witty and charming and certainly no stranger to these kinds of events. They danced to every western tune the band played, had a few drinks, and both were stuffed with the good food. Finally, they thanked the Baxters and said their goodbyes. They walked arm in arm through the marble pillared forum of the Senate Reception Area. Directly in front of the area stood the uniformed chauffeur beside an open rear door of the black limousine.

Wonder how he knows what time to be here? Thought Ted. *I didn't see anyone call—another pukey job—waiting out here for four plus hours, constantly on call for anything the Baxter's might dream up—at least Andy, the gofer, gets to be inside. It's amazing what a few billion dollars can buy, give or take a million or two.*

The ride back to Lieutenant Baxter's condo was beautiful. It was a clear night in the federal city and Ted was enjoying seeing the monuments and memorials all lit so brightly. Elaine pushed a power button closing the privacy window of the limo. She seemed right at home in here too.

She's probably been riding in limos her entire life. He thought.

"How about a bourbon and water, Ted?" she asked, reaching for the bar and selecting a bottle of Wild Turkey.

Oh, we're on first names now?

"Sure," he nodded, although he really didn't want the drink. Ted had sensed that she already had plenty to drink, probably too much. He was gazing out the window of the limousine when he noticed that her knee was touching his. Suddenly, he felt her hand resting on the inside of his thigh.

"You know," she whispered, "Washington is so big and there's always so much going on, but I still get kind of lonely and stuff. Don't you, Ted?"

Ted knew that he had to field this ball tactfully. "Sometimes I get a little lonely," he fibbed. "But I usually stay pretty busy and that makes it go away."

"Are you lonely now?" She asked snuggling against his shoulder.

Mercifully, the limo was pulling up to her condo at that moment. "I'll see you to your door Lieutenant," he said, as the chauffeur opened the rear door of the limo.

"Aren't you coming in?"

"Thank you, but no," said Ted. "I have a full day tomorrow so I'd better get some rest."

"But Ted, tomorrow is Saturday," she pouted.

"I know, but I have some things to attend to at the FBI lab over at Quantico," he said, lying through his teeth. I had a great time. Thank you. Goodnight, Lieutenant."

"Goodnight, Commander," she whined.

Ted's mind was racing and thinking, *Lord All Mighty, that's all I need, is for it to get around that I was bonking the admiral's niece—worse yet, what if she got pregnant? "Hey Admiral, I got some great news for you, I just knocked up your niece...." That would go over like a fart in a scuba tank—after my court martial I can see my butt hanging upside-down from the flag-staff at Quantico waiting to be drawn and quartered.... Evisceration scheduled at sunrise....*

Not to mention the daughter of Texas Zillionaire, who could pick up the phone and demand to speak to the president, or any other swinging dick in the world. He could have me shot or boil my ass in his "awl" in a heartbeat, even if she did have her eyes on me.... Well, the eyes of Texas can look somewhere else tonight.

I like sex as much as any man but not tonight—not tonight and certainly not with Lieutenant Elaine Baxter—ever....

And by the way, Elaine, it's "Lieutenant" Commander.

The fall in Washington D.C. was beautiful. It was early October and Ted was enjoying the leaves changing and that first bit of nip in the air that says winter is coming. The cooler weather demanded light jackets and seemed to put a bounce in everyone's step, truly, his favorite season of the year. Ted was busy at his desk when his intercom buzzed.

"Yes chief," he said to Gina Sawber, the Chief Petty Officer at the telephone switchboard.

"Call for you sir, on line two, a Mister Hendry."

"Who?"

"Hendry, sir, Wayne Hendry, says he's the District Attorney in Dallas."

"Oh yeah, yeah thanks Chief, put him through."

"Yes sir."

"Hello Mister Hendry."

The call from Wayne Hendry came on November fourth. January first found Ted in his Volvo at first light. Ted had felt a little guilty about leaving the Navy, especially with the war in Vietnam raging with no end in sight, but as Hendry had said, "You can do more for the country by putting criminals in jail then you can with the JAG Corps in Washington." Besides Ted wasn't really leaving the Navy, he had opted to stay in the Naval Reserve.

He steered the Volvo southwest on Interstate 81. Destination: Dallas, Texas.

This was all before Ted's confrontation with 'Mizz' Lili Perez. Now she haunted him. He could not get her out of his mind. He still stayed active in the community but his enthusiasm didn't seem to be the same. Ted's mind seemed to stay focused on the petite accountant.

"Why do I miss her so? I don't even know the woman—I've never touched her—I've never kissed her. We've never shared a meal together—we've never shared anything

together. Could it be that I'm in love with her? No—that's impossible—is it? Isn't it? I must have her.

Lili Perez stayed busy. She had plenty of work and absent a few good friends spent most of her time and evenings at home. Lili was content with her life except for lingering thoughts of the lanky prosecutor. Often she caught herself doodling his initials or drawing hearts around his name on her note pad. On occasion she read about him in the newspapers regarding some trial, or him giving a speech somewhere. She cut the clippings out and saved them.

Why?

Ted Barrett's biggest intrusion in her life was depriving her of what little sleep she could get. There was no explanation. Every night was the same. He was beside her, breathing, warm, her lifeline. She dreamed of his soft wet kisses, the passionate hugs. Every night the moisture was there.

CHAPTER SEVEN

L ili was exiting Lemmon Avenue and turning the corner on to McKinney Boulevard. Only two blocks ahead was her apartment. She was anxious to get home.

Maybe I have time, she thought. I need a couple things from the store and I am right here at the Safeway so I might as well stop.... I can pop in and out and be home before the storm, and it will save me from having to come back—Oh shoot, it's starting to rain—maybe if I hurry.

Her attention was not so much on her little apartment haven as it was on the dark blue, turning black, towering surge of cumulus clouds to the northwest that seemed to be subjugating the Texas sky like a boiling ocean of steaming purple tar. Lili felt the familiar queezing inside the pit of her stomach as the first tingling of fear ran through her body.

Kelaeno has found me.... Kelaeno, the winged Greek goddess of storms, the Black Goddess, the mother of Poseidon, the daughter of Typhon and Echidna, she knows where I am. Kelaeno, a goddess who can generate a storm with a mere thought, who can fling fire and lightning from her fingertips. Why is she after me again? Why isn't she at home in the Constellation Pleiades where she belongs?

Lili was back to that horrible day in Uvalde, her home town in southwest Texas about fifty miles from San Antonio. Lili was twelve years old, and her father and mother, Miguel and Rosemary Perez, had gone to attend to some business in San Antonio, depositing the younger sister, Gabriella, with Rosemary's parents and left Lili at home to watch her brother Enrique who was just barely seven.

That August day was not significant or different than any other blistering hot day in south Texas, except Lili noticed a rather strong surface wind and the gathering dark clouds to the north. It looked like a giant ice cream cone, but still nothing remarkable. She never saw it coming.

When Lili heard the first sound Enrique was playing in front of the house just beyond the steps of the Perez home. Suddenly, with no warning it began to pour rain. There was a screeching, howling sound that could strike terror in the boldest of hearts. The howling wind was deafening, blowing the rain and other debris sideways. Lili froze in fear.

She had heard about tornados. South Texas was certainly no stranger to them but she had never been in any violent weather other than the usual summer thunderstorms. Lili was brought back to her senses instantly when she heard the crunching growl of the corner of the living room roof as it was being wrenched from its mooring.

Oh my God, Enrique!

"Enrique, Enrique!" she screamed, as she charged through the ravaged and disappearing front door of the house. Her skin felt like it was being blasted by a thousand pellets as she dashed through the roaring tempest. Although she was barely able to open her eyes against the rain and wind she spotted Enrique still sitting in his play area screaming in terror. She flung her tiny body over her brother to shield him from the storm.

Lili heard a booming sound, like an explosion, as the entire roof of her parent's home was being torn from its roots. She covered her head with her arms, but she dared to look up and could see that she and Enrique were in great danger from the flying debris where they lay. "Come Riquie, the shed, Papa's shed!" she screamed. "A'ndale, a'ndale! Riquie, alejarse rapidamente!"

Papa's shed was twenty yards away and was not much more than a few fragile sheets of plywood covered with aluminum siding where Mister Perez kept his lawnmower and a few tools. Lili could see through the blistering rain that the roof of the shed was gone from the storm, but miraculously the sides were still standing. She grabbed her brother by the arm trying desperately to wedge against the screaming rain and debris. "A'ndale a'ndale, Riquie. We have to make it to the shed or we will be killed!" she cried.

Lili was able to cross the short distance to the shed which seemed like an eternity and quickly ushered Enrique inside. The roof was gone but at least the sides of the shed were still there and provided some shelter from the roaring tornado. Rain was pouring in like a waterfall but at least they were out of the raging wind. They huddled together praying that God would spare them and for the storm to pass. Lili held her little brother tightly knowing that she was his only sanctuary from nature's worst, a tornado, but at least they were safe—safe for now.

Lili's ears picked up a shattering sound, but she never saw the ripping shed as it was being torn apart nor did she feel the board that struck her head. Everything went black.

She came back to her senses minutes later, or was it hours? She felt her arms and legs. Everything seemed to be all right except for the huge knot on her head and a myriad of bruises, which she had no recollection of getting. The tornado had passed as quickly as it had attacked. It was still daylight outside but getting dark so she must have been out quite a while. It was still raining, but at least the wind had calmed to a strong breeze. Lili looked for Enrique. He was nowhere to be seen. "Riquie, Riquie!" she cried. "Enrique!"

Oh dear God, no! My brother…. How long have I been unconscious? Did he wander off? No, he wouldn't have done that…. He's only seven years old, did he think I was dead and went for help? No, he could not have known…. Oh dear God, please make him be alright—

Lili ran in a desperate search for Enrique. Her head was splitting with pain and her little body ached all over. Nowhere was any sign of Enrique. She burst into tears both from her pain and the thought of not protecting her brother. She intended to go to her grandparent's house, she knew the way, but first she must find Enrique.

A policeman found her wandering the streets a mile from her home late that night. She was lost, crying, and almost delirious. Her clothes were still wet and filthy and had been torn to shreds from the blasting wind.

"Come with me, little one, I will help you find your mom and dad," he said. She put her hand in his and he led her to his police cruiser.

Ordinarily she never would have gone anywhere with a stranger, as her parents had taught her, but they made exceptions for a uniformed police officer. She remembered the instructions in school that policemen and firemen are your friends.

When Lili arrived at the police station she was greeted by a frantic Manuel Perez, "Oh, mi bebe dulce!" he exclaimed with tears streaming down his face. "Te quiero tanto!" He hugged her so tightly he almost crushed her. "We were so worried about you little chiquita! We have searched everywhere for you. You are safe now."

"Riquie?" she whispered.

"Grandpapa found him a few hours ago. He is safe and sound. He was plenty scared but he's okay now. He was worried about you. You are a hero, Lili. You saved Riquie's life!"

This was a side of Papa that Lili had never seen. The Perez home was strictly run by an unemotional Mister Perez based on good catholic standards. At least that applied to the girls. It seemed the boys had pretty much a free reign and a long leash. It was an old Mexican tradition: chauvinism. Males ran everything and the women were subservient, and expected to stay in their place. Women's tasks were to have the babies, keep a home, and remain lily white virgins until they married; that is, marry the man of whom their father approved. Lili knew from early on that someday she would leave and be on her own. Somehow she sensed, even then that this archaic lifestyle was not for her. There was a big world out there and she wanted to be part of it.

The Perez family was forced to move in with Rosemary's parents until their home was rebuilt. It was crowded but no one seemed to mind and everything seemed to go back to normal. The change in Lili was not immediately noticed until her parents were summoned to her school one day.

Miss Dolores Wilcott was the school's associate principal and the town's spinster. She was very tall and thin and looked to be in her mid to late forties. Today, she was wearing a brown suit with a very wide matching brown belt. Because of her height she usually wore flats as she was today. She was convinced that the wide belt made her appear shorter.

"Mister and Mrs. Perez ever since the day the tornado struck Uvalde, we have noticed that Lili seems to drift off in class and sometimes she appears to be napping. Lili has always been a straight 'A' student and I'm afraid that her grades may be suffering."

Mister and Mrs. Perez looked puzzled, but thanked Miss Wilcott and assured her that they would look into it. The next day Rosemary scheduled an appointment with the family pediatrician.

Doctor Ramon Gomez, a plump and jovial man, gave Lili a through physical examination. Looking over his desk at the anxious faces of the Perez's he said, "Miguel and Rosie, I can't find anything wrong with Lili physically, but she is definitely not getting enough sleep for a twelve year old. My best guess, and I feel like it is a pretty good one, is that Lili was traumatized a bit by the tornado experience she had back in August. She told me that she has a dreadful fear of thunderstorms. That's understandable, but she'll grow out of it when she gets a little older. She's still just a child. I'm going to give you a prescription some Benadryl. It's a mild sedative. Let's see if that won't help little Lili get some rest."

That had been thirteen years ago. The dread of thunderstorms and the insomnia still dwelled within her.

Lili guided her car into the Safeway parking lot.

CHAPTER EIGHT

Ted Barrett was on the telephone.

"Okay Paul, round up Stan and I'll see you guys about six-thirty or seven. Remember kick-off is at eight o'clock. The Cowboys are playing the 49ers in San Fran tonight. Really should be a great game."

Ted listened for a moment and said, "Yeah Roger's healthy so it should be a close game. I'm going to go over to the Safeway and get some more chips and beer, so see you guys then."

Ted hung up the phone, rounded up his car keys, and made a run for his car. "Wow looks like Big 'D' is in for a stormy night," he muttered, as he looked at the darkening sky.

Ted pulled his car into the Safeway parking lot, and bolted for the entrance. Because of the on-coming downpour he was not looking around, concentrating on getting out of the rain. At that same moment, just as he was dashing between two parked cars, the door of a red Volkswagen Beetle swung open. Ted saw the movement, but it was too late. A collision was inevitable. The door of the Volkswagen cracked him on the right knee. Down he went.

Dazed, Ted looked up and was staring directly in the angelic face of Lili Perez.

"Oh I'm so sorry! Mister Barrett is that you?" Lili exclaimed.

Dear God, did I die…? Is this heaven? Is anyone on this planet really that pretty, thought Ted*?*

"Mizz Perez," moaned Ted, "we really must stop meeting like this. I'm going to run out of knees before you run out of cars."

His attempt at humor through his pain made Lili cast her majestic smile.

"Here let me help you," she said.

"Aw little lady, taint nuttin," said Ted, putting on his best John Wayne imitation. "I'll jest bite on this here bullet." Ted painfully hoisted himself up.

"Mister Barrett, you are hurt. Let me help you," cried Lili.

"Tell you what, little lady, I know what would make me feel a lot better," said Ted, still in his John Wayne character.

The last thing Lili wanted to do was to hit someone, but to clobber a lawyer? Especially this lawyer….

"Yes absolutely, anything Mister Barrett, uh anything within reason, of course," she said smiling and catching herself, reflecting on his alleged reputation as a philanderer.

"Mizz' Perez the only thing I can think of to make me feel better is for you to have a cup of coffee with me in the deli there," said Ted hopefully, nodding toward the store.

Lili replied, "I don't drink coffee, but I bet they have tea."

"I bet they do too, so it's a date 'Mizz' Perez. Shall we go? Let's get out of this rain."

She helped him limp into the store. Ted tactfully draped his arm over her shoulder, trying to get as much mileage out of the situation as possible.

Gad, she is tiny. Her smell just what I've been dreaming about....

His knee really didn't hurt all that terribly but he was not about to let her know.

An hour passed quickly. The coffee and tea were wonderfully exotic, but mostly they stared at each other.

Ted could only think, *Dear God, don't take me now.... Please Lord, let me finish this dream—*

Lili stared at him.

What a magnificent specimen of a man you are.... How many hearts have you broken with those brown eyes? Are you going to break mine...? Are you going to be mine or must I share you with a hundred others...? If I love you, and you love me back, and you take me, I have to be your one and only, it has to be forever—

"Mister Barrett, I think the rain is letting up a bit so perhaps I'd best go" said Lili, in a voice warm as honey. "I hope your knee is all right."

"Sure I understand. It's fine. Do you live around here 'Mizz' Perez?"

"Yes, I live in the Garden View Apartments just across the way. You?"

Ted's reply was instant. "I live in the Continental, two down from you. You mean to tell me that we have lived this close all this time and we haven't run into one another? We have lived this close and you haven't assaulted me with your car before now?"

Lili smiled displaying her beautiful white teeth. "Nice to see you again Mister Barrett; no need to walk me out, like I said, I hope your leg is okay."

"Oh 'Mizz' Perez," said Ted, "I know this is a long shot, but I noticed a Cowboy sticker on your car. I'm going to watch the game with a couple friends tonight. We'd love for you to join us."

"Thank you, Mister Barrett. I really don't like thunderstorms, they frighten me. So I am going to stay all tucked in my apartment. But thanks anyway."

"Suit yourself, 'Mizz' Perez, but if you change your mind, my unit is upstairs, 202."

Lili nodded. *Gosh, he's really human—and fun. He's funny—he makes me laugh. I like him—I think I love him....*

It was close to midnight when Ted bade goodnight to Paul and Stan. The Cowboys had won in San Francisco 24-21, thanks to the talented toe of place kicker Efren Herrera. Herrera kicked a field goal in the last seconds of the game, so everyone was in good spirits. Ted cleaned off the coffee table, tossed a few beer cans in the trash and emptied the ashtrays. He was not really a 'neatnik,' but he did like his home in order. He put some music on the stereo and elevated his leg. Earlier he had been using an ice pack on the paining knee so he put the ice back on and sat down to rest. Outside the storm raged.

"Man, I haven't seen a lightning show like this since I left Florida," he said to no one in particular. Ted was just about to drift off to sleep when the doorbell brought him alert.

"Now what did you guys forget?" He asked aloud limping toward the door. Paul and Stan had ridden together, so they had to have come back together.

Maybe it's the storm and they don't want to drive home. That's fine, I have plenty of room.

Ted opened the door and had to push a bit against the strong wind. His blood turned to ice water. There stood none other than Lili Perez.

"Why 'Mizz' Perez, you are drenched, soaked to the bone. Please, please come in," said Ted. "What on earth are you doing out in this storm at this hour?"

"I couldn't sleep and I was walking. I thought the bad weather had passed and was over. Then I got caught in this storm," said Lili almost in tears. "I was walking by the Continental trying to get home and I remembered your number and saw your light on, so I hope you don't mind."

"No, no please. I don't mind at all 'Mizz' Perez."

Lili Perez was beautiful no matter how she looked. Her hair was soaked and plastered about her face and neck. Her clothes were wet and clinging to her petite body. Water rolled off her and was making a small puddle on the floor. She was shivering and reminded Ted of a little lost girl who was just found.

Ted went back in his bedroom and rummaged through a drawer. He emerged moments later carrying a long white Dallas Cowboy Jersey and a fresh towel.

"Here 'Mizz' Perez, go in and take yourself a hot shower and put this on," he said handing her the jersey and towel. "I will make you some hot tea. It's okay. Go on now. You'll catch your death of cold. You can't stay in those wet clothes and you can't get home in this storm. A hot shower will do you good."

"What about the lightning?" she barely uttered.

"Don't worry about the lightning. You never see the one that gets you," smiled Ted. "If you like I can close the drapes. You won't see the lightning but we will still hear the thunder."

"No, I'm fine with the drapes open. I just didn't want to be alone. I was scared, but I feel better now."

Soon Ted could hear the shower running. He heated some water and got out a tea bag. It seemed like it took a long time for her to re-appear. Then she was there. Surely, this was an angel who just dropped in from heaven. Lili's hair was combed back and even with no make-up, of which she wore very little, her natural beauty was striking. Her eyes were larger than ever, deep brown eyes that seemed to drink in his every move. She was constantly beside him. Ted's Cowboy Jersey was the only garment she wore and hung down to her knees. The jersey did precious little to cover the two perfect breasts and erect nipples, which seemed to stare back at him.

"Here 'Mizz' Perez, please sit down," said Ted, indicating a large green sofa. "I'll get your tea. You don't have to be afraid of a little storm."

"I'm not frightened anymore," she barely whispered, wrapping herself in a blanket at the end of the sofa and folding her feet underneath.

They talked long into the night. They spoke of their families, college days, Ted's home in Florida, and growing up there, her home in south Texas, likes and dislikes, tastes in music, art, career ambitions, everything. Both were amazed how easy the other was to talk to, and how parallel and compatible they were, setting aside their rather awkward beginning.

Outside the rain came down.

Ted could see that Lili was tiring and said, "'Mizz' Perez, it's late and there is no way you can go home in this weather. I have fresh sheets on my bed. Please lie down in there and I will stay out here."

"No, no," Lili responded quickly, "I would never take your bed, Mister Barrett. I will stay out here. I'll be just fine. Thank you for the offer. I insist."

Ted could see that arguing with her would be useless. He rose and laid her head back against the pillow. He tucked the sheet about her and spread the blanket around her narrow waist.

Ted could not help himself. He leaned over and placed a soft kiss on her forehead. The enormous brown eyes looked at him.

"Night, night," he whispered. "I will be right here if you need anything."

"Mister Barrett would you leave the bathroom light on please?"

Sensing her fear he said, "of course I will. Goodnight, 'Mizz' Perez."

"Goodnight Mister Barrett," said a very soft voice.

Outside a bolt of lightning flashed followed immediately by deafening thunder. Both jumped.

"I've never stayed overnight in a man's apartment," was the last thing he heard her say.

Sleep was not to come easy for Ted. He stared at the ceiling thinking only of the majestic goddess not ten feet away. Yes, a goddess, the one I have been looking for my whole life. She is absolutely perfect. Scottie was right. All Miss Americas rolled into one—*flawless*.

Apparently sleep was not to come to Lili either. Ted could hear her tossing and moving about on the sofa. He started to get up and check on her but decided against it, not wanting to embarrass her or make her feel uncomfortable.

An hour later, Ted turned over on his side to relieve some of the pain in his knee and hoping some rest would find him. It worked and soon he was drifting off to sleep.

Lightning was bursting through the heavens, the thunder rolled.

Suddenly, Ted noticed a shadow from the corner of his flaccid eyes. Someone was in his room. He remained as still as a stone. He felt the covers of the bed being gently pulled back. Since he was lying on his side Ted could not see. He didn't move a muscle.

Ted felt a very warm body press against him. An arm was across him. A hand brushed the hair on his belly and stayed there.

The instant their skin touched Lili Perez was fast asleep.

Ted slowly turned and looked at the raven haired beauty as she slept. She was so peaceful and so lovely. He watched her for a long time and thought how much she reminded him of a little girl. Never did he ever dream that he could lie beside such a stunning creature as this, who absolutely reeked of sex appeal and not have sensual thoughts. But Lili Perez sleeping against him was innocent.

As innocent, as it might be Ted was sure Lili was not wearing the jersey he had given her. Her warm, natural breasts were pressing against his skin.

As Lili slept peacefully beside him, Ted didn't sleep a moment.

He started wondering what to make her for breakfast in the morning. Being a bachelor his pantry and refrigerator inventory was understandably sparse.

Let's see, I have some canned chili—Chili for breakfast? No, of course not.... Got some tuna, nah—got some Gator-Ade, she might like that—maybe we'll just go out. No can't do that she doesn't have any clothes, well she only lives up the street we could stop there first—We'll see....

Finally, Ted slept.

He awoke just after sunrise. The storm was gone and so was Lili Perez. The Cowboy Jersey was neatly folded on the pillow.

CHAPTER NINE

The week passed by quickly. Ted was buried in his legal work and Lili with her accounting, but thoughts of that stormy night burned in their memories. Neither could escape the constant thoughts of the other.

Lili wondered: *What must he think of me crawling into his bed like I did? I've never done anything like that before.... Ever! I must have been out of my mind—I couldn't help myself—I just couldn't help it, he was so sweet, so polite.*

Lili wondered if it was the same Ted Barrett she had seen in the courtroom. How could he be so gentle at home, and yet such a tyrant in court? He was so different. Lili was giving in more and more to her soliloquies.

He's not going to call me.... He would have by now—I want him—maybe I'm just another notch on his bedpost? But nothing happened.... Not really—it's going to be up to me to see him.... But what can I do?

Ted had spent most of his Friday morning trying to make some sense from the brief he was trying to read. He could not focus. All concentration was for naught. His mind kept drifting; drifting to the memory of a petite little accountant who spent a rainy night with him.

Ted pressed the intercom button, "Miss Susan would you find Ray Scott and ask him to come in here please?"

"Right away Mister Barrett," came the reply.

"Thank ya ma'am."

Ten minutes later there was a knock on his door. The head and shoulders of Ray Scott appeared from behind the door.

"Oh hi-ya, Scottie, come on in and sit down," said Ted, leaning back in his chair while rolling a pencil between his palms.

Ray Scott obeyed.

"Scottie," Ted began. "I sent for you because I need someone I can trust on a confidential matter."

"Sure, whatever you need sir."

"Scottie, I need a favor and it has to remain between us."

"Sure," nodded Ray Scott.

"I need you to go over to Oak Lawn Florists and pick out twelve long stem red roses. Now, you hand pick them yourself Scottie, don't let anyone else do it. They have already been paid for and Scottie, make sure they are red."

Ray Scott looked puzzled, but nodded, "Sure Mister Barrett, if that's what you want."

"That's what I want, Scottie. I know it's not your job, but it's a personal favor for me."

"Okay, consider it done Mister Barrett, but one small question: what do I do once I pick them out?"

"Oh yeah, I'm glad you asked that," exclaimed Ted. "See, my mind just isn't clicking and I've still got that freaking brief to finish. And by the way Scottie, deliver them personally to this person at this address." Ted handed him a note paper.

Ray Scott glanced at the paper. His eyebrows shot up to his hairline. "Ho! You got it 'baaaad,' boss-man."

"Never mind that Scottie, you're still a puppy, someday you'll understand. I didn't understand myself until a few nights ago. Once it hits you it's like a freaking avalanche. Now, have at it."

"Roger that boss," said Ray Scott heading for the door.

"Oh Scottie, put this in with the roses," said Ted, tossing Ray Scott a jersey. "And Scottie, no card, no names, nothing, just the roses and the shirt."

"Mister Barrett this is a Cowboy Jersey."

"Scottie just do it!"

"Roger boss, roger, roger. Ain't love grand?" laughed Ray Scott as he took off down the hall toward the elevators.

Ted grinned that boy has a future. He'll make a fine Governor or maybe even a U.S. Senator —

CHAPTER TEN

The following week had been long and difficult for Ted. By Friday the work was still mounting on his desk and he was driving his secretary crazy. It seemed as if the more he did the more he had to do.

He called his secretary on the intercom. "Miss Susan, I need a couple of those storage boxes and would you send Scottie in here."

"Yes sir," came an exasperated reply.

Susan found Ray Scott near the mailroom filing cases. "Scottie, the 'Pharaoh' wants you ASAP."

"On the way," said Ray Scott with a shrug. "What now?"

"Watch your step, Scottie. He's in one of his pissy moods. He's been a bear all week," said Susan. "We start the Huxley trial next Monday or Tuesday, I know that's on his mind. He's up against James Hicks, so it should be quite a battle."

"Miss Susan it's not the trial that's on his mind."

"Oh dear," exclaimed Susan, "Is somebody sick—his family? Is he alright?"

Ray Scott grinned from cheek to cheek. "Well, I'll tell you, Miss Susan. Nobody is sick and his family is just fine, but he ain't all right. No ma'am, he ain't all right!"

"Oh dear," Susan said again, "what's wrong?"

"Miss Susan," said Ray Scott, "our boss, the soaring Ted Barrett, Dallas' Don Juan, God's gift to women, the playboy of Texas is in love! That's right L-O-V-E, love. She is a gorgeous dish, a solid ten, and she won't have a thing to do with him."

"Love...? Ted...? Our Ted...? Ted Barrett? In L-O-V-E, love?" howled Susan.

They we both roaring with laughter and almost doubled over, when Ted stuck his head in the hall.

"Hey you two, this is not a freaking clam-bake. Scottie bring me those damn boxes!" He shouted.

The laughter stopped immediately but the grins were still there. Ray Scott trotted into Ted's office, boxes in tow.

"Scottie help me gather up these files and get them to my car. I'll have to work on them all freaking weekend. I can't seem to get a damn thing done around here. People, phones.... Damn it all."

CHAPTER ELEVEN

Lili Perez did not have a busy week and her usual workload was light. It was just as well. Enter Ted Barrett. She found herself straying farther and farther into her daydreams. She saw him everywhere. She talked to him frequently, and often pretended he was with her. His hands were so strong and yet so gentle. *This just can't be real, I have never been so taken with anyone like this ever before....*

I should have called to thank him for the beautiful roses but he's probably forgotten all about me.... I wanted to call, but what if he doesn't want to talk to me...? What if he didn't want to hear from me at all...? I can't stand the thought of losing him, but in truth, I never had him to begin with.... I can't bear the thought of him not wanting me. I want him so much. Are the roses an olive branch? If anything is going to happen—I will have to do something....

Ted Barrett leaned back in his easy chair and opened his first Budweiser of the night. The ten o'clock news was coming on, but Ted wasn't listening.

Screw the work, and screw the trial, I'm just going to sit here in my apartment and take the rest of the night off—I'll have a couple brews and start on that crap first thing in the morning.

After his shower, Ted was about to call it a night, get to bed and start on the trial prep material early, when he noticed a bolt of lightning out his east window.

"Jeez," he said to no one, "Dallas is getting more storms than Florida."

Looks like we're getting another one tonight.... Hope I put up the windows in my car—yeah, I did. I remember.

The doorbell interrupted his thoughts.

Now who can that be? Probably old lady what's her name looking for that dern cat again.

Ted opened the door.

"Why 'Mizz' Perez, what a nice surprise!" he exclaimed. "Must you always wait for a thunderstorm to stop by?"

Lili smiled at him. Ted could see the sparkle in her coffee brown eyes reflecting from the light. She was dressed in a pair of red Bermuda shorts and she was wearing the Dallas Cowboy Jersey.

"Here, this is for you," she said handing Ted a single yellow rose.

"Thank you, 'Mizz' Perez, thank you! How thoughtful," he managed through his surprise.

Lili said, "Mister Barrett, it's raining, may I come in?"

"Yes, yes of course, of course, 'Mizz' Perez please come in. I'm so sorry," Ted exclaimed. "I was just so surprised to see you."

Lili entered his apartment rather shyly, as Ted busied himself looking for a vase, which he was sure he did not have. Finally he put some water into a champagne flute and in it the yellow rose.

I wonder if he knows. She thought. *In my culture, flowers have a language—a meaning—flowers speak. The giving of an Amarillo Rose—a yellow rose" says: "I long for you, I want you, and I need you."*

"Have a seat, 'Mizz' Perez, I'll get some hot tea," offered Ted.

As the rain fell outside they talked into the night. Deep subjects, light subjects, funny things, their wants in life, and what they didn't want, but mostly they talked about each other.

She was never far from him, always touching, a knee against his, a shoulder, always some kind of contact. Ted wondered.

Finally, Lili covered up a slight yawn.

"Oh no," thought Ted, *"she's going to go now—I don't want her to leave."*

Lili turned and looked straight into his eyes. "Mister Barrett may I sleep with you tonight?"

Ted could not believe what he had just heard. It was as if a professional wrestler had cuffed both his ears at the same time. Ted didn't say a word. He rose and turned off the lights, took her dainty hand and together they walked into the bedroom.

"Can we leave the bathroom light on?" she asked.

"Of course we can."

Ted was stumbling and mumbling wondering what to do next when Lili came out of the bathroom completely nude. Her nakedness didn't appear to concern her at all. She peeled the covers back from the queen-size bed and gracefully slid in not saying a word. All of Ted's thoughts and questions were answered in that second. He quickly striped off his shorts and his sweat jersey and climbed in beside her.

Lili snuggled her head against his shoulder as she stroked the hair on his belly. She found it softer than the thick mat covering his chest.

"I'm in love with you, Mister Barrett," she whispered.

"I love you too, 'Mizz' Perez," Ted responded.

"That's not what I said," Lili firmly replied. "I said that I am 'in love' with you, Mister Barrett. Please don't say anything; just let me stay here in your arms."

Ted kissed her deeply, his tongue caressing her lips, her shoulders, her neck, and her breasts. The back of his fingernails made circles ever so lightly around her navel. They searched lower.

Lili made no move to restrain or to stop him.

She closed her eyes not wanting to dispel the intoxicating warmth of his body. Her entire being was throbbing with hunger for him. Lili felt like every nerve in her body was a raging inferno, flushing her cheeks. Ted's eyes moved slowly over her naked body. She felt no reluctance or shame. His lips covered hers sending her into a hypnotic state. She reveled in his embrace, her lips parted easily for his tongue. His lean muscular body moved over her sending her to the depths of ecstasy and she could only savor in skin touching skin. Lili lost all awareness of everything except Ted.

She was oblivious to the pouring rain outside, only the seeking, arousing feel of his body against hers, and the gentle caress of his hands. His mouth explored her neck and breasts.

Ted's breathing was as labored as hers. They were wet with sweat. Ted was softly kissing her. His state of arousal was becoming increasingly apparent. He ran his fingers through her thick black hair, pulling her close to him. She could feel his hardness against her. His kisses were soft and gentle.

Ted's lips kissed little circles around her nipples as his fingers made long strokes on the inside of her thighs, touching her ever so softly. He touched her there. She was incredibility wet. No one had ever touched her there before.

Lili sank farther into her pillow. Her breathing tightened as the outcome of their moment became increasingly predictable.

With a moan, Lili brought her mouth to his as she threw her arms about his neck and shoulders. His lean, muscular body moved over her, but she could only glory in the nakedness of their touching skin.

He was hers at last—

Exploding shivers of ecstasy made Lili tremble until she lost all awareness of anything except Ted Barrett. His mouth explored her neck, first nuzzling, then nibbling at the sensitive areas until Lili thought she could stand it no more. She was like a wad of dough, he could knead her anyway he wanted. Tossing her head back, she freely let him have his way with her.

Ted Barrett was one hundred per-cent male.

Lili was about to explode. It felt as if ten thousand needles were touching every inch of her skin.

Outside the rain came down.

Lili's arms were outstretched clenching the sheets into a ball with her fists. "Oh Mister Barrett, take me. Take me now!" she cried as she arched her back.

Ted gently eased on top her, keeping the bulk of his weight on his arms. He tried to enter her.

"Ow, ow" she moaned. He could barely hear her.

He tried to enter her again. "Wow," she whimpered again as she slid back.

Ted rose up on his knees. "Mizz Perez, are you new at this?"

After a pause came an embarrassing whisper. "Yes."

Ted leaned up and kissed her lightly on the forehead, and then he kissed her softly on the lips. "Let's rest for a few minutes, okay?"

"No!" cried Lili. "Make love to me now, oh Mister Barrett now!"

"We will," he said. "We will in time. Let's take a few minutes. I'll get us something to drink."

Ted was at the bar in the kitchen when she came out dressed only in the Cowboy shirt. Her lovely brown eyes were red and her cheeks were streaked with tears.

"Mister Barrett, I'm not good enough for you. I'm so sorry," she bawled.

"Oh no 'Mizz Perez,' you are fine, just fine," he kissed the salty tears in her eyes, and hugged her close. "These things take time. Everything is going to be just fine. Trust me. Now, let's see a smile on that pretty face."

Lili did her best to manage a weak smile and reveled in him holding her so close to his bare chest. His chin was resting on top of her head. They took a few sips of tea, then Ted took her hand and they walked together back to the bedroom.

"Come on, let's get some rest," he said.

Lili walked to the left side of the bed, which she had already claimed as her own personal fiefdom, and slipped off the jersey. Ted followed, stripping off his shorts. Together they lay there naked. Lili snuggled under his arm, her leg was across his middle, and her arm rested on his chest.

Their skin touched. Lili Perez was fast asleep.

Ted watched her sleep as she snuggled deeply into his armpit.

Ted thought, *how could she breathe...?* He made a vain attempt to move her, but she was instantly back in the same position.

The weekend came and went. Ted finished his brief easily and had time to enjoy the company of Lili. They were together every evening, talking and teasing each other. Laughing together, touching, and always touching. Loving, hugging, and kissing.

Ted had never been happier. His days were filled with bliss and his love for Lili grew and grew. He was constantly finding notes pinned in his underwear, a love note in his briefcase, a lipstick kiss on the mirror. Lili was everywhere and hovered over him like a mother hen, wiping shaving cream from behind his ears that he had missed. Did his clothes match? Lili checked. Was his hair parted with care? Yes, because Lili brushed it. Was his tie on straight, yes, because Lili straightened it? Where is that "thingamajig," I was looking for? Ask Lili, because Lili knew. Lili took good care of Ted and managed her own business as well.

She tried to cook for him, but cooking was not included in her accounting major. She gave it a valiant effort. He pretended it was wonderful, and he loved her all the more for trying.

In bed, they would kiss deeply and hug each other. Ted's skillful hands would explore her, the fingertips found their way around her nipples and to her flat belly. They often found their way to the inside of her legs and to the special place.

Lili did not resist him. She never did.

She began touching him.

Since that first night, Ted had not tried to make love to her again.

One night as they lay in the darkness holding each other, Lili was snuggled in her usual position with her head on his shoulder, her hand tweaking the hair on his belly. "Mister Barrett when can we finish what we started?"

"Whenever you feel that you are ready," he said. "I wanted you to think it through and not allow something to happen that you might regret later. I figured you would let me know when you are ready."

Lili's skin was touching his. She drifted off to a sound sleep. She was at peace. He was her lifeline, her haven of peace and security, her anchor.

The week passed quickly for Ted, it was Friday and he was glad to be leaving work and the stacks of files at work.

Now I know what T.G.I.F. really means, he mused. Thank goodness for Scottie, I've been piling a lot on him lately—it's good for him.... If he thinks he's got a heavy workload now, just wait until he becomes a real lawyer.

Ted pulled into his apartment building's parking area and eased into his parking spot. Sure enough, right beside his space, sat Lili's little red Beetle. Lili was there every afternoon waiting for him when he got home. She was there every night too.

Every day was the same. He couldn't wait to see her. She was so bouncy and full of energy. Lili always jumped around like a puppy when she saw him. His apartment took on a new air. Everything was spotlessly clean and everything was in order. Sometimes it annoyed Ted because Lili had everything put in its place according to where Lili thought it should be. Often Ted spent time looking for things.

Dern accountants, everything's just gotta be perfect— everything's just gotta match—everything in a column....

After swearing under his breath, she would say, "Why don't you just ask, you silly?" They would smile at each other and hug. Everything else was forgotten.

Lili was in the kitchen when she heard Ted's car door shut. She reached in the fridge and grabbed a Coors and half skipped, half ran, to meet him at the door. Reaching way up, she flung her arms around his neck and gave him a kiss, almost knocking him over. "Oh, Te amor de mi vida!" she exclaimed. Ted had no idea what that meant, but he thought it must be something pretty good—maybe not?

"A beer for my hero, my champion, my lover!" she exclaimed, giggling.

Ted looked at her and his heart melted. She was so happy. He knew there must have been a great deal of sadness in her past.

Lili never said much about it.

Ted didn't ask.

Lili was clad in one of Ted's dress shirts, no bra. The tail of the shirt was knotted at her waist. Moreover, she wore a pair of Ted's baby-blue boxer shorts, also tied in a knot at the waist.

"Nice outfit. Neiman Marcus?"

"No, you silly," came the curt reply. "These are a special order from 'Teddy Marcus,' and I am modeling this new line of fashion just for you."

"I think you'd rather wear my clothes than your own," sighed Ted. "You look like a pint in a gallon container!"

Lili was giggling and laughing. She jumped in his arms and kissed him again and again. She had never been this way with anyone before, but Ted Barrett had changed everything, well, almost everything.

Then Lili stopped and kissed him deeply. "Mister Barrett, I'm ready," she whispered in his ear, easing down from her tip-toes.

"Are you sure sweet love?" he asked.

"I'm sure."

"Well, then why don't you get out of your 'Teddy-Marcus,' and change into a "Neiman-Marcus", and what say we go to Rosalita's for a nice Mexican dinner?"

"Oh Papasito, that is perfecto!" she squealed. "Just give me a sec."

Rosalita's was not crowded for a Friday night and Ted was able to get them a good table. They sat and laughed, and as usual stared at each another.

Ted was thinking. Just look at those big brown eyes and how they sparkle in the light from the candle—everywhere I go, I'm with the prettiest girl there.... She doesn't have a clue how beautiful and perfect she is.... I don't think she has ever thought about it....

Lili ordered the Quesadilla and Ted had the Chicken Enchiladas. It was the perfect evening. Ted started to order some wine but could not decide what was fitting with Mexican food. He forgot all about it. He was completely absorbed in Lili.

"I love candles," she said, looking into the flame of the table candle.

"Me too," said Ted.

Dallas was enjoying beautiful fall night. It was crispy cool and the moon was shining bright. As they were taking the exit off Central Expressway, Ted said. "May I have a dance with you, 'Mizz' Perez?"

"Oh yes, Mister sexy, handsomest of all lawyers, in the wholest widest world," she giggled. "Dance me until dawn, Mister Astaire." She had both hands gripping his arm and her head rested the shoulder of her life's anchor.

Lili thought he was making a joke until Ted pulled into a small supper club called, Ricardo's. "That's not Ricky Ricardo is it?" she laughed.

Inside a small trio were playing some of the oldies they both remembered from high school and college. Ted led her upstairs to a small balcony overlooking White Rock Lake, where they could see the moonlight reflect off the water like a thousand ribbons. He held her close and they swayed to the music neither said a word. They didn't need to. Lili could not get close enough. She would have climbed inside him if she could.

This wonderful, gentle man—how could this ever happen to me? I will never be sad or lonely again—I have never been so happy—I have Ted Barrett.

They had rarely danced together. Ted found it easier to place his arm on her shoulder instead of around her small waist. She was so little he would have had to bend over. Lili didn't mind. She had both arms wrapped tightly around him, her nose in the middle of his chest. Ted rested his chin on top of her head. It was a perfect fit.

For more than an hour, they stayed wrapped together in the moonlight keeping time with the music. The night air was cool and crisp, just perfect. It was a bit cool but they didn't notice. He kissed her. Ted reached under her arms and lifted her straight up until they were looking face to face. He kissed her again, a deep long sensuous kiss. As he lowered her back down she could feel the firmness of him slide against her.

"Mister Barrett, I think we'd better go now."

"Go now? They will be playing for another couple hours," he said. "Why do you want to go?"

Lili leaned against him arched on her tip-toes. Ted bent down. She whispered in his ear, "Because my panties are soaking wet."

No further explanation was necessary.

Back in Ted's apartment it was still a bit chilly, but neither seemed to mind. Lili changed into her Cowboy Jersey.

Ted said. "Just give me a couple minutes, sweet love," as he went into the bedroom and shut the door.

That's strange, she thought, *we never close that door,* but she said nothing.

Ted emerged minutes later closing the door again.

Lili's mind was turning, *that is so odd.*

Ted walked over to the stereo and put on a Sil Austin, Saxophone album. "Moonlight for Lovers."

He held out his hand to her, "Mizz' Perez."

She took it.

Together they opened the bedroom door. Lili stopped, taking in the sight of four candles spread about the bedroom. The music played. There was a single yellow rose on her pillow. Her eyes were larger than ever. Goose bumps covered her skin. She burst out in tears.

"Don't cry 'Mizz' Perez," he said embracing her.

"Oh Mister Barrett, no one has ever been so wonderful to me!" she wailed. "This is so romantic and you have four candles; that's exactly how many months we have known each other."

"I know," he softly said as he eased her gently on the bed.

Ted slipped off her jersey drinking in the richness of her body.

This beautiful creation… She could have anyone she wants… Why me?

Lili made no resistance.

In the candlelight, Lili could see him bare-chested, as his muscle-toned, body pressed against hers. She could smell the distinct aroma of his maleness and the latent power of his touch tingled through her.

Lili's heart began to race as she reacted to his embrace and she could feel his hot breath on her breasts. All the desires she had ever known rushed through her body like a raging tsunami.

Ted cupped her face in his large hands and kissed her softly. His eyes looked into hers with a love he had never known before. He held her warm body against his own, his mouth opened sensually over her lips. Lili's arms were around him as she hugged him.

I will never, never let him go —

Her breath was coming in gasps, he could have her anyway he wanted. She would do anything to please him. Lili completely surrendered herself to him. The bed sheet was soaked from her wetness.

Lili was delirious. She was totally unaware of the world, just the candles, the music, and Ted Barrett. She reached down and took him, guiding him into her. She wrapped her arms around him and arched upward to join his gentle and slow thrusts inside her.

"Easy baby," he whispered, as he tenderly eased into her until he was all the way inside. Ted made slow and deliberate movements inside her. He was very gentle.

Lili felt a bit uncomfortable but she experienced no pain. Her only thought was to please this magnificent man, whom she adored, making love for her first time. She pushed upward matching Ted's easy and tender motions. They were in perfect rhythm with each other.

Lili let out a cry as her very first orgasm thundered through her body. Her blood was boiling. She arched her back to the ceiling. She had never known or imagined such ecstasy. Her climax went on and on, sending a pleasure she had never known before.

Finally it waned. Lili couldn't breathe, but was finally able to gasp a few breaths. She knew that Ted was trying to bring pleasure to her and not to himself.

"Oh, Papasito, I love you so much. Amor de mi vida!" she exclaimed.

Although making love was a new experience for her, Lili could tell from Ted's breathing and his tightening muscles, that he was nearing his climax.

Oh no, what if he gets me pregnant—he won't.... I know he will take care of me—he is my Amor de mi vida...!

Ted felt the pressure of a thousand geysers building within him. A pleasure he had never dreamed of raced through his body. He had had sex before, but this was his first time at making love. This little accountant beneath him had changed everything in his life.

Ted was still on top of her supporting his weight on his arms. Their lips locked, the kiss was warmer and more loving than ever.

"I'm in love with you, 'Mizz' Perez," he whispered.

"I'm in love with you too, Mister Barrett. I think you can call me Lili now."

"Call me Ted."

CHAPTER TWELVE

A nd the couple spent that night together, and the next night, and the next night, and the next night, and the next night, and the next night, and the next night, and…

Edgar Alan Poe probably said it best in his classic *Annabel Lee:*

"She was a child, and I was a child,
In this Kingdom by the sea,
And we loved a love that was more than a love,
I and my Annabel Lee…"

So it was with them. If ever there was a deep, true and binding love, Lili Perez and Ted Barrett were the poster couple.

They were constantly together laughing, talking, teasing each other and jesting. Not only did they love each other immensely, they were best friends. Their love had no stipulations. It was unconditional.

It seems as though Lili and Ted shut out the entire world when they were together. They had friends and they socialized with others. But even in a group they would pair up completely absorbed with each other.

She was always beside him, constantly. No matter what Ted was doing, washing the car, working at home, reading the paper, or watching television Lili was there. She never left him. They would never fail to touch each other. At home or out and about, you could bet on it, they would figure out a way to touch, sometimes subtle, sometimes not so subtle. They could communicate without words. Often all it took was a look, sometimes just a touch.

Neither Ted nor Lili had ever been so happy and contented. It seemed to Ted that Lili walked around with a bright light over her head like a halo. Her smile was permanent and her big brown eyes sparkled. Lili always seemed to have a bounce in her step, and her mission in life was to take care of her man. She was always fussing over him. Their love for each other was complete. It was safe, secure and a love like no other.

Ted had a decidedly authoritative way about him. Obviously, a man accustomed to giving orders and have others obey. Ted liked being "on stage," as a lawyer, he liked being in control of a situation. This could not have been further from the truth when he was with Lili. There were no rules, there were no orders. They shared everything equally.

Lili loved to tease him. She would creep up behind him, especially when he was working at home, or concentrating, then she would stick her tongue in his ear, or pinch him then dash off. Ted right behind her. They would tussle on the floor, he would tickle her. She would shriek with delight.

Needless to say, this led to passionate love making more often than not.

Frequently, she would leave the bathroom door open when she was sitting in there just to get a rise out of him.

"Lo there, 'lady modesty," and he would cry, "close the door!" Lili would just smile one of her big smiles and wave. Sometimes she would make a face at him. He loved it, and he loved her.

Lovemaking was not something reserved only for the bedroom. They made love in the shower, in the kitchen, living room, the chair, and even once in Lili's little red Volkswagen.

Lili would stand on the balcony in her Cowboy Jersey, and cry: "Oh kind and noble sir, if you don't come ravish me this instant, I shall fling myself from this yon balcony! O Buen y noble Senor Encsanteme!"

Ted would rush out to get her hoping to keep the neighbors at bay. Then he would lead her toward the bedroom to fulfill her wish.

One afternoon Ted came home and she was not at the door to greet him.

Umm, where's Lili? Her car is here.

Then he saw her busy in the kitchen, stark naked, except for the necktie she was wearing.

"Ah nice tie," he managed.

"Te amo mucho!" she cried as she flung herself into his arms.

I still wonder what she is saying. Ted grumbled.

He grabbed her hand. They didn't make it to the bedroom.

It was a nippy winter day that Saturday and Dallas was overcast but no rain was yet falling. "Hey baby, I'm going over to the Safeway," said Ted. "Anything you need? Wanna go?"

"Are you going?"

"Yep."

"Then I'm going too," she flatly replied, with her hands on her hips and her face tilted upward as only Lili could do.

Kris Truax, the head cashier, was balancing the cash in her drawer at the Customer Service Counter when she looked out the glass door of the Safeway.

"Hey Cindy, psst Cindy," she loudly whispered to Cynthia Atwater, the nearby Customer Service Rep. "Remember that couple I was telling you about?"

Cindy shook her head yes.

"That's them," Kris nodded toward a tall man and a striking brunette, coming through the electric doors of the store. "Now you watch Cindy. They will get a cart and by the time they get to produce she'll stick her fingers in his back pocket, I'll betcha."

Cindy was glad she didn't take the bet. Because sure enough, Lili released the grip she had on Ted's little finger and put most of her small hand in his rear pocket, where it stayed as they walked about the market.

"How'd you know that, Kris?"

"I've watched them before, lots ah times. He's crazy about her; he never takes his eyes off her. He never gets more than a few feet away."

"Gad, she is beautiful," said Cindy.

"He ain't no throwaway either," returned Kris.

Kris pointed toward the deli. "Now, you watch, if they go to the deli, he'll feed her some of his off his fork and she will feed him some of hers."

On aisle six, Lili was desperately trying to reach a box of crackers on the top shelf. She was hopping on her tip-toes to get the crackers when Ted leaned over her and got them.

"Okay five foot nothing, here are your crackers," he said, placing them squarely on her head.

Lili didn't miss a beat. She balanced the crackers on her head and swished down the aisle.

"And now ladies and gentlemen, here is Miss Texas, modeling her string bikini at the County Fair," she announced, as she see-sawed her hips from side to side.

Ted was beside himself laughing. He thought *cute itself couldn't get any cuter than my Lili.* He relieved 'Mizz' Perez of her cracker-box tiara and tossed them in the shopping cart.

She flung herself against him and said, "Mister boldest and bravest lawyer man in the whole wide world, my hero, give me a smooch!"

Ted obliged.

By the time they got to aisle eight, Lili signaled him to bend over. On her tip-toes she whispered, "Teddy Bare," using her favorite cognomen for him, I think we need to go."

"Go? Baby we still have stuff to get on our grocery list," he answered. "Why do you want to go?"

"Because Papasito," she whispered in his ear, "you got me all wet down there and I don't want to get all icky." She pinched him, making Ted twitch. "And it's your fault, Mister cracker-getter!"

Checking out was done in record time. Not a thought was given to the deli.

As they left, Cindy turned to Kris. "Can you imagine loving anyone that much?"

Kris replied, "And be loved back like that? Only in my dreams Cindy, only in my dreams."

Ted was buried in work the following Wednesday morning. His desk was stacked end to end with papers, notes, and every kind of trial preparation. The telephone rang.

"Good morning, Ted Barrett," he answered.

"Hi baby," Lili cooed, using her favorite salutation.

"Hi sweet love," he said back. "Why are you calling? You know I'm in trial all week. And to make matters worse the judge is 'Send-um Home Jerome'," he said, referring to a widely known nickname for a liberal judge.

"Oh, I just wanted to tell you something," she purred.

"What is it baby? I've gotta go. I gotta be in court in an hour."

"Okay Teddy Bare," she purred again, "I just wanted you to know that I am here in our bed. I'm really wet down there and I'm all nee'ked! I love you," she giggled and hung up the phone.

Ted couldn't think. His brain had turned to oatmeal.

"Ah Judge, if it pleases the court," he stammered, "the State would like to move for a brief continuance, if it fits Your Honor's docket calendar, say a couple days?"

Judge Jerome Green peered over his granny glasses, he was not pleased. "Mister Barrett this is the second time this week the State has moved for a continuance and it's only Wednesday. Does the State have a problem?"

"Yes Judge," replied Ted. "It appears that something rather urgent has just come up and needs my ah, the State's attention."

"You say something urgent has arisen Mister Barrett?" queried Judge Green.

"Yes Your Honor, something has definitely arisen," Ted replied.

"Okay then," said Judge Green, "if the Defense has no objection, I can fit you in, let's see, how about next Tuesday the 18th at two o'clock?"

"That's fine Judge," everyone agreed.

Ted was out of the courthouse like a Kentucky Thoroughbred at Churchill Downs. His mind set on finding a solution to his rising problem.

CHAPTER THIRTEEN

Winter passed and spring arrived. Not much changed with Lili and Ted. They were a very adoring couple, deeply in love, and very attentive and affectionate to one another, always together, always touching each other. They played like a couple of school kids, laughing together, teasing and making love.

Then one day it happened.

Ted had accepted a speaking invitation in Austin for the Travis County Bar Association's Annual Conference. Lili was folding some clothes that had just come out of the dryer when Ted told her that he would be out of town for a couple days. She asked, "Where are you going?"

"I've got to go down to Austin and talk to the bar association. I plan to leave Friday, the conference is Saturday evening, and so I should be home sometime Sunday afternoon."

Lili wrinkled her nose, pouted her lips and whined, "Teddy Bare that means I'll be home all alone without you for two and a half whole days."

"Oh sweet love, I think you will manage somehow," Ted teased. "Hey baby, I just thought of something. Didn't you say that your parent's anniversary is coming up?"

"Yes, it's on Saturday and I'm going to be here all alone," she said putting on her pouting face again.

"Well then," said Ted, "why don't you go to Austin with me? You can drop me off at the hotel and take my car on down to Uvalde. It's only an hour or so from Austin and it will give you a chance to see your folks on their anniversary and visit with your family."

"Oh yes, yes!" she squealed. "I love you so much! Te amo mucho! What a grand idea. I'm so glad you thought of that, Teddy Bare!"

Ted was proud of himself for making her so happy but he had a sneaking feeling that she had already thought of it first. He was right. Ted smiled. It seemed that she was always a step or two ahead of him.

Friday found them packed and ready to make the four hour trip to the Texas capital. It was a lovely spring day and both Ted and Lili were enjoying the ride. They especially liked seeing the Texas Bluebonnets blooming so densely beside Interstate 35, and the myriad of wild flowers and spring foliage. They laughed, talked, and as always enjoyed just being together.

Lili was chattering away and pointing out many of the Texas towns with Spanish names; Cisco, Salado, Hutto, and was explaining about some of the battles that took place there during the Mexican-American War of 1846-48. Although the war was a defining event for both countries and transformed the continent, by the time Lili got through "esssplaining," he was sure that Mexico had won the conflict.

Ted laughed to himself. Lili's rendition of the Mexican-American War reminded him of a very southern professor he had at Florida State, Doctor Madeline Vandergriff. After taking her class in American History, and if he hadn't known better, Ted would have been certain that the South had won the Civil War. "We whooped them Yankees and chased them back across Bull Run not once, but twice!" so said, Doctor Madeline Vandergriff.

Too soon, the city limits of Austin appeared and Ted steered his car on to San Jacinto Avenue toward the Omni Hotel and Convention Center. They pulled up in front of the hotel and a bellman appeared instantly. "Just one bag," said Ted, opening the truck of the car. "The name is Barrett."

"Yes sir," said the bellman and quickly disappeared inside the Omni with Ted's overnight bag.

"Okay sweet love, do you know how to get back to I-35 from here?" Ted asked, as he gave her a deep kiss.

"Of course I do, you silly," Lili said, doing her best to bring the seat up and adjust the mirrors. "Oh here is my sister's phone number, you can reach me there or leave a message."

"Why can't I call your parent's house?"

"Oh no, Papa would never understand. He thinks he has to approve of whoever I fall in love with and he would never approve of you."

"Never approve of me? Why? What's wrong with me?"

Lili smiled her special smile, "Because you are a gringo, Teddy Bare, you silly!"

Well I can't change that," he laughed. He kissed her again. "I'll see you here Sunday at noon, be careful."

Lili waved as she drove off. "I love you Teddy Bare! Te amo mucho!"

Ted waved back. "I love you too, sweet love," he mouthed.

If you only knew how much I truly love you.

CHAPTER FOURTEEN

Ted walked into the main lobby of the Omni soaking in the elegance of the high ceilings and brightly lit chandeliers. As he approached the mirror polished reception desk the clerk said, "Good evening Mister Barrett, you are in room 532, your bag is in your room. Here's your key," handing Ted a computerized plastic card.

"Thank you," Ted muttered and started toward the elevators. "Oh Mister Clark," said Ted, turning and reading the clerk's name plate, "Would you kindly see that the bellman gets this?" Ted handed him a folded five dollar bill.

"Thank you, but that is not necessary," said Clark refusing the lagniappe and pointing across the lobby. "The elevators are right over there sir. Please use the car on the left."

"Okay thanks," said Ted.

What's going on? If that guy Clark is a hotel clerk, than I'm the Pope, and I'm dern sure not the Pope.... Maybe he's some sort of manager or something—whatever? And that bellman—a little too smooth—how did they both know my name? I'm not a big wheel or anything.... Something isn't right....

The elevator responded immediately and to Ted's delight traveled non-stop to the fifth floor. He read the sign: "Rooms 520-532 indicating a right turn.

Crap, they've stuck me all the way down at the end of the hall by the stairs.... Well can't complain, I'm not paying for this, besides, if there is a fire at least I'm by the stairs.

Ted arrived at his room and inserted his room card into the slot by the blinking red light. He watched it turn steady green and heard the usual "click." The door swung open.

Ted was startled and took a step back. Two men were standing in his room. The tall immaculately dressed one was a light-skinned African American wearing a dark blue suit obviously tailor made. His yellow cuff-linked dress shirt was accented with a perfectly constructed Windsor knotted lighter blue tie. The other man a Caucasian was considerably shorter and a bit overweight. He was not nearly as neatly or expensively clad as his companion. He reminded Ted of a big city detective like you see in the movies. He had on a gray suit, which had seen some wear in its day, the usual white shirt and dark tie, and the standard Scot-Irish closely trimmed blond hair, and watery blue eyes. Being a prosecuting attorney, Ted was accustomed to being around big city detectives in Dallas. He knew well how to recognize a suit that had been cut to accommodate a shoulder holster. Both of these men were armed.

"Oh guys I am so sorry!" he exclaimed, looking again at the number on the door, which still read 532. "There must have been a mistake. I...."

"No mistake Commander, please come in." said the gray suit. Ted was suddenly aware of two men standing behind him, the bellman and Clark, the clerk.

"Commander Barrett," the gray suit began, "my name is St. John, Robert St. John. I'm with the FBI." He showed Ted his government shield and identification. "This is Major Douglas Lynn of the United States Marine Corps. Major Lynn is currently on assignment as a special agent to the Office of Naval Intelligence. He nodded, indicating the tall well-groomed man on his left.

Neither man smiled or offered to shake hands. Likewise, neither did Ted. Special Agent Lynn flashed his ID and said, "Behind you Commander, is Captain Trent Steele of the Austin Police Department and Colonel J.D. Moore of the Texas Rangers."

What could they possibly want with me? The FBI? The ONI? What is a Ranger doing here? The Austin PD?

"Hey guys, there is a big mistake," exclaimed Ted. "I'm just a country lawyer here for a county bar association conference. I've been off active duty for two years."

The black man pulled a thick file from his briefcase. "Aren't you Theodore Fredrick Barrett, born in Stuart, Florida, and raised on the Seminole-Miccosukee Indian Reservation in the Big Cypress Swamp, south central Florida, four years undergrad at Florida State, three years law school there, and four years with the JAG Corps in Washington?"

"Well yeah, all that sounds about right, but what could you guys want with me?"

"Ah Commander, we don't know," spoke up Agent St. John. "My assignment is to escort you and Major Lynn has been sent down here from Washington to accompany you.

This must be important though, my orders came straight from the Director."

"Yeah mine came from the top man too, said the major.

"Escort me where?" Ted burst out. "Accompany me? Bullshit! I'm not going anywhere with any of you. Screw you and the John Deere you rode in on. I can't go with you guys even if I wanted to, which I don't! I have to give a speech tomorrow night, I've got a job, cases pending, and I've got an apartment. I just can't pick up and leave. My girlfriend is picking me up here on Sunday and...."

Special Agent St. John interrupted, "Commander, we don't know any more about this than you do. Those things you mentioned are being attended to. But for now we have a job to do and we have our orders from the top, so...."

Ted butted in, "Top? Top of what? I'm not on active duty in the Navy anymore, I'm in the Reserves. How can my personal affairs and my job be attended to? By whom? How is my girlfriend supposed to know? Will I be back here by Sunday? And for the last freaking time it's 'Lieutenant' Commander!"

"Not according to this," said Major Lynn. "It came through last night, also from the top dog himself. At 0001 hundred hours, this morning you were promoted to O-5, a full commander."

"What? Let me see that," said Ted. He read through the file and sure enough, he had been promoted to the rank of commander a few hours before. The file contained his entire history, but most of it had been sanitized pursuant to Naval security regulations. A lot of lines had been removed with a razor knife or otherwise blacked out with ink marker.

"Okay," sighed Ted, "escort me to where? I have to be back here by Sunday noon, positively without fail. Understood?"

"We don't know," said St. John. "My job is to get you to Bergstrom Air Force Base."

"I don't know either," spoke up Major Lynn. "I am ordered to go with you, but I've got no idea to where."

"Let's get on with it. All I've got is that overnight bag. Where is it?" he said looking at Captain Trent Steele, the bellman.

"Your bag has been taken care of Commander," said St. John.

"All right let's go," said Ted.

"We can't move you until it gets dark sir," said Lynn.

What? More government bullshit!

"Commander," said Lynn, "I'm afraid I have to ask you to change your clothes and slip into these," handing Ted a pair of olive green coveralls. "Put your clothes, all of them, in this duffle bag."

"In that bag?" asked Ted looking at a U.S. Navy sea bag on the table.

"All of them?"

"Yes sir, all of them. Watch, skivvies, wallet, ring, everything.

"Look, I've had about enough of this crap," said Ted.

"Commander please. We all have a job to do; let's make it as easy as possible," said Agent St. John.

Finally, Ted gave in and changed into the ugly coveralls. Everyone sat back and waited for dark.

Ted waited. It seemed like forever then precisely at 12:30 A.M., Agent St. John's beeper sounded. Looking at Major Lynn, he said, "Let's move."

Lynn looked at Ted. "Sir," he said, "one more thing. Please put these on." He handed Ted a Kevlar bullet proof vest and a ski mask.

"Now I've had about enough of this cloak and dagger bullshit," Ted exclaimed.

"Sir just do it," snapped an impatient Major Lynn. "We have our orders Commander."

"Look," said Agent St. John, "it's been a long day for all of us and we're getting a bit testy. Let's all pull together and get this over with."

Ted decided that acquiescence was better than argument so he did as the major asked and donned the Kevlar and the ski mask. Ranger Moore cleared the hall and signaled for everyone to move. Ted started toward the elevators.

"No sir, not the elevators," said Agent St. James quietly, "the stairs."

The stairs...? We're on the fifth freaking floor! This is getting ridiculous.

Ted could see through the eye holes in the ski mask that every landing of the stairwell was guarded by U.S. Army MPs. He admired their snappy dress with the silver helmets, white pistol belts and white leggings.

Probably from Fort Hood over at Killeen, thought Ted.

At the bottom of the stairs, an armored truck was waiting to whisk him away and he was soon standing on the dark side of the airplane taxi ramp at Bergstrom. Seemingly, out of nowhere an Air Force C-21-A, Learjet taxied up its engines screaming.   The hatch of the airplane opened and Ted climbed in.

CHAPTER FIFTEEN

The Learjet started to taxi before Ted could get in his seat. ONI Special Agent, Major Douglas Lynn was behind him. Ted could choose any seat in the airplane. He selected the left rear seat facing forward and strapped himself in. Major Lynn sat opposite him facing aft. The major occasionally glanced out the window but didn't say anything. Ted had already accessed him as not much of a conversationalist.

What a tight-ass, thought Ted, *strictly business. No smile, no jokes, no talk... all business*—the jet had apparently been cleared for an immediate take off. No waiting, no run-up, no anything.

Oh my sweet Lili, you are never going to believe it. Just wait until I tell you all about this on Sunday—

The Lear climbed like a home-bound fighter and soon they were at a cruising altitude of 41,000 feet. In spite of his inconvenience, Ted was almost enjoying the ride. The co-pilot opened the accordion door, which separated the cockpit from the cabin. Turning in his seat said, "Commander

Barrett, there's some sandwiches and finger food in that cooler over there," he pointed to a small Styrofoam ice chest.

Hardly military, probably got it at Wal-Mart…. How does he know my name?

"There's some ice and sodas in there too."

"I was hoping for something with a little more kick than soda," said Ted having to raise his voice over the engines, and causing Major Lynn to bolt upright in his seat with an assiduous look of disapproval on his face.

"Sorry sir, this is a government airplane, United States Air Force. No alcoholic beverages are allowed on board," said the co-pilot.

Ted sulked. *No alcohol allowed my butt…. Do you think I believe that for one second? Do you really think that all the generals and admirals and other self-assessed royalties who tool around up here in the friendly skies on the taxpayers money do it without booze? You ever heard of Air Force One? Who's blowing smoke at whom?*

"Hey Lieutenant," said Ted.

"Sir?"

"What's your name?" There was a pause and Ted could see there was a brief discussion with the other pilot.

"Broster sir, First Lieutenant Joe Broster."

"Who is in the other seat?" Ted asked.

Another pause and another brief discussion, "That's Captain Franklin, Captain Neil Franklin sir. He is the aircraft commander."

Lieutenant Broster looked to Ted to be about sixteen years old.

Wonder if he's shaved yet?

"Well Lieutenant Broster would you be kind enough to ask Captain Franklin just where the hell you two are taking me?"

The accordion door was immediately closed. Even over the roar of the engines, Ted could hear the lock being snapped into place. ONI Special Agent Lynn gave Ted an icy stare.

Ted didn't want anything to eat or drink although it had been a while since he last had anything. He was tired so he tilted his chair back and propped his feet up in the seat across the aisle. He drifted off dreaming of his beautiful Lili.

CHAPTER SIXTEEN

On Saturday, the Perez anniversary party was nothing short of an extravaganza. A pavilion was rented because of the growing population of the Perez family and grandkids, in-laws and guests. Lili danced with her brothers, brothers-in-law, and many others to the Mexican band playing many of the favorites from the old country, and of course, western swing. No one in the crowd could keep their eyes off her. Lili could have cared less or perhaps didn't notice. Her mind was never far from her man who she thought was in the Omni Hotel in Austin.

I love him so much…. Te amo mucho—

Lili walked past the food stands treating her nostrils to the familiar aromas of her childhood. The enticing redolence of burritos, enchiladas, chimichangas, tamales and an array of other scrumptious Mexican treats filled the air.

I've had too much to eat already, she thought. I have to stay nice and trim for my Teddy Bare.

Lili finally spotted her sister, Gabriella. "Gabbie, I've been looking all over for you."

"Oh sister, you're not going to tell me more about that Dallas lawyer are you?" moaned Gabriella. "You kept me up almost all night talking about him. You know the one who is faster than a speeding bullet and can leap tall building in a single bound, the most handsome man in the whole world?"

"Aw come on, Gabbie," said Lili. "I love him and I'm going to marry him. I want to tell mama and papa."

"Don't you dare!" cried Gabriella, never shy about mincing words said. "Mama might be okay with it, maybe? But papa would have a cow. Se volvi'o loco!"

"But Gabbie, I love him so, so much, and he loves me."

"Lili look," said Gabriella. "Papa still insists on the girls having chaperones when they go out, much less your living arrangement in Dallas with that lawyer."

"His name is Ted."

"Okay Ted then. If papa had the slightest inkling of your life style, and that you are not the snow white virgin who left here a few years ago, why he would drive to Dallas and shoot up half the town, starting with the DA's office. Your precious Ted Barrett being number one."

"But, Gabbie, I love him and he loves me."

Gabriella was patient. "Lili, besides all the good things you told me about him, the fact remains that he is a gringo. Papa would have another cow. Maybe you should wait until your next trip home. Give yourself a chance to think things through."

Lili said, "Gabbie, look around, lots of people in our family married gringos."

"Yes, that's true," said Gabriella, "but if you remember, every single time papa threw a fit. Mucho loco!"

"Oh okay," agreed Lili. "I'll wait until the next time I'm home. I don't want to spoil their celebration." If Papa Perez were going to explode and have a cow, it would have to wait.

I'm going to call the hotel tonight…. I want my Teddy Bare to know how much I love him—I miss you Teddy Bare— Te amo Mucho….

CHAPTER SEVENTEEN

The sound of the engines in the Learjet quieted as the pilot reduced the power bringing Ted awake. He could tell by the pressure popping in his ears that they were losing altitude. He glanced at his wrist to check the time. No watch. It had been taken from him back at the hotel, but he chanced a peek at Major Lynn's watch. *Ten minutes after four in the freaking morning...?*

Ted looked out the window and saw nothing but black darkness.

Where are we...? Are we landing in a bowl of ink...? Let's see, we took off at approximately one a.m. in Austin, and we have been in the air for a little under three hours we could be anywhere. Had the major changed his watch to the appropriate time zone? Are we in a different time zone? I want some answers.

Ted felt a slight jolt as the Lear's landing gear touched down on the earth. He felt the airplane decelerate as the crew threw the engines into reverse thrust to help brake it. As he looked out the window, Ted noticed that each runway light was immediately extinguished as the plane rolled past. Soon the airplane stopped and he could hear the engines being spooled down but were not shut off. The door hatch opened.

"Commander Barrett," said an immaculately dressed Marine, as Ted stepped outside into the dark chilly morning. The light from the airplane's interior was the only illumination, allowing him barely to see.

"Yes?"

"I am Captain Galvan sir," he said, greeting Ted with a snappy salute. "I'm here to escort you sir."

Captain Galvan was a Marine right out of the textbook. Perfectly attired in his uniform of blue slacks with the red stripe, a khaki shirt, tan tie and the ever-present white hat. Captain Galvan was armed. A wide white pistol belt adorned his waist.

Ted returned the salute. "Escort me where?" he demanded.

"Please come with me Commander," said the captain.

"What? No ski mask? No flak jacket?" Ted snidely asked glaring at Major Lynn who was still in his seat in the airplane.

"Not required here, Commander," replied Captain Galvan. "Please come with me sir," he said as he ushered Ted toward a waiting station wagon.

Not until Ted was walking toward the station wagon did he notice two other armed Marines standing in the darkness. Just as he was getting in the car, Ted heard the roar of the Learjet departing on the unlit runway.

So long, Lieutenant Broster and Captain Franklin—I see you are taking ONI Special Agent Major Lynn with you. Good riddance—Bon Voyage.

Ted was driven to the front door of a very plain one story farmhouse. He knew from the boring architecture that it had to be middle twentieth century and he noted nothing remarkable about it. Inside Captain Galvan led him to an elevator and down they went. Ted guessed about three stories. Exiting the elevator the captain led Ted to a plain door.

"These are your quarter's sir, you will find clothes, toiletries, and most anything you need inside."

"I need to know where I am and what the hell's going on," said Ted sternly.

Ignoring the question Captain Galvan said, "Commander someone will be here for you at 0700 hours. That's about two hours from now sir; try to get a little rest if you can. This is, Corporal Sinclair. He will be outside your door if you need anything."

Corporal Sinclair...? He just appeared.... How is it possible that I didn't see him before? This place is weird— Corporal Sinclair is not there in case I need anything.... Corporal Sinclair is there to make sure I stay put.... I am a prisoner—why me?

The first thing Ted noticed in his room was a telephone.

I must get in touch with Lili....

He was pretty sure that he had committed her sister's number to memory.

I know it's a crazy hour to be calling but I've got to try while I can.

Ted picked up the phone and immediately a voice said, "Yes Commander Barrett, how may I help you?"

Surprised, Ted stuttered. "Ah, I need an outside line."

"I'm sorry sir; this line is only for use within the building." Ted slammed the phone down in its cradle.

Ted's mind was racing. He had heard back during his time in Washington that the CIA had a training facility somewhere a couple of hours out of town known as, "The Farm." Nobody seemed to know where it was or about anything. Ted was not too eager to believe any the stories and rumors about the clandestine activities of such a secret place. More Washington gibberish was Ted's opinion.

Maybe I'm at the CIA "Spy School." Whatever the hell this place is... Ted tried reasoned. But why on God's green earth would I be here? No telling where I am—I could be anywhere for all I know. When we landed, there wasn't even a light bulb in sight.... They all seem to know who I am.... That Learjet didn't stay on the ground more than three minutes. People just appear out of nowhere.

Ted plopped on the bed and closed his eyes the events of the day swimming in his head. He must have dozed off for a moment because the ringing of the phone startled him alert.

"Ted Barrett," he said.

"Good morning Commander," said a voice who did not identify itself. "Your escort will be at your door in exactly one hour.

"Thank you," Ted muttered.

Ted decided he'd best shave and take a quick shower then call and try to have something sent for him to wear to wherever he was being taken. He detested the olive drab coveralls he had been given by the major, but that was all he had. He was surprised to see that in the bathroom, or "the head," as it was called in the Navy and Marine Corps, was almost identical to his bathroom at home. The shaving cream, toothpaste, deodorant, and even the green Irish Spring bar of soap were exactly the same brands. Something caught his eye. A jar of Jergen's Hand Crème was off to the side of the sink, the exact same hand crème that Lili used and kept in their bathroom and exactly in the same place where she kept it at home.

Ted's mind raced: *This place is getting stranger by the minute—if someone is trying to duplicate my bathroom they have screwed up.... I don't use hand crème, Lili does.*

Ted looked in the closet of his room. To his dismay there were several uniforms hanging in perfect order, whites, blues, fatigues and even some civvies. They were all perfectly tailored and his name was neatly stenciled in each uniform. Complete set of underclothes was aligned on the top shelf of the closet and three pair of shoes, eleven Ds, rested on the floor in a perfect row.

Ted chose the dress blues. He knew that it was still cool outside and felt sure the uniform of the deck would be blues. He admired the new three solid gold stripes adorning his sleeves. At exactly 0700 hours, not one second before or after seven, but precisely at seven a quiet but firm rapt came against his door.

"Good morning, Commander," a warm voice greeted him. "My name is Captain Lisa Finnegan, please follow me." Ted nodded and fell in behind the captain. She was in her Marine Corps Dress Blues and quite a stunning figure with big blue eyes and long silky honey-blond hair.

Probably long enough to just under regulations—maybe not.... Yes ma'am, I am happy to follow you—I love to watch you walk.

Captain Finnegan led Ted through a maze of hallways and up two floors on the elevator. "This place is a lot bigger than it looks from outside," he said. The captain was silent. She led him to a pair of tall oak doors and gestured. "In there."

Ted entered a high ceiling room and all conversation stopped. He was looking at a large horseshoe shaped table and a map of Southeast Asia on a screen behind it, clearly a war room of some sort.

Around the table sat officers from every branch of the armed forces including a Four Star Admiral, Four Star Generals and the Commandant of the Marine Corps. The Chief of Staff from the White House was there, as well as the Director of the FBI and the CIA. Ted hadn't seen this much brass since he visited an ore mine in Minnesota.

"Please sit down Commander," said the admiral, indicating the one remaining chair at the center of the table.

Ted was petrified being in a group like this. These were the highest ranking military officers in the world. He was only a mere commander, a brand new one at that. He was a lawyer for crying out loud.

Why am I here? I don't know anything about war.

In an attempt to break the ice, Ted nervously joked. "Why isn't the president here?"

"Ask him yourself," said the admiral, "he's listening."

"Good morning Commander Barrett," came a very distinctive and recognizable voice over the speaker.

Oh, my gosh, it is the president! The President of the United States knows my name! The President of the United States!

"Thank you for coming in this morning, Commander," the president continued.

Yeah like, I had a big friggin choice….

"Yes sir," was all Ted could manage.

"Commander, I know you must be puzzled about all this. The gentlemen there with you are going to explain everything to you. They have been in my office every day for a week or so and I think we have come to a solution to a most urgent situation."

"Yes sir," was again all Ted could say.

"Very well then Commander, I will leave everything in their capable hands, but I wanted to take a minute to thank you personally. I know you will do your duty. Goodbye and Godspeed, Commander."

Do my duty…? What duty…?

"Goodbye Mister President."

Ted could hear the high squeal of the telephone scrambler as the President of the United States rang off.

"Is the SDS activated?" asked one of the colonels.

"Yes sir," came a sharp reply from an Army MP standing just inside the large doors.

Noting the question on Ted's face, the colonel said, "The SDS stands for Sound Disruption System. It slightly vibrates all the walls and windows in the building to prevent eavesdropping by unfriendlys who may have sophisticated equipment. It's not detectable to us. We are two stories underground, but just to be safe…."

"Where am I?" asked Ted.

The colonel looked at the admiral who gave an approving nod. "You are at Camp Peary, the Central Intelligence Agency's Training Academy, Commander, commonly referred to as 'The Farm'."

"The Farm?" Ted asked.

"Yes Commander," said the admiral, "'The Farm'. We have designed it to appear exactly like a working farm with crops, livestock and so on. If any counter-intelligence tries to spy on us or take photographs from satellites or wondering aircraft all they will see is a farm. We are about an hour or so out of Washington. I'm afraid that's all I can tell you."

This place is huge—all underground. From the surface it looks like an average one story building, only thing there was a small desk and some elevators…. No telling how many stories it goes down…. I'm not going to ask.

"Commander Barrett." The admiral began, "My name is David Petersen."

David Petersen…? "The David Petersen…?" The Chief of Naval Operations David Petersen…?

"On my right is William Sellers."

Four stars. The Commandant of the whole freaking Marine Corps…? Four stars. Holy cow!

The admiral stood and if by magic the oak paneling began to move back, a movie-sized screen appeared with a large slide image of North, and South Vietnam replaced the map of Southeast Asia.

"Commander," he said, "a couple months ago General Vo Nguyen Giap, the Commander-In-Chief of the North Vietnamese Army, along with the Communists put together and executed a major surprise attack on South Vietnam. Our high altitude reconnaissance aircraft photos showed a massive movement of enemy troops and supplies to this area," he indicated with a pointer. "This was on 21 January. We knew something big was going down, we were just not sure exactly what."

He continued. "The Communists made a diversionary attack on our base here at Khe Sanh. Caught us totally by surprise and really grabbed us by the short hairs," again he indicated with the pointer. "However, the real attack which we call the Tet Offensive came on 30 January. Tet is a Vietnamese holiday celebrating the Lunar New Year. The Cong, and Communists, literally ravaged South Vietnam, attacking over a hundred major cities and over 45,000 dead, thousands of others wounded or maimed."

"They seized and occupied Saigon and they had our embassy too," barked Commandant Sellers.

"Yes they did," said the admiral, "but we were able to take it back in eight hours or so, but it took us over two weeks to take back Saigon."

Commandant Sellers stood up in his Marine Corps Dress Greens, and said, "In military terms, Commander, the United States won but we were stunned at the size and ferocity of the attack, but I'm happy to say we were able to keep them from gaining any foothold in the south."

"But sir," Ted said, "what's this got to do with me? I'm just...."

"Just a minute Commander," said the admiral. "The Tet Offensive showed us another side of the war which we don't like. The enemy is much stronger than we had anticipated and the coordination and surprise instigated by the Communists caught us off guard."

Rising Ted said, "Well gentlemen, this is all well and good and I am sure most this is classified, but I've…"

"Damn it, sit down Commander!" snapped Admiral Petersen. "We are just coming to answering any questions you may have. I'm going to turn this meeting over to the Director of the CIA. Mister Payton if you please—"

Ted sat.

Curtis Payton walked over to the front of the map. Ted guessed him in his early fifties, slightly balding and a bit paunchy.

So this is the head spy-guy, mused Ted.

"What I am about to say here and the facts revealed can never be mentioned outside this room," Payton began.

Everyone nodded they understood.

"Commander Barrett our research has revealed that you are fluent in the Seminole Language."

"Yes sir," Ted acknowledged.

"Good," said Payton. "We have searched through all military personnel records and have been able to only come up with six Seminoles that we believe would qualify for our assignment. They are from all branches of the service, but now they have been inducted into the Navy SEALS on a volunteer basis only."

"What assignment?" asked Ted.

"I'm coming to that," said Payton, "bear with me please, Commander. Of these six men we selected you are the only officer except for a Marine Major named, Gary Wildgoose."

"Gary Wildgoose!" exclaimed Ted. "I know him very well. We always called him 'Goose'. I played high school football with him. Matter of fact, I think Goose went to the Naval Academy. He played football there."

"Yes, we know," Payton continued. "Major Wildgoose and three other Seals, all Seminoles, were air dropped at night in the South China Sea, just off the coast of Qui Nhon, approximately here," Payton indicated with the pointer. "Their mission is to swim to shore and disappear into the jungle undetected. From there they are to proceed to just north of Tay Ninh and stay here in the swampy areas by the river just east of the mountains."

"River sir?" asked Ted.

"Yes, Commander, the Mekong River runs right along here," he said pointing, "and it divides Vietnam and Cambodia. Major Wildgoose and the other Seminoles are to establish an observation post somewhere in this area," again tapping the screen with his pointer. "They are to advise us on General Gaip's troop movements, strength, supply and fuel depots and anything else we might need to know. They are also under orders to eradicate the general."

"Eradicate sir?"

"Yes, eradicate Commander," spoke up General Sellers. That's some fancy word the CIA uses for taking his ass out. For some damn reason they think eradicate is more ear-friendly then kill the son-of-a-bitch."

"Assassinate sir?"

The general said, "Damn right, Commander. Kill him. Kill the bastard!"

"Sir," said Ted, "if you don't mind me saying so, a rifle shot in that jungle would be a dead give-away of their position."

"We've thought of that Commander," said Director Payton. "Our men have been trained and are armed with

Swiss made crossbows. They don't make a sound and they are deadly accurate."

The admiral stood again, "Alright Commander, I'm sure you have questions. Let's hear them."

"Thank you, sir," Ted began. "I have noticed you said Seminole several times. Why Seminoles?"

"I believe the CIA has the best information on that," said the admiral, "Director Payton."

"Thank you, Admiral," said Director Payton standing again. "Commander, the Communist Cryptologists have somehow been breaking our codes lately. We are sure it's the Russians who are behind it. It's damn sure not the Cong. They are not sharp enough nor do they have the technology or the equipment to decipher our more sophisticated codes and radio transmissions. So we are kind of stymied right now because we can't move troops or offer any counter-offensive or anything else that is classified in case the Cong are listening, and they are."

Ted leaned forward and placed his elbows on the table. He steepled his fingers and said, "But Mister Payton, I asked you why Seminoles and most of all why me?"

"I'm coming to that Commander," said the Director. "We chose Seminoles because they are the only ones in the Armed Forces who could stand a chance of surviving in that terrain. It is much like the Everglades. Full of swamps, a few rice paddies, mosquitoes, bugs, snakes and all kinds of vermin. You name it."

"But sir, why me?"

"I'm coming to that too, Commander," said Payton extending his arm with the flat of his palm out indicating stop. "There is no writing for the Seminole language. It has a structure and sounds that do not exist in any other language. The Seminole language has always been handed down from one generation to the next. It is totally learned by ear and by association. You, Commander, speak Seminole perfectly. It is a language that could never be understood or decoded by the enemy."

"Yes," replied Ted, "I learned it as a boy. As I'm sure you already know I was raised in The Big Cypress Swamp, an Indian Reservation, in south central Florida."

"Yes, we know Commander," spoke up the admiral. "Your orders are in here." He nodded at Payton.

The CIA Director held up a sealed white envelope. Big red letters read: FOR THE EYES OF THE PRESIDENT ONLY. "I have prepared this for the president. Once he approves, you will be dispatched to one of two locations in Vietnam. I can't tell you where yet. It's up to the president."

"Why? Because I speak Seminole" Ted exclaimed.

"We need you to establish radio communication with the major. Their lives depend on it," said the Marine Commandant. "The Seminole translator, an Army Sergeant Jesse Osceola, we had near Da Nang disappeared. We are pretty sure he was taken out by a sniper. With Osceola gone Major Wildgoose has no way to get messages to us."

Admiral Petersen spoke up. "Commander, Major Wildgoose and the others are under strict orders not to break radio silence under any circumstances until they hear a transmission in Seminole. We desperately need the information that Major Wildgoose can provide. We haven't heard a word from him, or any of them since the drop. We don't even know if they are alive or not. I cannot begin to tell you how urgent it is for the Army and Marine Corps to have that information."

An Air Force General stood up and said, "Commander, we need that info badly too. So does the Navy. We can't call in our air strikes without knowing where General Giap is and where his troops are located. We need to know where the fuel depots and the supply lines are located."

The admiral still standing said, "Commander Barrett, here is the bottom line. We need you, the country needs you. If the Cong Army is as strong as we think they might be and if they hit us, again we are looking at maybe a half a million lives lost, a lot of them Americans. We have to get to Wildgoose. He is the only one who knows exactly what the enemy is doing, where he is, and which way they are moving. There are countless other things we need to know."

"He can't communicate without you," broke in Payton. "All radio transmissions are in Seminole."

Ted sank in his chair. *I've got no choice—too many lives at stake here. It's for God and country—*

"Okay gentlemen," he said, "I'll go on one condition."

The admiral and the Marine commandant both looked over the top of their reading glasses and peered at Ted like two schoolmarms glaring at a naughty pupil.

"You'll what?" they said in perfect sync.

"I'll go on one condition," answered Ted.

"Commander, there are no conditions," snapped the Commandant.

"Hang on a minute, Bill," said the admiral, "What's on your mind son?"

"Well sirs," Ted began, "I have a job, I have a home, bills, I have a thousand responsibilities. My dad died a couple years back and my mother moved to West Palm Beach, I keep an eye on her, and I…."

"All those things you mentioned will be attended to, Commander," said Admiral Petersen.

Ted was angry. He didn't care if he was in the largest brass melting pot in the world. "Admiral, General," he almost shouted. "You had me taken out of a damn hotel room in the middle of the night and flown here to God knows where. Now you're going to send me to the other side of the fucking world, rip my entire life and career from me, and now you tell me my things are going to be attended to?"

It was obvious to Ted that neither the admiral or the commandant, or anyone else in the room was any stranger to salty military language.

"Commander," the admiral said softly, "we know you have been under a lot of stress. We have been too. We are talking about thousands of lives here. Not only the South Vietnamese, but our own boys as well. GIs, Airman, Sailors, Marines and American civilians."

The admiral continued, "There was no bar association meeting in Austin. We had to get you out of Dallas so we could move you quietly and safely. All your things have been packed and are being flown to Langley for storage. Your mother has been advised that you have been called back to active duty. That's all she knows."

"But Gentlemen, there is something else," said Ted.

"Gentlemen if I may," interrupted a voice from across the table. "Commander Barrett, my name is Daniel Macaphee. I am the Director of the FBI." Macaphee was not a tall man, but he was nice looking and extremely well groomed in his tan slacks and a darker brown coat. Ted thought he looked too young to be the Director of the FBI.

The old saying rang out in Ted's mind: *not "what," you know; but "who," you know*....

"Yes, sir, Mister Macaphee, I recognized you," said Ted.

The director continued, "Gentlemen, I am sure Mister Barrett, excuse me, I mean Commander Barrett, would like to inquire about how this news will reach his lady friend."

"I sure as hell do!" exclaimed Ted.

Director Macaphee reached in his briefcase and produced a large manila file. "That would be a Miss Perez? Miss Lili Perez?" he asked opening the file.

"Yes," said Ted. "We have talked about getting married maybe later this year."

"I'm sorry Commander," said Macaphee. "Miss Perez cannot be privy to any of this."

"Why? Why the hell not?" Ted urgently asked. "I can't just up and leave her. No explanation, no goodbye, no nothing!"

"I'm sorry Commander," that's the way it has to be," said the FBI Director.

"Why?"

"I think I can answer that if I may," spoke up Payton. "Commander our sources tell us there is more than a good chance the Communists know about you and have already placed a price on your head, a bounty, maybe as much as a million dollars in their money."

"What?"

"Let me finish sir," said Payton. "The Seminole translator we had in Saigon, Sergeant Osceola, we think was taken out by a hidden sniper. We don't know if it was a clean kill or if the Sergeant was merely wounded; we never found his body. If he was wounded, he might have been captured and tortured for the Seminole codes. So there is a better than even chance the enemy knows about you."

"That's bullshit," said Ted.

"Bullshit?" asked the Marine General, his eyes popping wide open over his granny glasses.

"Yes, General, that's bullshit and I can tell you why. To begin with, even with a severe wound Osceola would have made it to cover and trust me, sir Davy Crockett and Daniel Boone together could never find a Seminole Indian in that jungle. They are like ghosts, they just fade into nothing. I have seen it too many times."

"And?" said an Army General.

"And gentlemen, all the torture in the world would never break a Seminole. Now what about Lili?"

"We are going to extract Miss Perez," said the FBI Director.

"Extract? Just what the hell does that mean? Extract?"

"That's the ear friendly word again Commander," said Commandant Sellers. "The CIA and the FBI like to use the word extract, which really means relocate." Ted detected a hint of animosity between the two agencies.

"Extract? Relocate?" exclaimed Ted. "Move her how? Where? She will never go and besides, why would you want to?"

"Commander," said the admiral, running out of patience, "we wouldn't do it unless absolutely necessary. We are afraid if Miss Perez knew anything about this or your whereabouts, her safety might be challenged. The enemy would use her to get to you, and of course, your mission compromised. Simply put, we can't afford to run that risk."

"Yes sir," Ted said quietly thinking of Lili's safety.

"Don't worry son, the FBI, and the CIA are teaming together to work out a coordinated arrangement to have your Miss Perez safely relocated. She will never know anything about it."

"Yes sir," Ted mouthed, but no sound came from his lips.

The admiral pushed a button under his desk and four Marines immaculately clad in fatigues, entered the room and stood at attention. "Commander Barrett these gentlemen are your escorts. Two of them will be with you 24 hours a day constantly. No matter where you go, or what you do, there will always be a least two of these Marines with you. They are for your protection. We can't afford to lose you. That's why we had to exercise so much secrecy moving you."

In the real world, they are called bodyguards, thought Ted.

"Gentlemen," spoke the admiral, "is there anything else?"

"Yes, Admiral," said Ted, "just one thing."

"Of course, what is it, Commander?"

"Sir," said Ted, addressing the admiral, "may I have a moment with Director Macaphee?"

"Certainly Commander please go ahead."

"I would like to speak with Director Macaphee in private sir," said Ted.

An icy hush settled in the room. "Commander Barrett that would be highly unusual; this meeting is of the highest priority and extremely top secret. Everyone here is privy to whatever you might have to say," said the admiral.

"Sir," said Ted, "what I have to say to the director is of a personal nature and nothing to do with this mission."

Admiral Petersen seemed to think over Ted's request for a long time. "Very well," he said. "You two may retire to the conference room over there." He pointed to a small room on the side of the area. "Please be brief Commander."

"Yes sir."

Once inside the conference room, Ted said, "I don't know how I am supposed to address you, Mister Director?"

"Why don't you try Dan?" said Macaphee.

"Good," said Ted. "Dan, in Dallas I have in my apartment a small mahogany box about so big," he indicated with his hands.

"A box?" shrugged the FBI Director?

"Yes, a box, Dan. I need a favor."

"Sure."

"I know your guys and probably the CIA too, are going through my place. Would you please get custody of that box and keep it for me somewhere that it is absolutely safe?"

"Glad to Commander." said Macaphee. "What's in it?"

"Sorry Dan. Can we just leave it at that? It has nothing to do with any of you or the integrity of this mission."

Macaphee said, "Fine by me we will do it your way. Must be something valuable though?"

"Totally worthless to you," said Ted, "but to someone else it could not be bought with all the gold in Fort Knox."

"Okay, Commander, I'll get it for you. If it makes you feel any better, I will lock it in the security vault at FBI headquarters. Only a couple others and I have excess to the vault. We are the only ones ever allowed in there."

The two made their way back to the large table and the waiting officers. Admiral Petersen gave Ted an acerbic look. "All right gentlemen, if there is nothing else."

No one moved or spoke.

"Very well," said Admiral Petersen, looking at Ted he said, "you may be gone just a few days or it could be a bit longer. No one knows for sure. Your code name for this operation is Ooki Nakni."

Ha! How appropriate...? "Swamp man," or "Water Man," depending on how you said it. I guess Ooki Coacoochee, "Swamp Panther," was a little too tough for them. That's okay, Goose will know....

Admiral Petersen leaned back in his chair. "If there is nothing further Commander you are dismissed. You will wait in your quarters here until the president approves your orders, which should be within the hour. A helicopter is standing by to take you to Andrews Air Force Base, in Washington. From there you will proceed accordingly, pursuant to the directions in your orders. That is all."

Admiral Petersen gave Ted a sad smile. "Good luck son and God be with you."

Ted saluted, turned an about face and headed for the large oak doors, his Marine escort in tow.

CHAPTER EIGHTEEN

L ili was excited. In fact, she was ecstatic, as she steered Ted's Volvo off Austin's I-35 at Exit 238A. She negotiated the confusing labyrinth of the highway cloverleaf and headed north on Barton Springs Road. At Lamar Boulevard, she turned north. She drove past the Governor's Mansion and found herself on San Jacinto Avenue, and soon at the Convention Center.

Lili parked the Volvo in the guest arrival area where Ted would be sure to see her. She loosened the top button of her blouse and pulled down the vee as far as she dared exposing as much cleavage as possible. *Teddy Bare would like that.*

If papa could see this, he really would have a cow!

She knew that it was hardly necessary because it seemed to her that Ted was in a constant state of arousal anyway. He never needed any encouragement. Lili often teased him saying he popped up like a Jack-in-the-Box.

She was on time. Where was Ted?

These lawyers, she thought, *they are worse than a gaggle of old women... talk, talk, talk....* Lili waited. Soon it was 12:30 and still no Ted.

Come on Teddy Bare, I want to see you so much....
Quiero ver usted tanto!

Lili had seen a very neatly dressed woman sitting on a guest bench just outside the center's lobby doors. She appeared to be engrossed in the *Austin American Statesman*, the morning newspaper, but Lili had noticed that she seemed to be looking at her more than she looked at the paper. The woman stood up and started walking toward her. Lili quickly buttoned the top of her shirt. The woman was dressed in a dark red business suit, with a white blouse, and matching dark red shoes approached the car. "Miss Perez?"

"Yes?" said Lili in surprise.

"Mister Barrett has left."

"Where did he go? We are supposed to ride back to Dallas together. Where is he?"

"I'm sorry ma'am, I don't know," said the woman truthfully.

Lili looked at her lap. That's impossible.... He would never do that....

"How did you know my name," she asked looking up.

There was no reply. The woman was gone.

How could that be?

Lili checked everywhere. Even the hotel manager had said, "Sorry ma'am, but we have no record of a Mister Ted Barrett. He didn't check in here."

"That's impossible!" she exclaimed. "I dropped him off myself two days ago, on Friday."

"I'm sorry ma'am."

There was only one thing left to do. Drive back to Dallas and find him. He will be home, or at the DA's Office. Somebody will know where Ted is. Maybe there was an

125

emergency? Maybe his mother? Did he go to Florida? No, he would have gotten word to her somehow.

He wouldn't do this to me—never...! Never in a million years.... Am I going crazy...? Muy loco?

Lili drove back to I-35. Ignoring the speed limits, she accelerated toward Dallas. I-35 was adorned with acres of Pecan orchids. The Interstate was lined with beautiful Red and Gold Sweetgum trees, festooned with Texas Bluebonnets and a kaleidoscope of wild flowers. Lili didn't notice. Her mind was in a hypnotic state, she could think of nothing except Ted.

Arriving in Dallas, she drove straight to Ted's apartment, the haven they had shared together. Bounding up the steps two at a time, she tried the door. It was locked.

That's okay I have my key.

The key didn't fit; the door lock had been changed. From the apartment's balcony, she tried to see inside though the sliding glass door. The same glass door that she and Ted had spent so much time together sitting on the sofa holding each other and gazing out at the small creek running behind the apartment building. Sometimes they sat and watched the moon, sometimes the rain.

The drapes had been pulled closed. *We never closed those drapes except at bedtime—wait a minute.... Those aren't our drapes—those drapes are new!*

Lili was sitting at the bottom of the steps sobbing wondering what is happening to my life. Has the whole world gone crazy? Has my whole life been turned up-side-down over the week-end? *Muy Loco?*

"What's the matter, little Missy?" ask a deep voice from behind her.

"Oh Mister Crozier, you startled me," she said to the apartment handyman, Pete Crozier. He was a rather distinctive man dressed in paint-streaked coveralls and his standard white tee shirt.

Pushing back his straw hat, he said, "I'm sorry little lady, I didn't mean to come up on you like that. I didn't see you until just now."

"Oh Mister Crozier, I am so glad you are here. I was looking for Ted. Have you seen him?"

"No ma'am, kain't says that I have. But there is something mighty, mighty strange going on though."

"What, Mister Crozier? Please tell me, please."

"Well," he drawled, "come the other night an eighteen wheeler pulls up right over yonder." Crozier pointed with the handle of the paint brush he was carrying. It was bout three or four in the morning. The only reason I know is cuz I heard them air brakes come on. Woke me up. I didn't think he was gonna make it there in the driveway but he did. Pretty tight fit it was."

"Why? Why was there an eighteen wheeler here?" Lili asked.

"Kain't say little Missy. All I know is they went into yawl's place there and loaded up everything. Must've been a hun'ert of um. Didn't take more than a few minutes and man, they was out of here."

"When did all this happen?"

"Well like I said, ma'am; it was Saturday real early, long about three or four in the morning."

"And that is all you know?"

"Yes ma'am, cept that same morning, Saturday, when this feller comes up there to the office," said Crozier, again pointing with the handle of the paintbrush. "He was all nip and tuck in a big fancy suit saying Mister Barrett wanted to extend his lease fer a year."

"For a year?" quizzed Lili.

"Yep for a whole year, paid cash for the whole year he did, all in hun'ert dollar bills."

"Mister Crozier would you let me inside please?"

"Nope fraid I kain't do that little Missy. Same feller told me that no one was to be allowed inside. They changed the locks, the door and deadbolt both. They even took the keys."

"Oh no, I can't believe this." Lili began to cry.

Lili knew Crozier liked her. She had seen him watching her as she moved about the apartment grounds. She looked at him with her beautiful face; still sobbing she said, "Oh dear Mister Crozier, what I am going to do? I had clothes and lots of things in there."

"Tell you what little Missy. Can you keep a secret?"

"Sure."

"I kept a spare key. You know, what if the place caught on faar, or a busted water pipe or sumthin' like-at? I would need to get in to fix things wouldn't I?"

"Of course," Lili nodded.

"Tell you what little Missy, why don't me and you go upstairs and check on them water pipes?"

"Oh Mister Crozier, would you?"

"Sure. Come on."

Once inside the empty apartment she could smell the fresh paint. The whole apartment had been painted. Nothing looked the same to Lili. The carpet had been replaced; the drapes and curtains were not what they had left on Friday.

The place was spotless. Not so much as a fingerprint remained anywhere.

As Lili looked around her mind was flooded with memories. It was here she thought.

It was right here in this apartment that I found so much joy. I found true love with the man of my dreams. I was able to sleep the whole night through when I was with him. Even the storms didn't bother me when I was in his arms.

She looked into the bedroom.

In here is where I spent the first night of my life with a man. We shared everything. I shared my virginity with him————in here.

Lili's eyes flooded with tears.

What's happening? Make everything all right again— you always did.... Come get me.... Come get me now, Teddy Bare.

CHAPTER NINETEEN

Ted relaxed in his seat as the Air Force C-141 Starlifter eased off Andrews Air Force Base Runway One-Nine Right. He sat back and closed his eyes. He finally had been able to comprehend some of the things that had happened to him in the past twenty-four hours. He was bone-tired. Ted hadn't slept in what felt like years. Everything seemed like a blitz.

"Commander, before you nod off sir," said a handsome Air Force Steward. "What can we serve you when you wake?"

Ted glanced at the menu in the pocket of the seat in front of him. "The steak and eggs sure sounds good."

"Yes sir, it will be ready whenever you want it, sir."

The Steward was walking away when Ted said. "Say Corporal, you folks in the Air Force ever heard of grits?"

"Yes sir, of course, sir. I'm from South Carolina and the aircraft commander up there is an Alabama boy. Why he'd have me shot if I didn't stock up on grits."

Ted smiled.

"I'll make sure they are on your tray, Commander."

"Good, I'll take it now please," Ted said and thanked him.

"Yes sir, medium rare on the steak, sir?"

Ted bobbed his head saying yes without using words.

They even know how I like my steak....

A whole Air Force Transport for just a handful of us...? Menus—Steak and eggs—Grits. Why did I go in the Navy?

The food was excellent. Ted had forgotten how hungry he was. He ate the meal then nodded off into some much needed sleep.

Lili, I miss you so much.

We've been apart for just a few hours but it seems like forever.... I have to reach you but I can't.... I can't take a chance on someone trying to get to me through you. Director Payton was right. You cannot know anything about this.... I love you so much.

The jarring of the transport's wheels hitting the concrete runway jolted Ted awake. "Where are we?" he asked sleepily.

"Guam sir," said the Air Force Steward.

"Guam?" Ted asked. "Jeez, Sacramento, Hawaii, now Guam, what's next, the South Pole?"

"Yes sir, Guam. Andersen Air Force Base. It's a quick stop for fuel."

The aircraft commander appeared. Ted could see on his flight suit that he was a full colonel. "Commander, I'm Colonel Byrd."

What an appropriate name.

"It is regulation that we always deplane when taking on fuel. However, our orders are that you must stay on board, so we've had to leave you here during all three stops." Ted

131

shrugged and nodded. "We will be back in the air in less than an hour," said the colonel.

Ted bobbed his head but said nothing.

Soon the huge transport was back in flight. Ted was dozing off to sleep again. As always, the thoughts of Lili danced in his head. He was smiling thinking of his Mexican beauty when he felt himself being shaken awake. "Commander," someone said. He had heard the voice before.

"What?" he said sitting up. "Oh! My old friend, ONI Special Agent Major Douglas Lynn what a nice surprise," Ted said facetiously. Ted noted the major had no more, or less of a sense of humor than he did in Austin.

Lynn, I bet you are always the life of the party.

"Please sit up Commander, we are only an hour or so out and I have to brief you."

"Where did you come from? I didn't see you at Andrews?"

"No sir, I got on at Andersen. For security reasons they didn't want us riding together." Ted nodded.

"Okay sir, your name is Michael Fletcher," Lynn continued. "You are a registered nurse assigned to the Red Cross in Saigon. You will be working out of the American Embassy."

"A nurse? Major, I don't know the difference between an enema nozzle and an ass thermometer."

"Don't worry sir; you won't have to do any nursing. You will be working in the embassy. The staff has been alerted. They don't know exactly what you are to do, neither do I for that matter, but you are relieved of any nursing duties except, of course, emptying and washing a few bedpans." Lynn's lips parted with the slightest hint of a smile.

Major Lynn, you son-of-a-bitch, you do have a sense of humor buried in there. You would like nothing better than to see me scrubbing bedpans.

"Your status as a nurse is strictly a cover Commander. Here are your credentials, photo ID, wallet, pictures, everything," he said as he handed Ted a plastic zip bag. "Here are your nurse clothes. You will have to change before we land."

"What about my Marine quartet over there?" Ted asked.

"They will never be very far away from you, sir. They will be changing too."

The airplane touched down on the Saigon runway.

CHAPTER TWENTY

L ili was frantic. She searched all over Dallas for anyone who might have any knowledge about Ted. She called his mother only to have her calls re-routed and a strange recorded voice telling her that number was not available. She went to the police, the sheriff, the FBI; no one knew anything. She waited in the District Attorney's parking lot for Ray Scott. He was not hard to find because usually he was dressed like a float in the Easter Parade.

"Scottie, you have to tell me," she begged. "I'm going crazy not knowing. I don't know anything! It's been almost two months now and I'm losing my mind. I love him so much, Scottie, and...."

"Lili, I swear we don't know a thing," said Ray Scott looking into her elegant face. "Mister Barrett just disappeared. Even old man Hendry doesn't know where he is. It's got us all baffled. When we came to work that Monday, a month or so ago, his office was completely cleaned out. No papers, no files, that picture of you he liked so much, gone. Everything is gone. Nothing."

By summer Lili's family was starting to worry about her. Finally, her sister, Gabriella, came to Dallas. Sitting in Lili's little apartment she was stunned at how gaunt Lili looked and the amount of weight she had lost.

"Lili, you have to come home with me to San Antonio. There is nothing for you here."

"Gabbie, I can't leave," exclaimed Lili. "When Ted comes back he will be looking for me. What if he can't find me?"

"Sister it's time for you to face the cold hard truth," Gabriella said. "Your Ted has obviously found someone else and, Lili, he's not coming back. He is a serpiente."

"No! My Ted is not a snake. He loves me and he will be back," insisted Lili. "I will never, ever leave him."

Lili thought some things through during the next week and eventually did succumb to the idea that maybe it would do her well to be back among family and friends. She reluctantly agreed to move to San Antonio under the stern condition that she would continue to search for Ted.

While Lili was packing her things for the move, she went into her closet for her most valued possession. She got on her footstool, reached to the top shelf of her closet, and brought down a large photo album. "Look Gabbie, here's some pictures of Ted and me. See? You go ahead and look at them. I'll get us something to drink. Be right back."

Gabriella began thumbing through the album. "Lili," she called. "What did you want me to see?"

"Pictures you silly," said Lili coming back in the room carrying two glasses. "See there's some of Ted and me skiing and playing in the snow in Aspen last winter, of us at Lake Dallas in Sammy's boat, at the mayor's barbeque, the office Christmas party, lots of things Gabbie."

"Where?" Gabriella asked. "There is nothing here."

Lili tore the album from Gabriella's hands. There were no photos of Ted. Everything had been removed.

Lili moved back to San Antonio and easily found work as a freelance accountant. She settled into a comfortable apartment but refused date or have any social life. It was not because she wasn't asked often enough; she simply did not want to go anywhere without Ted.

Lili was devastated. She cried for days and days, and weeks, and months. Without Ted beside her, the sleeplessness returned. She did not feel as if she had any reason to go on living. Without him, her world had ended. Her depression grew. Ted was her universe, her life-line, her standard bearer, her security, the love of her life, her first everything. She never got over him, she never stopped longing for him and she never stopped loving him. She would love him until the day she died.

Lili's parents, Miguel and Rosie Perez, grew considerably more apprehensive and worried about her. It was Gabriella who stepped in to help.

"Sister," she said softly to Lili, "things are just not right with you. You don't eat, you don't sleep. You were always so peppy and full of energy, now you seem so despondent, like you're at a funeral or something."

"Si, a mortuorio, my own," sighed, Lili.

"Lili, here is someone I want you to see," said Gabriella handing Lili a business card.

"Him?" Gabbie, "you are not serious are you? He's been retired for years."

"Even so sister," said Gabriella, "if your name is Perez he will see you. Here is his number he is expecting you to call."

Lili made the call and a few days later, she was sitting on the porch at the home of her childhood pediatrician, Doctor Ramon Gomez.

"Chica, I have known you since the day you were born. I have treated you, your brothers and sister your whole lives. I can tell when something is troubling you. So what is on your mind little Amando?"

"Doctor Gomez, what I have to tell you has to remain in the strictest of confidence. My papa must never know."

"Of course Lili, the Hippocratic Oath is still alive and well, even in Texas," he smiled. "How can I help you?— Co'mo puedo ayudarle?"

Lili related the entire story of her relationship with Ted to the doctor leaving out nothing. If Doctor Gomez was surprised or shocked, he didn't show it.

"Doctor Gomez, I love him so much and I know he loves me."

"Lili," said the kindly old doctor, "always before when you had a problem I could reach for my prescription pad and fix it, but these problems are emotional and considerably out of my league. I know someone I want you to see. I will make a call."

A few days later Lili arrived at the office of Doctor Nicole Larson, a psychologist. Doctor Larson showed her into a tastefully decorated room that didn't look anything like Lili had expected. Instead of the proverbial couch was a brown leather La-Z-Boy recliner, soft lights and a coffee table. Across from her chair was a console adorned with nick-knacks and two framed photographs. One was of an elderly couple and Doctor Larson looking out over an ocean; the other showed her with a handsome man in an airline pilot's uniform. On the wall was an oil painting of a beautiful valley. A creek with a voluminous field of flowers blooming on each side ran in front of snow-capped mountains. The mixture of the blues, greens, browns, oranges and many other colors the artist created was eye catching and beautiful to Lili.

In the corner of the office rested a well-worn tennis racquet and a gym bag.

Doctor Larson was a surprise to Lili as well. She was very attractive with a cute button down figure. She was bright and witty and seemed to be full of life. *Most likely in her mid-thirties,* Lili thought. Her light brown hair was fashionably treated with blond streaks. Lili admired her style, but was a little taken by her casual appearance. She was wearing chic white slacks and a pair of low cut tennis shoes, no socks and an orange University of Texas sweater, which read: "Hook-Um Horns." It was obvious Doctor Larson was athletic.

Doctor Larson motioned for her to take a seat. Looking at Lili, she thought:

She has got to be the most beautiful woman on the planet.

"Doctor Larson, I...."

"Let me stop you right there, Lili," she broke in. "My name is Nicole. There is no doctor-patient atmosphere in here. I don't work that way."

"Um okay," Lili quietly said.

"I have a lot of respect for Doctor Gomez," she continued. "He is very fond of you and your family. He spoke highly of you."

"And of you as well," replied Lili, glancing at the photo of Doctor Larson and the handsome pilot.

"His name was Gene, or guess I should say, his name is Gene. He dumped my ass back when I was in graduate school at UT," said the doctor reading Lili's thoughts. "I even stopped studying for my PhD for a while just to be with him and he still dumped me." He used to insist I go on his motorcycle with him. I never did. I hate those damn things."

"Motorcycles?"

"Yes. Motorcycles, bikes, hogs, whatever they call them. Damn things scare me to death."

Lili liked Nicole's directness. Nicole was one of those rare people who could use peppered language without it sounding offensive.

She's been hurt too — maybe, she understands how I feel.

"You still keep his picture?" asked Lili with her eyes.

Reading her thoughts Nicole said, "I keep that picture around just to remind myself of how much I don't miss the son-of-a-bitch. But I know all about me, let's talk about you."

CHAPTER TWENTY-ONE

Nurse Michael Fletcher strode into the American Embassy in Saigon. A Marine clad in dress blues stood, took his papers in his white-gloved hands, and said. "Welcome to the Saigon Embassy, Mister Fletcher, are these other gentlemen with you?" he asked indicating the four trailing Marines.

"Yes Sergeant, I am an R.N. these gentlemen are CNA's."

"CNA's, Mister Fletcher?"

"Yes, Certified Nursing Assistants, Sergeant."

"I'll take it from here," said a neatly dressed man approaching them. The sergeant shrugged with a look that said, "If you say so."

"Gentlemen, my name is Henry Carson, please follow me to the Infirmary. Thank you, Sergeant," he said, waving to the Marine.

The sergeant turned and whispered to the other Marine manning the front desk. "CNAs my ass. Those guys look like the starting linebackers for the Green Bay Packers."

Henry Carson led Ted down a narrow hall and into a makeshift infirmary. Behind a discreet door at the rear of the infirmary was a small two-person elevator. "Gentlemen," said Carson, "we need to go down to the basement. After you, Mister Fletcher."

One of the Marines took a step forward. "I'm sorry, Mister Carson, Nurse Fletcher is not to leave my sight."

"But we are in the American Embassy, and…."

"I'm sorry sir. No exceptions."

Carson could see arguing would be useless. He stepped aside and said, "Of course after you, Mister Fletcher. Please send the car back up for the rest of us." The Marine got on the elevator with Ted.

I've seen that guy before, thought Ted, eyeing Carson.

The elevator car bumped to a stop and the doors rattled open. "Just a minute sir, then follow me," said the Marine.

"Roger."

"Commander Barrett," said a man approaching with his hand extended. "I'm Clayton Grant, CIA."

Ted shook the man's hand. "Yes, I remember you. I saw you in the War Room during my briefing." Then it dawned on him, the other man, Carson, he was there too. Just then, the elevator arrived with the others.

"Mister Fletcher, this is Henry Carson, with the FBI," said Grant.

Ted nodded. "We have met. Yes, Mister Carson, I remember you too."

"Okay," said Grant, if you will come this way I'll…."

"Hold it!" exclaimed the Marine, placing his hand inside his coat where Ted knew there was a sidearm. "I don't want to be rude gentlemen, but may we see some credentials?"

141

"Of course," said Carson. Both Grant and Carson identified themselves then led them to a small room in the rear of the embassy basement. Inside was an array of radio equipment. "This one is yours Mister Fletcher," said Grant. "It is all set up on a special UHF military frequency."

"No time like the present," said Ted. He put on the headset and keyed the microphone. "Chobee-who-non-wah, this is Ooki Nakni listening."

The response came right away in perfect Seminole. "Ooki Nakni, we thought you had forgotten us." Ted knew Major Wildgoose's voice instantly.

"Never," said Ted. "We had a bit of difficulty. Your contact here has been compromised. I just got here this morning."

"Yeah, I recognized your voice. Sorry about the contact. He is a good man, sure hate to lose him."

"We hate to lose anybody," Ted said quietly, still speaking in Seminole.

"Ooki Nakni, do you remember when we used to skip school and go swimming bare-ass down there, on the south side of that old dirt road, at Gator Slough?"

"Yeah, I remember."

"Wonder what ever happened to Frank's little brother?"

"Frank?"

"Yep, he had a little brother. Last I heard he teamed up with Mary's husband and took to robbing banks out by the Big Mo somewhere."

"Frank?" A confused Ted asked again.

"No, Ooki Nakni, not Frank, his little brother—the little brother," he emphasized. "He was living outside St. Cloud. Frank told me that he went into the service."

"The Cong are probably listening," said Ted.

"So, let um listen," Wildgoose continued in Seminole. "We call them Charlie. I kinda figured they would send you."

"Why?"

"Who else?"

"What do you have for me, Chobee-Who-Non-Wah?"

Major Wildgoose had invaluable information and lots of it. "We have been tracking the whole damn North Vietnamese Army for months. You will find them heading south in Grid Area Sixteen."

"Number?" Ted asked.

"Near as we can tell probably 45,000 or more strong, but here is something you have to know."

"Go," said Ted, "I can copy."

"Their fuel dumps are in Toi Ping, just east of Grid Area Sixteen. They've got it camouflaged. From the air, it looks like more of the jungle, just like flying over broccoli. Tell our air boys to lay their eggs just north of the village; they can't miss it."

"Roger, got it," said Ted.

Wildgoose said, "Guess I'd better sign off now, I gotta save my batteries. I don't want to give Charlie time to get an ADF fix on me with this radio going. Make sure and get this info to the Ho Tah Lee."

Ted sat back in his chair chuckling. "What's so funny?" asked Agent Grant.

"Wildgoose just called the president, 'The Big Windbag.'"

"Roger that, Chobee-Who-Non-Wah, are you guys able to maintain your cover?"

"Are you kidding?" said Wildgoose. "These idiots couldn't find their own ass with both elbows and a radar compass. I got one of my guys sitting in their camp right now, not eight feet from their chow table. They will never spot him."

"Roger that, Chobee-Who-Non-Wah. I will be on this frequency at eighteen minutes past every third odd hour, but someone will be monitoring it around the clock."

"Roger. Pleasant memories. Chobee-Who-Non-Wah clear."

"Same here. Ooki Nakni clear," said Ted.

Has Goose gone nuts…? Frank? Frank who…? Who the hell is Frank? Maybe surviving in that jungle swamp could make a man loony—no, not Wildgoose.

He's trying to tell me something and he doesn't want anyone to see it translated. But what…?

CHAPTER TWENTY-TWO

A s the weeks melted into months, winter came and went. As the first hints of spring appeared Lili, found herself becoming more and more attached to Doctor Nicole Larson. Likewise, Doctor Larson was very fond of Lili, but still she kept things at a professional distance. They played tennis together, rode their bicycles, and often had lunch at San Antonio's River Walk, but she never mixed any business during their outings. Nicole was beginning to wonder if she would ever break through Lili's uncompromising and stubborn resistance to facing the truth about Ted. He had dumped her. Simple as that, and he didn't have the guts to confront her. Lili's love for Ted was unyielding and unshakable.

Lili's respect for Nicole grew. She found that her doctor was a fierce competitor on the tennis courts and a warm compassionate person on the inside. Lili trusted Nicole, but she would never give up her belief in Ted, no matter how deep their sessions would get, she would say: "He will come for me; he will come someday soon. I know he will. I will never stop loving him. He loves me. He loves me like no other."

The warm days of early summer were cloaking San Antonio. Sometimes there would be a light breeze and cooler cloudy days but for the most part it was just plain hot. Nicole called Lili. "Oh Lili, I'm so excited, I have something perfect for you!"

"What?"

"I don't want to talk about it over the telephone. Can you come by my office later?"

"Sure," said Lili. "How about five or so? I can stop on my way home."

"Great," said Nicole, "see you then."

"K," said Lili.

What can she want that's so important? It's not like Nicole to get all excited.... Hope it's not another man she wants me to meet.... If it's not Ted, I'm not interested.

"Lili come in, come in," exclaimed Nicole.

"Nikki, what's so blamed important?"

"Oh Lili, I have the perfect thing for you. My cousin works in the U.S. Embassy in San Jose and...."

"San Jose, Costa Rica?"

"Yes, now listen. I was talking with him this morning and he said they need a Spanish speaking accountant-bookkeeper, to audit things for the State Department. The person they had got married and moved away. Lili, this is perfect for you."

"Move to Costa Rica? That's insane!" said Lili. "That far away from my family and San Antonio? Ted would never think to look for me in Costa Rica."

"Lili," Nicole sighed, "this is a change you need. A new place, new job, different friends; it would be great for you. You have the education and you have the language skills. What are you waiting for, girl?"

"But it's so far away."

"Lili, San Jose is a little over three hours from Houston and there are several flights that go there every day. It would take you more than two hours just to drive to Houston."

"It's worth thinking about. Let me talk to my sister. Mama and papa would never understand but maybe Gabbie would."

Lili did talk it over with Gabriella and her parents too. Oddly enough no one seemed to put up much resistance, except the predictable Papa Perez. She stopped by to see Doctor Gomez.

"Little Chiquita this might be just what you need," said the kindly old physician. "A change in your life would probably be most welcome. You are young, try it. There is no rule that says you can't come back."

Lili thought, *Maybe a change is exactly what I need. Maybe the embassy can help me find him. We can be together again—I'll be back in the arms of my Teddy Bare— then I can sleep again.*

She picked up the telephone. "Hello Nikki, I have decided to do it."

"Oh Lili, that's wonderful!" Nicole exclaimed. "I'll call my cousin and tell him you are going to take the job. You can say goodbye to everyone here and I will drive you to the airport in Houston."

The documents for Lili's new venture were completed quickly, cutting through the usual tangle of government paperwork with blazing speed. In a few days she was waving goodbye from the jet-way to her dear friend Nicole. Nicole was smiling bravely as was Lili, but what she didn't see were the tears streaming down Lili's face when she entered the airplane.

Ted will find me.... I know he will. I know he loves me.

As always, everyone starred at her beauty. As usual, Lili was oblivious to their attentions.

On the drive back to San Antonio, Nicole was feeling blue. Lili had turned out to be such a good friend. Nicole knew she was going to miss her tennis partner, the bicycle rides and the lunches together. However, she knew moving to Costa Rica was best for Lili.

Nicole could always make the guys look twice. She was attractive and slim, but nothing like when she was with Lili. It seemed everyone gawked and the earth stopped turning when Lili appeared. "I'm going to miss her," she said aloud.

I should have never gotten so close.... It's not professional.... In my line of work I can't be friends, I cannot be close to anyone.... No exceptions—but, Lili was so special.... It was my fault.... I should have never allowed it.... It's just not professional.

Nicole parked in the driveway beside her office. Once inside she went to a closet and dialed the combination to a hidden wall safe. Opening the safe she took out an aluminum case. It was a telephone. A different kind of telephone.

She pushed 'ACT,' for activate, there was no ring nor did any voice respond, just a series of clicks and beeps. When the phone fell silent she said," Foxtrot, Tango, Juliet, niner, eight, four, three."

"Payton," said a gruff voice.

"It is done," she said.

The line went dead.

Nicole waited a few seconds and a tape the size of grocery store receipt ticked out from the bottom of the phone. She read:

REPORT LANGLEY THIS DATE—FURTHER BRIEFING--NXT ASSIGN SALT LAKE CITY— READ AND DESTROY.

In Langley, Virginia, Director Payton dialed the phone. "Hello, Baxter, it's done."

Both men hung up.

CHAPTER TWENTY-THREE

Ted leaned back in his chair. He was deep in thought.

"Is everything okay Commander?" asked Grant.

"I think so. It's been a long couple days, you know?"

"Sure has been. A couple of long days for us all."

Still sitting, Ted leaned toward the young Marine nearby. "What's your name, Corporal?"

"Culpepper sir, Corporal Culpepper."

"What's your first name?"

"Theodore sir."

"That's a good name Corporal. I bet your Dad calls you Ted and your mother calls you Teddy."

"Ah sir, yes sir," replied the corporal.

"Somehow I knew that," smiled Ted. "Corporal Culpepper, how long have you been in the service?"

Corporal Culpepper came to attention. "With all due respect to the commander sir, I am not in a service."

"You're not?"

"With all due respect to the commander sir, I am not in a service. I am a United States Marine, sir."

"I see," said Ted. "Then once you get out you will be an ex-Marine?"

"Sir, with all due respect to the commander..."

"You don't have to keep saying that Culpepper."

"Yes sir, begging the commander's pardon sir, once you are a Marine, you are always a Marine. No such thing as an ex-Marine, sir."

"Thank you, Corporal Culpepper. Stand easy."

The Corporal relaxed a bit. "Aye, aye sir."

Ted thought: *You have to hand it to the Marines.... They certainly are a dedicated lot. Wildgoose is a Marine but he had said "service...?" A Marine would never say that.... To a Marine it is always, "The Corps." So what was Goose trying to tell me...?*

"Commander Barrett, I know you and your boys must be worn out. Let me show you to your quarters," said Agent Carson.

"Good idea," replied Ted. "I guess we could all use some shut-eye. At least we have made contact with the major."

Ted was pleasantly surprised with his quarters. There was a double bed looking very inviting. A full dresser and chest of drawers occupied one side of the room and a private bathroom on the other.

Nice, Ted mused. *But after all, it is the embassy.*

All his clothes had been placed in the dresser and his white nurse uniforms were neatly hung in the closet. Ted noticed his personal items in the bathroom had been arranged just as they had been at home in Dallas. On the side of the sink, just like always, was a jar of Lili's hand lotion.

Those folks at the CIA really do their homework.

Ted was dead tired. He didn't bother undressing. He peeled off his shirt, stepped out of his shoes and flopped on the bed but he couldn't sleep. He folded his hands behind his head and starred at the ceiling. The hum of the air conditioner droned.

What was Goose trying to tell me...? Frank...? Who the hell is Frank?

Ted got up from his bed and stretched.

Can't sleep anyway.

He walked down the hall, still in his tee shirt, to the radio room. Corporal Culpepper two steps behind.

In the radio room, Ted saw a Marine Gunnery Sergeant attending to the radios. "Hey Gunny, have the tapes from my transmission with Major Wildgoose been transcribed yet?"

"No sir, I don't believe they have," said the sergeant looking about the long table, but we have notified Washington and the Pentagon."

"I translated them and wrote everything down in longhand," said Ted.

"I have them," spoke up CIA Special Agent Grant.

"Good," Ted said. "Would you have them copied and sent to my room Gunny?"

The Sergeant gave a quizzical look at Grant, who nodded his approval and rolled his eyes.

"Yes sir," said the gunnery sergeant. "They will be ready for you in the morning at 0700, sir?"

"No. I want them now."

Again, the gunnery sergeant looked at Grant. Again, he nodded his approval. "We can do it for you now Commander," said Grant.

Ted left the radio room and got a few steps down the hall then stopped. Turning around he bumped into the ever-present Corporal Culpepper. They both excused themselves at the same time. Ted walked back to the radio room.

"Gunny."

"Sir?"

"How long have you been in the service," Ted asked?

The Sergeant stood. "Begging the commander's pardon sir, I am not in a service. I am a Gunnery Sergeant in the United States Marine Corps. To answer the commander's question sir, I have been in the Corps eighteen years."

Ted smiled to himself. "Thanks Gunny."

"Aye, aye sir."

Back in his room, Ted spread out the transcribed copies of his conversation with Major Wildgoose, which he had translated into English. With a yellow highlighter he marked: Frank, little brother, Mary, Mary's husband, Service, Big Mo, St. Cloud, Gator Slough, dirt road. Beside each one, he marked a large question mark.

What is Goose trying to tell me…? What is here that I'm not seeing…? Who is Frank…? Who is Little Brother…? Mary…? Mary's husband…? St Cloud…? St Cloud what…? Maybe Goose was getting mixed up…. Gator Slough where we all went skinny-dipping, was on the north side of a little dirt road—not on the south side like Goose had said—Goose would never have put things like that out over the radio unless he was trying to get a message to me…. Why not just say it in Seminole…? No, he was afraid someone here in the embassy would intercept his message and read the transcription…. It was for me only.

The following morning Ted was shown to a designated area for breakfast away from the general population of the embassy cafeteria. It was pleasant enough and the food was good. He could tell his two Marine escorts enjoyed it by the way they wolfed down the ham and eggs.

As they were leaving, Ted passed by the second security check point well inside the embassy lobby. He noticed a tired looking Army Sergeant at the security desk. The sleeve of his dress green uniform was abundantly adorned, indicating many years in the military. His chest was covered with medals and ribbons awarded to him in the service of his country.

"Sergeant Major, good morning."

"Good morning Mister Fletcher, did you Red Cross fellows sleep well?"

"Yes. Everything is fine Sergeant Major. Thank you," said Ted.

As Ted was walking away, he paused and said, "Sergeant Major how long have you been in the service?"

"Too long Mister Fletcher," the Sergeant Major laughed. "Twenty-eight years. I only got fourteen months to go to make my thirty, then I'm going fishing; I'll be out of here."

"Well good luck Sergeant Major, I wish you well," said Ted.

"Thanks Mister Fletcher, likewise to you."

Ted's mind was a maelstrom of activity. *The sergeant major had joked and talked about his time in the "service…" Marines never did that…. Marines were adamant about the Corps; "Semper Fi de Corps." Goose was talking about the Army not the Marine Corps. That's got to be it—but, what about all this other nonsense, Frank, whoever Frank is, Mary, husband, St. Cloud…? Little Brother…?*

Ted went back to the radio room and spread his notes, trying desperately decipher whatever message Goose was sending him. Addressing a young Air Force Airman he said, "Airman, are there maps of Vietnam here in the embassy?"

"Yes sir."

"Could you get them for me please?"

"Yes sir."

"Oh Airman, while you are at it, would you get an atlas of the United States as well?"

"Yes sir, I'm sure the ambassador has one in the library."

"Good. On the double if you please, Airman."

"Yes sir."

CIA Agent Grant said, "Commander, you have been here for hours. It is late. Wouldn't you like to hit the bunk for a while and get some shut-eye?"

"I will in a while Agent Grant. Right now I'm trying to figure out a few things."

Ted used a heavy black marker and copied the buzz words he had marked from his transcript of his conversation with Major Wildgoose. He pinned them on the bulletin board in front of the desk and was staring at the one marked "Big Mo," when the young airman spoke.

"Going to Missourah sir?" asked the young airman.

"Missouri?" said Ted, baffled.

"Yes sir, I'm from Missourah, and we always called the river, 'Big Mo.'"

"Big Mo?"

"Yes sir. Missourah is bordered by both big rivers. To the east, it's the Miss-ah-sip and on the west side, is the Missourah. We always called her, 'The Big Mo'. I was raised in a little town on the Big Mo."

"Where?" asked an astonished Ted.

"Right here, sir," he said, pointing with a pencil to a little spot on the map. "Little town called Fairfax sir, about thirty-five or forty miles north of St. Joe."

"St. Joe?" Ted asked.

"Yes sir, St. Joseph, Missourah," he said dragging the pencil down the river to St. Joseph. "Not much going on there. That's one of the reasons I joined the Air Force. I wanted to get away and see some of the world. Bout the only thing we're known for is Jesse James. You know the outlaw. He was from the St. Joe area. He lived there too."

Holy Moses! This young airman just stuck a needle in the puzzle balloon. Joseph! Saint Joseph was Mary's husband.... Mary, the mother of Jesus was married to Joseph! Goose wanted me to find St. Joseph, but why?

Wait a minute.... The James brothers, Frank and Jesse James robbed Union trains and banks right after the Civil War. Jesse was Frank's younger, "little," brother. Jesse James was driving the Union Forces crazy by robbing their payroll trains—this was right after the war and it is questionable if they knew the war had ended.

Thank you, Professor Madeline Vandergriff—without you, I would never have known how Jesse James aided the South by robbing Union trains....

Ted literally tore open the atlas and quickly found Florida.

I know there is a St. Cloud, Florida. But, where is it?

"I found it sir," said the young airman.

"Where," Ted demanded.

"Right here," he said, marking it with the same pencil, "Just a tad out of Orlando, in Osceola County."

"In what county?" Ted almost shouted.

"Osceola sir."

Goose, you son-of-a-bitch I got it! You were telling me Frank's little brother was Jesse.... Now you made me find Osceola County.... I got it—Jesse Osceola! He was in the Army, not the Marine Corps—that's why you said service.... You didn't say he "was" a good man; you said he "is" a good man. Jesse Osceola is alive!

CHAPTER TWENTY-FOUR

L ili loved Costa Rica from the moment she stepped off the airplane in San Jose. Her predilection of the Central American Country was proving true. The cool mountain air was refreshing compared to the sizzling hot breezes blowing across the Texas Hill Country. At home in San Antonio with its high density of Spanish speakers, being Hispanic could be a plus, but more often than not, a minus. Here, everyone was Hispanic. The Spanish language flowed from everywhere and was like a symphony to her ears.

Most of all she liked the laid-back traditions of the people. It was like stepping fifty years back in time. People were friendly as they spoke and waved their happy salutations. It seemed everyone greeted her with a smile. The locals did not seem as anxious as what she was used to in the States. Lili was certain she would fit in well in her newly adopted home.

One thing that never changed no matter where she was, people stared at her, especially the gentlemen. Some gentlemanly, some not so gentlemanly. It was a truth as old as the sea. It is called biology. Her natural beauty was overwhelming. People noticed her.

If only my Teddy Bare was here…. He would love Costa Rica too. I know he will find me. I know he will—I love him so much….

Costa Rica is where a mixture of Mesoamerican and South American cultures meet. It enjoys the luxury of two oceans, the Caribbean to the east and the Pacific on its western side. She is bordered by Nicaragua to its north and Panama to the south.

Christopher Columbus landed on Costa Rica's Caribbean coast near Limon in 1502, on his third and final voyage to the new world. The indigenous Indians gave him huge gifts of gold and silver—a big mistake.

In, *McTeague*, author Frank Norris creates a repugnant dentist named McTeague, whose gold imagery and lust for riches brings about his demise. McTeague does achieve great wealth, but shows the kind of personal doom one can face on account of greed. He finds that he has burglarized his freedoms and prostituted his values and integrity. He has riches but in the end, he finds himself handcuffed to a dead man in Death Valley, with miles of nothing in every direction except blistering hot sand and not a drop of water. All because of his overmastering craving for gold.

So, it was in Europe. The lust for gold and riches was akin to a giant magnet drawing European adventurers to the area in droves. They were met by inhospitable coastal swamps and hostile Indian tribes and they suffered great losses at the hands of the natives. Eventually, the persistence of the Spanish Conquerors, the Conquistadores, prevailed in the mid-1600s.

Lili had arrived in San Jose on a Wednesday and spent the rest of the week getting settled and acclimated to her new surroundings. She enjoyed her long walks drinking in the natural beauty of Costa Rica. She made a mental note to buy a bicycle as soon as she had steady money coming in again. She was going to be paid in American dollars, which would go much further here.

Lili had always kept plants in the apartment she shared with Ted. She loved them. The blooming wild orchids and the red and white petunias of Costa Rica enchanted her. Lili's eyes filled with the splendor of the mountain foliage, the crotons, the wild grapes, and so many others.

Costa Rica's degree of equanimity did not seem to be jeopardized with the crime and violence as its neighbors to the north. Lili loved it here but memories of Ted were always on her mind.

Lili reported on time to the American Embassy at Calle 120 Avenida Pavas, Monday morning. The embassy compound was beautifully landscaped and "Old Glory," the American flag, waved proudly from the flagpole. The embassy was tastefully furnished with red carpet lining the entrance hall surrounded by a white tile floor. The American eagle was prominently displayed on the center wall.

"Good morning Miss Perez," said a handsome Marine, in a dress blue uniform. "Please come with me. Mister Casers is expecting you," after examining her identification.

In an inner office, a man stood and walked around his desk. He was rather short, dressed in a crème colored suit with a dark maroon shirt and a suit-matching crème tie. "Miss Perez so nice to meet you, my name is Antonio

Casares." He was balding and his honey colored complexion looked to be of Latin descent.

"Nice to meet you too, Mister Casares. You are Nicole, ah, Doctor Larson's cousin?"

"Nicole?" He looked at her quizzically. "Oh yes, Nicole, Doctor Larson. She told me about you and she recommended you very highly."

"Thank you," said Lili. "I have tried to call her several times but I haven't heard back."

"I'm sure Nicole will get back to you. She stays pretty busy up there in Houston," said Casares.

"How are you two related?" asked Lili, not seeing the slightest hint of any family resemblance between Nicole and Casares.

"We're cousins, I was born in the D.R., the Dominican Republic, but I grew up in New York City."

"This is really strange," Lili said to herself.

"Nicole never mentioned her cousin was dark-skinned or from New York. Nicole was a farm girl from Iowa. Why did he say Houston? Didn't he know Nicole lived in San Antonio…?

Confused, Lili decided to try something. "Mister Casares, did Nicole always like to ride her motorcycle?"

"Boy, I'll say. She used to zoom all over the place on that thing. Come with me, I'll introduce you to Ambassador Thomas."

Something is very peculiar… thought Lili. *Nicole loathed motorcycles.*

Casares led her to the opposite end of the embassy. The entire side of the building was the ambassador's office. A large archway led through a reception room and into the main entrance of the office. The floor was covered by a powder-blue carpet with the Great Seal of the United States perfectly embroidered in gold. Lili knew the American Bald Eagle always faced to its left, toward the arrows, during times of war. In peace time, it faced the olive branches on its right side. A concept bantered back and forth by the Continental Congress in 1782, midway between the Declaration of Independence and the Constitution. Lili noted the Eagle's head facing right.

The ambassador's office was roomy and it was splendid. An American flag was hanging to the right of a large executive Cherry Wood desk and a State Department banner hung from the left. A sofa and several comfortable looking chairs were placed tactfully about the room. Books occupied the shelves. There were flowers, picked daily, in vases on both sides of the room.

"She hasn't come downstairs yet," said a matronly looking woman looking up from the reception desk.

"She?" asked Lili.

"Yes she," said a pleasant voice behind her. "Hi, I'm Julie Thomas and you must be Lili Perez. I am so pleased to meet you," she said extending her hand and waving off Casares, who was about to speak.

Lili turned and was looking at a slim, extremely pretty woman with dark Chestnut hair and crystal blue eyes.

"Yes ma'am, I'm Lili Perez. Are you, are the ambassador?"

"I think I am. At least that's what they keep telling me," laughed Ambassador Thomas. She shook Lili's hand and continued to hold it placing her left arm around Lili's shoulder. "Come on in, honey, and let's have some coffee and get acquainted. We have the best coffee in the world and it comes right from here in Costa Rica." Lili detected the ambassador's slight southern accent.

Lili felt at home instantly with the ambassador. She was immaculately dressed in a pink suit trimmed in black. She was wearing a hint of light pink lipstick and black heels. The ambassador did not sit behind her desk. Instead, she sat in a chair and motioned for Lili to do the same on the adjoining couch. Lili found her down to earth and a very likeable person, who laughed heartily and quickly. Lili guessed probably in her early forties.

Ambassadors are hand-picked and appointed by the president. Usually ambassadorships are handed out as rewards for political favors, but sometimes the right person is picked for the job. Lili felt it was certainly the latter in Julie Thomas' case.

The refreshments came right away. "What do you take in your coffee, Lili?"

"To tell you the truth Ms. Thomas, I don't drink coffee."

"What? You don't drink coffee. Well then, how about some tea?"

"That would be fine, thank you."

Ambassador Thomas made no motion nor did she indicate any signal to order tea, but in a matter of seconds, a young Costa Rican boy in a white waiter's coat appeared with a cup of hot water and a teabag.

The ambassador and Lili visited and chatted for over an hour. Lili liked the ambassador. She was smart and fun. "Ms. Thomas, I'm sure you have appointments and people to see." "Oh phooey on them, Lili. They can wait. But guess we should get you started. I'll get Casares back over here."

"What does he do here in the embassy?" Lili asked.

"Good question, Lili. Who knows? We have a Human Resources Director who does our hiring and firing. But some personnel are sent down here from Washington. I don't have any say in that. Casares is one of them."

"Oh."

"Lili before you go, do you have a significant other?"

"Ma'am?"

"You know a significant other. Someone you're seeing. A boyfriend?"

"Oh, yes!" Lili exclaimed. "He is the most wonderful man in the whole world."

"Where?"

"Ma'am?"

"Lili, where is he?"

"I don't know," Lili's voice was barely audible. "But he loves me and I love him. He will come for me. I know he will."

Ambassador Thomas squeezed in her cheeks like she had just sucked on a lemon.

Washington didn't brief me on all of this…. Poor kid. Some bastard dumped her and she still believes in him. I can help fix that—who would ever walk out on a gorgeous creature like her…. She's got brains too.

"Lili, I tell you what."

"Ma'am?"

"We are having a dinner tonight for the President of Chile. I want you to come. You can be my guest."

"Oh, Ms. Thomas, I would love to," Lili exclaimed pressing her hands together.

"Done," said the Ambassador. See Casares and have him put you in touch with Kylee Navarro. She will fix you up with a wardrobe. See you tonight at eight."

Ambassador Thomas showed Lili to the door. Watching her disappear down the hall, she turned to the receptionist. "Margaret, please ask Mister Brodbeck that if he is not too busy, I would like to see him."

Edward Brodbeck stayed busy running the embassy's protocol and social event schedules. When he wasn't worried about something, he worried because he had nothing to worry about. Tonight a state dinner for the Chilean President was already bringing him migraines. Was security tight enough? What wine went where? Is anyone a diabetic? Who sits next to whom? Who gets to sit next to "El Surpremo, besides El Presidente?" And now she wants to see me.

"Yes ma'am?" he said standing outside the large office.

"Good morning Ed, please come in," said Ambassador Thomas gesturing.

"You wanted to see me, ma'am?"

"Yes Ed, thank you," she began. "We have a new accountant who just joined us today. She's an adorable little thing; her name is Lili Perez."

"Yes ma'am?"

"I invited her to the dinner tonight. Would you please make sure she is seated at the same table as Don Velazquez?"

"Anastasio Velazquez, ma'am?"

"Yep, the Don himself. Thanks Ed."

Just as Brodbeck was leaving she said, "Oh Ed."

"Yes ma'am?"

"Please make sure Orlando, the Don's son, is seated next to Miss Perez."

"Yes ma'am."

Lili was very excited. This was her first time at such an event. As she walked through the tall embassy doors that evening, a handsome Marine in dress blues appeared at her side.

"Miss Perez, I am Sergeant Taylor. May I escort you to your table?"

"Certainly Sergeant," she said, slipping her arm in his.

He led her to the end of a reception line where the ambassador was greeting guests and making introductions to the Chilean President.

"Lili," said the ambassador. "Thank you for coming. Mister President, this is Miss Lili Perez. Lili, President Salvador DeVeccio of Chile."

"A great pleasure," said the President, struggling with his English, slightly bowing to kiss her hand.

"Senor Presidente, este un gran honor," Lili replied.

President DeVeccio beamed with pleasure at being spoken to in his native language. He smiled broadly at Lili.

Wow! thought Ambassador Thomas. *Not only does she make a stunning appearance, but also she can talk to them in their own language. This little doll is dynamite!*

Lili did indeed make a stunning appearance. Kylee had done an excellent job. Because of her petite size, the Embassy Boutique's inventory of dresses was slight. However, Kylee found a size four. It was perfect.

Sergeant Taylor walked Lili arm in arm into the ballroom. It seemed as if everything stopped. The purr of polite conversation hushed. Everyone turned and gazed at the handsome couple. Lili's floor length, shoulderless white gown seemed to flow with her like a reverie. In her white-gloved hand, she held a small black purse. Her nigrescent hair hung down below her shoulders and gleamed in the light from the chandeliers.

Sergeant Taylor showed her to table two and pulled out the chair in front of her name, which was neatly printed and encased in a small silver frame. The gentlemen at the table were instantly on their feet.

The dining tables were covered with deep red tablecloths and set with white bone china gracefully etched with the great seal of the United States. The table candles were placed in the center of the table among a tasteful arrangement of flowers. A deep red cloth napkin was in the center of her plate and tied with a same colored ribbon in a bow. An array of silverware was set beside the china plate.

I hope I can remember what Kylee told me…. What fork goes with what…? I'll just watch the others.

"Miss Perez, if I may? I am Anastasio Velazquez," said a tall man with silver hair. He was very good looking, dressed in a casual tuxedo, with black slacks, white coat and the standard bow tie. Lili thought he looked much like the movie star Cesar Romero. His English sounded more British than American. He bowed and kissed her hand.

"Mister Velazquez it is a pleasure to meet you," she smiled, her white teeth gleaming.

"Thank you. Miss Perez may I present my son, Orlando?"

Orlando was also a handsome man, an exact duplicate of his father, except with jet black hair and thirty pounds lighter.

He too bowed and kissed her hand.

Marine Sergeant Taylor seated Lili and quickly departed.

"Miss Perez," Velazquez said. "You will forgive my English. I have not had the benefit of being educated in the Ivy League Universities of the United States, as my son, Orlando."

"Oh Mister Velazquez, your English is very good," said Lili.

"You are too kind Miss Perez."

Lili said, "Podemos hablar en Espanol si le gusta."

"Maravilloso, Maravilloso! That is wonderful Miss Perez. Yes, of course, we can speak in Spanish." Velazquez exclaimed very pleased. "Mucho Gracias."

Ambassador Thomas looked past President DeVeccio from her table. Her eyes were on Lili Perez and the Don, Anastasio Velazquez.

Lili, you beautiful little Angel, you have the richest man in Costa Rica eating out of your hand like a puppy with a milk bone.

The orchestra began to play.

CHAPTER TWENTY-FIVE

"Mister Grant may I take a moment of your time privately please?" Ted asked.

"Yes, certainly Commander, of course."

"My room," said Ted.

Once in Ted's quarters, he had just begun to speak when CIA Special Agent Grant held up his hand. He placed his index finger over his lips signaling Ted to be quiet. He scribbled on a note pad. "This room may not be secured."

Ted nodded and shrugged with his palms up. Grant crooked all four fingers at him indicating follow me.

They were soon back in the radio room when Agent Grant said, "Commander, this is the only room in the embassy that we are sure is secured. We can talk over here," he pointed.

"Mister Grant," Ted began, I need to know who would be in charge of any special missions for Army personnel around here.

"Army?"

"Yes, Army," said Ted.

"Umm. That would be most likely Colonel Abernathy."

"Full bird?" Ted asked meaning was he a full colonel.

"No Commander. He is a lieutenant colonel, silver leaf, just like you."

"Okay Mister Grant. I need to see him. It's urgent. Can you take me to him?"

"Commander you know I can't do that. I can't even take you topside, much less out of the embassy."

"Then bring him to me here," Ted ordered.

"Sir it might not that easy. No telling…."

"Mister Grant, I'm not asking you, I'm telling you. Just get it done," Ted barked.

An hour later, Army Lieutenant Colonel Abernathy was shown into the radio room. "Colonel, my name is Michael Fletcher. I'm a Registered Nurse here with the Red…."

"Relax Commander. The colonel has a Top Secret Security Clearance. He knows who you are and why you are here," said Grant.

"Very well," Ted said.

Abernathy interrupted. "Commander, we are the same rank. If it's all the same to you, my name is Josh."

"Fine with me, I go by Ted."

Ted continued, "Josh, I need your help. I need a jeep or a truck; something with a flatbed on it."

"No problem. Where are you going?"

"I'm afraid I have to leave that up to your people, Josh. I need to go to the approximate area where we lost Sergeant Osceola."

"Yeah, we can get you there. It's a radio outpost about fifty miles of bad road from here," said Josh. "Lots of Charlie out there you know."

"This is outrageous! You know I can't let you out of the embassy. Do you know who this man is?" shouted Grant jabbing a thumb in Ted's direction.

"Take it easy Grant," said Ted calmly. "We will be out of here and back before anyone knows a thing. Your job is to get me out of here and back quietly and as surreptitiously, as possible."

"Bullshit! I have my orders from the president on down. No exceptions."

"Agent Grant don't force me to pick up that phone and talk to Payton," bluffed Ted.

Grant gave Ted a chilling stare.

That's all I need…. The director chewing on my ass like a Great White…. I've only got a couple years to go to retirement…. Embassy duty is plush, most always for senior agents…. I can just see myself doing my last two years in freaking Bangladesh or on some God forgotten iceberg in Greenland…. I'm screwed if I do, and screwed if I don't….

Agent Grant fell silent.

Ted turned to Colonel Abernathy, "Josh, one more thing."

"Yes sir."

"Do you have someone in your outfit who was raised in the rural south or maybe out west? What I'm getting at is someone who is comfortable in the wild. Someone who has hunted and been exposed to the outdoors. I have to have someone really good—a hundred-percenter."

"Yeah Ted, I have the perfect man."

"Who?"

"Me."

"You?"

Abernathy said, "Yes, me. Does that surprise you? Before I went in the Army, I was a hunting guide back in Montana. Led a couple hunts over in Idaho and one down to Wyoming."

"Perfect," said Ted. "Can you pick me up here, say 0330 hundred hours? We need to get there exactly at daybreak."

"Sure," said Josh. "But where can I pick you up? This damn place is lit up like Times Square on New Year's Eve."

Ted was starting to answer a question with a question when Agent Grant said, "Don't go near the front, too well guarded. Pull around on the west side by the fire escape. I'll rig the motion lights for five minutes before and five minutes after. That's all the window you'll get. I'll get you past the Marines and to the fire escape, but from there you're on your own."

"That's all we need. Josh, anything else?"

"See you at 0330," he replied, popping a quick salute.

When Lieutenant Colonel Josh Abernathy said fifty miles of bad road, he wasn't making a joke. Ted thought the fillings in his teeth would be jarred out.

I thought some of the roads on the Reservation were bad, but this….

"I guess the Vietnamese Department of Roads and Highways took the day off," said a smiling Abernathy.

"Maybe they didn't come to work at all," Ted said, looking out over the folded down windshield.

After a long jolting ride, Josh said, "Alright, Ted, the radio outpost was over there." He pointed to the dense jungle.

"I don't see a thing," said Ted.

"That's the idea. The Indian did it. It's supposed to be hidden and camouflaged. It's gone now," said Abernathy. "He would probably have lived somewhere between this point here and the outpost. What do you think? A mile maybe?"

Ted shrugged, "I dunno."

He was watching the road. On his right, Ted kept a sharp eye on the thick high ground growth of the Vietnamese jungle back-dropped by mountainous terrain. The major was right; it looked like a cluster of broccoli.

To his left, Ted was watching more closely. On his left, the south side was a swampy marsh with dense growths of jungle and swamp vegetation. Deep brown murky water covered the area, giving off a foul smell, completely uninhabitable for humans.

Goose had said the old swimming hole, Gator Slough, was on the north side of the old dirt road, which was on higher ground and dry. But Gator Slough was on the south side by the swamp. Goose had said "pleasant memories," he was telling me to think of those days; I remember that old dirt road just like this one. Goose was telling me to look south toward the swamp.

"Turn around Josh," Ted said.

As Josh turned around he said, "But we were almost to the outpost, Ted."

"I know, but if Osceola was hit, he would never have led them to the outpost. He has to be over here," Ted said, waving his arm at the swamp in a sweeping motion.

Josh looked at Ted grievously. "Hey guy, I hate to say this, but there's no way the man is alive. It's been too long Ted. Nobody in their right mind would go into that sewer when they could easily go to the other side. It may be a jungle, but at least it's dry."

You don't know the Seminole Indians, Colonel.

"That is exactly what he wants you to think, Josh."

After a while Josh said, "I don't see a thing."

"That's exactly what he wants you to see. Nothing. Slow down Josh."

Josh slowed the truck.

"Wait a minute. Stop!" exclaimed Ted. "See that broken leaf there?"

"No sir, I don't see anything but swamp."

"Look closely Josh. See that leaf that's bent over a bit?"

"Nope. I don't see a thing."

Ted got out of the flatbed and walked over to where the leaf was hanging. He gazed at it briefly then he pulled the limb back. He saw what he was looking for. Carved in the tree was a "2" with a single line crossing through its center. It was no bigger than a man's thumb. "Here," he said.

Josh joined Ted as he entered the swamp. Ted did not make a sound, but behind him, all he could hear was the gurgling sucking sound of Colonel Abernathy's boots with every step as he tried to break them free from the mucky glue-like mire. "Josh, why don't you wait here for me?"

"Okay", he readily agreed. But Ted remember, this place is infested with Charlie. They are bound to know we are here."

Ted nodded. He spotted another broken leaf, then another.

"Ma-Chamee," Ted said in a loud whisper.

"Over here," came a quiet voice speaking in Seminole.

Ted was straining his eyes in the overcast canopy of the quagmire; still he couldn't see anything resembling a man. "Where?"

"Right here," said a clear voice right beside him in English.

Ted leaped. Osceola was practically invisible less than an arm's length from his side. He was hidden in the mud and jungle sludge. Osceola looked like a jungle plant growing on the side of a small swamp island.

He said, "I knew you were coming." Ted didn't ask how he knew. Seminoles had a way. They just knew. As a white man, Ted never was never able to acquire such a skill.

"I knew you were U.S., I smelled you both a half hour ago."

"How bad you hurt Sarge?"

"Pretty bad, sir, they shot me up good. I made for the swamp. They looked everywhere for me for a couple days. Mostly they were searching the other side of the road. Couple of them came close. I could have bit them on the ass. One of them even stepped on me. He never knew it."

"Can you walk?"

"I don't think so sir, not anymore. I can't feel my legs."

"Okay Sarge, we'll get you out of here. Josh!" he yelled.

Ted and the colonel were able to get Sergeant Osceola out of the mire and loaded onto the flatbed of the truck.

Osceola said, "Hey guys we'd better get going. Charlie is all over the freaking place."

"No worries," said Josh. "We're outta here!"

Josh had no sooner uttered the words when a rifle bullet tore off the side mirror next to Ted, followed by a torrent of gunfire. "Crap!" exclaimed Josh. He stomped the little truck's accelerator to the floor.

They were flying down the narrow dirt road like an out of control juggernaut, throwing a volcano of dust and debris in the air. Ted heard the sizzling sound of bullets as they buzzed all around him. A few mortar rounds exploded nearby, but none close enough to cause any harm, except petrifying them with fear.

Suddenly a mortar round exploded in the middle of the road directly in front of them, obliterating any semblance of what was already barely a road.

"Hang on to your ass, this is gonna be all or nothing!" shouted Abernathy. He slammed the jeep's gears into four-wheel drive and veered off into the swampy edge of the road, avoiding the crater left by the mortar. Ted could hear the motor of the little jeep straining as it tried valiantly to pull against the mud and slime of the swamp.

Abernathy was trying to climb up the incline back to the road. The flatbed was barely moving. "Shit! We are sitting ducks," Ted shouted. At that moment, the folded over windshield of the flatbed bounced high and slammed back down on the truck's hood shattering it and sending slivers of broken glass in all directions.

So far, we've been lucky, but we aren't going to make it this time, Ted thought. *This is just what Charlie needs, to capture not one, but two, Seminole Translators…. Chances are they don't know who I am, but they damn sure know who Osceola is!*

The little flatbed jeep made a herculean effort and managed to barely get up the bank and back on the road.

Ted thought, *Whoever makes this thing, remind me to write them a good letter….*

Just then, a bullet passed between the two officers and smashed into the console of the jeep, exploding the speedometer and RPM Gauge, splattering glass and jagged metal toward the two men.

"You okay?" shouted Abernathy.

Ted signaled with his thumb up.

"Is our passenger all right?"

"Don't know. He's still there. We can't stop," Ted yelled back.

Sergeant Osceola was silent.

Miraculously all three were unscathed except for cuts from the broken glass and bruises. At the Saigon city limits Josh grinned, "I think we are okay now?"

"Maybe you are but I've still got to figure out how to get back in the embassy."

As Ted was getting out of the flatbed Josh said, "If you can get out, I'm sure you can get back in. So long Ted, it has been an experience."

"Yes, it has. Please make sure Sergeant Osceola gets good treatment."

"Of course, the best."

Osceola groaned, "Ah-Yah-Lee Ma-Chamee."

"Yes, goodbye to you too my faithful friend," Ted replied.

Ted was exhausted. He tried to be as inconspicuous as possible, but looking at his reflection in the embassy's glass doors, he knew that would be impossible. It was difficult to tell if his nurse's uniform was actually white. He was covered from head to toe with mud and sludge from the jungle and he was bleeding from the glass of the shattered windshield. "I'm bet I smell like a morning gardenia too," he muttered, as he got behind the crowd entering the embassy.

The ever diligent Sergeant Major spotted Ted and quickly motioned toward the basement elevator. Ted gave him an appreciative glance and quickly stepped into the elevator.

"Commander sir!" was the first thing Ted heard when he exited the elevator. "I have looked everywhere for you! You had us all in a panic sir! The Corps would court martial me or have me shot for losing you sir. The next time you go anywhere, I... Good God Commander, sir, what happened to you?"

"Shut up Culpepper...."

CHAPTER TWENTY-SIX

As the months passed Lili grew more and more at home in Costa Rica and with her work in the embassy. The pain of not having Ted beside her was getting more endurable, but the memories of him were never far from her mind. Insomnia still plagued her. If she could only feel his skin against hers, she would drift off to sleep like a hibernating kitten, a deep, peaceful, soothing sleep in the arms of her aficionado.

The late summer rains trekked across Central America, bringing with them lightning and thunder. Lili would go down to the basement of the embassy pretending to be busy. She was secretly getting away from the storms.

Lilith, from the Epic of Gilgamesh.... Lilith is stalking me.... Lilith is the hunter. I am her quarry. Lilith, the Mesopotamian Demoness of storm and wind. She is with Kelaeno, the Black Goddess. They have found me. If I were with Ted, he would protect me.

Ambassador Thomas was leaving her office when she saw Anastasio Velazquez.

"Don Velazquez how nice to see you."

"Ah Ambassador Thomas, always a pleasure," said Velazquez, kissing the Ambassador's hand.

"How can we be of service to you, Don Velazquez?"

"No, nothing, thank you, Madam Ambassador," said Velazquez. "I am here strictly on a social call."

"A social call?"

"Si, Ambassador Thomas. Miss Perez and I are having lunch on the veranda."

"The veranda? But we don't have any food service on the veranda."

"Si, Madam Ambassador, I know. I have made arrangements. I am hopeful someday soon you will visit me again at the Corobici, my hacienda."

"Why Don Velazquez, your El Rancho Grande. What a lovely place. That would be splendid. Thank you," she smiled.

"Perhaps it would be most enjoyable if Miss Perez could join us," said the Don.

"Yes, that would be nice, thank you."

What's going on here? she thought.

"Well okay then, nice to see you again, Don Velazquez."

"And you as well, madam."

Ambassador Thomas quickly made a left turn down a hallway with offices on both sides. Taking long strides, she stepped into the office of the constantly fidgeting Edward Brodbeck.

"Ed, what's going on here?" she demanded, jabbing a thumb over her shoulder toward the veranda.

Brodbeck gazed out the window at the dining couple. The veranda was a lovely spot, a perfect place for lunch. It was surrounded by the flower beds of the embassy and shaded by the lovely Guanacaste Trees, the National Tree of Costa Rica. Two of Velazquez' workers were serving Lili and the Don smoked salmon and steamed rice with vegetables.

"Can't say ma'am. I can tell you this: Mister Velazquez is here a couple, maybe three times a week. Always sniffing around Miss Perez like a hunting dog pointing a bird."

"Well, we've got the right bird Ed, but the wrong dog!" exclaimed the ambassador.

"Ma'am?"

"I had you seat Lili at the Velazquez table so she could take up with Orlando, not the Don."

"Madam Ambassador," said Brodbeck, "I think there is something you should know."

The Ambassador's eyebrows shot up. "Oh?"

"Yes ma'am. From what I hear Orlando is, shall we say, is a little light in the loafers."

"A little light in what?" she exclaimed. "Oh you mean he is…."

"Yes ma'am. From what I hear he is gay."

"Now isn't that just great?" said the exasperated ambassador.

"I guess that explains why he is not interested in Lili, but the Don sure as hell is. Look at them!"

"Yes ma'am."

"He is twice her age and then some," she exclaimed.

"Ed get with Antonio Casares," said the ambassador. "I think he has a bit of Tinkerbell in him too. Anyway, find out what the hell is going on. He seems to know everything that is happening around here before I do."

"Yes ma'am. Ah ma'am, I can only tell you what I see and hear, but…."

"Yes Ed, what is it?"

"Well ma'am, from what I hear the Don is very interested in Miss Perez, but I don't think she is a bit interested in him. She keeps talking about some lawyer in the States and how she loves him and he loves her. She says he is going to come for her someday."

"Oh?"

"Yes ma'am and like you said there's the age thing with the Don."

"Thanks Ed. I want you to get with our resident FBI Agent. The agent's name is Stockwell. Alex Stockwell."

"Yes ma'am."

"Let's get Stockwell with Casares and find out about this lawyer Lili is so crazy about. Also, find out what's going on between those two," she said motioning toward the veranda.

"Yes ma'am, if you say so."

"I say so."

On the veranda, Don Anastasio Velazquez was saying: "Miss Perez, we are having a big cook-out, gran parte hacer una barbacoa, weekend after next. It would give me great pleasure for you to join us."

"Don Velazquez that is so nice of you. But I fear your hacienda is too far for me to travel and besides, I don't think it would be proper for me to…."

The Don was well prepared. "Miss Perez no worries," he interrupted. "My plane will pick you up at San Jose's,

Juan Santamaria Airport, at what? ah say, five o'clock Friday, the 24th? My hacienda is less than an hour by air."

"But Señor Velazquez, I…."

"And please Miss Perez, feel free to invite the person of your choice to accompany you as a chaperone," the Don said, making a clear disambiguation of any despairing thoughts she might have had.

Friday the 24th found Lili and Kylee Navarro standing outside the general aviation facility of the Juan Santamaria Airport. A Beechcraft Baron taxied up to the ramp. The airplane was solid white, trimmed in a deep burgundy color. Lili could see the Don's logo neatly painted in the tail of the Beech and "Corobici," printed in bold burgundy beneath the logo. The pilot alit and approached them.

"Hello ladies, my name is Ray Corbin. May I fly you to the Corobici please?" said the handsome pilot in perfect English. He had on black slacks and a white shirt. On each shoulder was an epaulet with four gold stripes. Lili thought he was probably from the States.

"Yes, thank you," Lili said. Corbin helped her and Kylee climb aboard.

What a beautiful airplane, she thought. *This is so nice. I wish my Teddy Bare could be here.*

"Shall we go?" asked the pilot. "The Don is waiting and Mister Velazquez doesn't wait for anybody."

Both girls were very excited. This was such a rare treat for them. They were impressed how quickly the Baron left mother earth and how smoothly it climbed to a safe altitude to clear the mountains. No more noise than a steady hum filled their ears. Lili was sitting beside the pilot in the front seat and she could see the cluster of instruments. One got her attention.

"What is that instrument with the white and the green arcs?" she inquired. "And I think I see yellow and red in it too."

"Yes ma'am. That is the ASI, ah, the Airspeed Indicator. Right now, it's telling us that we are flying at 175 knots. Ah, that is a little over 200 miles per hour, ma'am."

It seemed a matter of moments then Lili could see the pilot slightly retard the power on both engines and lower ten degrees of flaps. As the airplane began a slow decent, he made a steep bank to the left.

"That is the Corobici Hacienda under the wing there, ma'am," said the pilot.

Lili looked out, the hacienda was enormous. *Muy Grande!*

She thought it looked more like a hotel than a private residence.

"I thought the Corobici was a river," spoke up Kylee from the one of the rear seats.

"Yes ma'am, it is," said the pilot. "It originates in the Guanacaste Mountains here in northwestern Costa Rica and flows south until it reaches its estuary at the north end of the Gulf of Nicoya."

"So the Don named his house after the river?" she asked.

"No ma'am. His grandfather did. It's been in the family for generations. The hacienda, the farms and the ranch all have the same name. The Corobici is one of the most beautiful rivers in the world. It is so lovely here the Don's grandfather named everything after it.

Thought Lili:

All the farms...? Farms, as in plural...? The ranch...?
Lili tapped the pilot on the shoulder. "Did you say farms?"

"Yes ma'am. Mister Velazquez is one of the largest coffee growers and exporters in the world. He raises prize beef cattle, too. Better button up your seat belt Miss, we're about to land."

"I don't see an airport," said Kylee.

"No ma'am. The Don has a private airport. We land right next to the hacienda."

The Baron touched down smoothly.

As the airplane's engines shut down, Don Velazquez stepped up on the wing and opened the hatch door.

"Welcome ladies. Bienvenido!" he exclaimed. The Don kissed Kylee's hand, as was the contemporary custom. However, he kissed Lili on both cheeks, European style.

Strange, she thought, *bizarro.*

He led them to a six passenger golf cart. No mention was made of their overnight bags. "This is all the Corobici, as far as you can see," he said, gesturing with a sweeping wave.

Lili was enthralled with the lush greenery and the array of beautiful flowers. The Corobici appeared to be in a valley encompassed by the most captivating mountains she had ever seen. In the near distance, she could see thousands of coffee plants rising about six feet in height. The coffee plant is actually an evergreen shrub and they were lovely as they dotted the hills with their jade color.

Don Velazquez drove the golf cart up a sloping circular driveway. A large fountain stood in the center of the driveway spewing water into the air and back down to a pool filled with goldfish. It was surrounded with blooming flowers.

"Welcome to my casa ladies," said Don Velazquez.

Lili thought: *Calling a grand hacienda like this a casa is like calling Buckingham Palace a summer cottage. This sure is a long way from our little house in Uvalde. It would be so much better if my Teddy Bare was with me.*

"Ladies would you care to join me in the library for a drink?"

"Yes, of course, Don Velazquez," said Lili. "We would love to."

They were soon seated in the dark brown leather chairs, which adorned the Don's luxurious walnut library. Neither of them had ordered a drink when a white coated, Costa Rican waiter appeared carrying iced tea with a slice of lime for Lili and a Lime Daiquiri poured over cracked ice for Kylee.

"How... how did you know?" asked Kylee.

"You will forgive me for being so presumptuous Miss Navarro. I inquired about your beverage of choice. I wanted your visit with us here at the Corobici to be as pleasant as possible," replied Don Velazquez.

Kylee gaped.

After visiting together for the better part of an hour in the Don's library, he stood and said, "I know you ladies would like to freshen up after your journey."

He motioned toward the door and immediately two very pretty young ladies appeared. "This is Lucy, Miss Perez; she will show you to your room. Miss Navarro, this is Juanita, she will show you to yours. Dinner will be at eight o'clock in the main dining room."

They both thanked him and Lili followed Lucy up a wide "L" shaped marble stairway and down a long carpeted hall.

"This is where you will stay, mum," said Lucy in Spanish, opening the door to a large suite.

Lili said, "Lucy, usted hablar Ingles?"

"No mum," she replied.

"That's okay," said Lili. "We will get along just fine in Spanish."

Lucy said, "You are very beautiful, Señorita Perez."

"Why thank you Lucy, so are you."

Lucy smiled broadly.

"Yes mum, I will be in the hall if you need anything."

"No need Lucy, thank you. I won't be needing anything."

"Señorita Perez," said Lucy. "I don't think you understand. I am your mujeres siervo, your demestico, mum. I must stay within your call or I will be in trouble."

"How old are you, Lucy?"

"Catorce. Fourteen, mum."

"And you are my what?" Lili asked sternly.

"Your demestico, your servant, mum. I am to stay with you and attend to anything you might desire."

"We'll see about that," said an agitated Lili. "I am an American. We don't have servants in America, we have employees. We don't have servants!"

That's something I have to get straight with the Don right away.

"And furthermore, call me Lili."

CHAPTER TWENTY-SEVEN

As the seasons changed Lili became more and more a frequent visitor at the Corobici. She started looking forward to seeing the Beechcraft taxi up to fly her for another weekend with the Don. They would walk hand in hand around the farms and often they would go up the mountain, which overlooked a herd of white-faced Hereford Cattle the Don raised.

Often they would go about the Corobici on horseback, a skill Lili acquired during her weekend visits. She truly loved the riding and the horses. She would always take treats of sugar lumps with her when she went to the stables. She cherished the time she spent curry-combing and grooming the animals.

To Lili there was no place on earth as beautiful and as peaceful as the Corobici.

Don Anastasio Velazquez no longer kissed Lili on the cheeks. He kissed her lips. During their walks about the grounds, he often draped his arm over her shoulders and held her close. She would slip her arm through his.

Lili felt an attachment to Anastasio Velazquez. She genuinely liked him and could readily see how any woman would be attracted to the polished aristocrat. She loved the Don, but it was not the same. Something was missing.

With Ted, a kiss was nothing short of a crashing tsunami. It would start at the soles of her feet and travel up through her body like a giant explosion of atomic energy. Her heart would race like a locomotive at just the sight of him. She often thought her heart was going to leap out of her chest when she heard his voice. Orgasms were like the top of Mount Kilimanjaro erupting into a volcano. Everything about Ted was special.

Teddy Bare, I will always love you.

Back in San Jose, Lili continued to keep the books and tend to the vast accounting duties of the embassy. She was a stickler for detail and had everything in perfect order. Still things weren't right in her mind. It was always Ted.

Lili had befriended a Catholic priest who frequently held Mass at the embassy. When she confided in him, he referred her to Doctor Mildred Shuenberger, an American Psychiatrist, who had retired in San Jose.

Lili began a long series of visits with Doctor Shuenberger. During one of her visits, the Doctor said, "Lili we have talked about this enough. You are not a child. It is time for you to realize that this Ted of yours is gone and he is not coming back. You are a beautiful young woman with your whole life in front of you. You cannot waste any more of it waiting on a ghost."

"But Doctor, if you only knew how real and true our love is…."

"Lili, you are not listening. You are hearing only what you want to hear and you are living in the past. I am going to give you some exercises. You must stop this pining over this Ted Barrett. He is a memory. A good memory, yes, but nevertheless a memory."

"If only you could talk to Nicole, Doctor Larson. She understood, but…."

"Lili, we have exhausted that subject too. I cannot tell you why Doctor Larson never got back to you. Remember? I never could find her listed in the any of the professional registers. Maybe she got too close. It happens. It's not professional."

"Okay."

"Here Lili, take this list and the next time Ted Barrett enters your mind do the exercise."

"Yes ma'am, thank you, Doctor."

What actually entered Lili's mind was Shakespeare's *"A Mid-Summer's Night Dream,"* Lysander speaks to his lover Hermia: "The course of true love did never run smooth."

No list of exercises will ever make me forget my Teddy Bare.

It was a perfect fall morning at the Corobici. The air was fresh and filled the unmistakable aroma of the burning piñon logs in the fireplace. Lili was bouncing down the stairs just as Don Velazquez entered the foyer. He was dressed in his riding clothes.

"Good morning, my little dove."

"Good morning to you, Anastasio." Lili exclaimed, as she gave him a kiss on the cheek. "What a wonderful day!"

"Come with me," he said. "I have something for you to see."

"Of course kind sir," she teased, slipping her arm into his.

Outside by the steps she recognized Carlos, the stable boy. He was holding one of the Don's favorite horses and the reins of the most beautiful Palomino mare she had ever seen. The mare was a dark golden color with a silver mane and tail.

"Oh, she is so beautiful!" Lili cried. "Where did you ever find such a magnificent animal?"

"It took some time but I knew exactly what I wanted," he said.

"What are you going to do with her, Anastasio?"

"I don't know. That is up to you."

"Up to me? How could it be up to me?"

"Because she is yours," he said beaming a wide smile.

"Mine! Oh, Anastasio, this is so wonderful!"

The stable boy, Carlos, cupped his hands beside the mare. Lili stepped in them and he hoisted her 110 pounds up onto the saddle.

"She needs a name," said the Don.

"I have it already," said Lili. "She is my Golden Belleza. My Golden Beauty!"

Lili and her mare were inseparable. Every weekend and holidays, they were together, galloping around the Corobici.

She was always excited to see her Golden Beauty. The palomino would trumpet and begin to paw the earth in her stall whenever she heard Lili's voice or caught her scent.

Don Velazquez watched in awe as Lili would thunder past, the horse at a full gallop. He marveled at how she and the animal melted into one as Lili leaned forward, her legs tightly gripping the saddle and staying in perfect sync with the mare.

This is what the Corobici needs, he mused. *Youth.... Life...! Here before me is the finest horseflesh in the country.... And astride her, the most exquisite raven haired beauty I have ever seen. Magnificent—Maravilloso!*

After an early dinner, one November evening, Don Velazquez said, "Come Lili, it is time we talk."

"Sure Anastasio,"

He led her to the front door and down the steps where Carlos held the horses. They were saddled and waiting. Golden Belleza bobbed her head and let out a whinny, sounding her pleasure at the sight of Lili.

A nipping chill was in the air announcing the incipience of a biting winter. Lili looked about at the colorful foliage and the falling leaves from the dense woods. To her, this was when the Corobici was at its most beautiful.

They rode in silence for a while. Lili's spirited and impatient mare pranced and crow-hopped from one side to the other, as if she was saying: "Come on, let's go! Let's race!" Lili kept the reins tight remaining in complete control of her steed.

They stopped on the east side of the mountain overlooking the serpentine Corobici River below, winding its way through the valley and the farms of Don Velazquez.

"Anastasio, you look so sad. What's wrong?"

"No not sad, my love, perhaps a better word would be pensive."

"Pensive, Anastasio?"

"Yes Lili. I have had many things on my mind for a long time. I am sure you know by now the truth about Orlando."

Lili looked at him and tilted her chin slightly.

"I have been a widower for almost fifteen years. It is most difficult raising a child even with all this," he said waving both hands toward the river, "but something is lacking in my life. I have no one to share my home, here... I did not completely focus on these things until you came into my life, Lili. The Corobici must always remain in my family. I am the third generation to own it, but my doubts about Orlando are quite troubling."

Lili gave the Don an understanding look, but still said nothing.

"We have come to a point in our relationship," he continued, "where we must move forward, we cannot continue our relationship as it is."

"Anastasio, what are you trying to tell me?"

Anastasio Velazquez turned in his saddle and looked Lili squarely in the face. His eyes riveted on hers. "Lili, I want you to marry me, to move here to the Corobici, and be my esposa."

Lili thought her ear drums had exploded. "Anastasio, you want me to marry you?"

"Is that so strange? I love you, Lili, and I know you love me."

"Yes, I love you, Anastasio, but marriage? It is such a huge decision."

"I know," he said. "I have thought it over well. As I mentioned a few moments ago, the Corobici must always remain in my family, but I would care for you and I would leave you extremely well off. Perhaps you would give me an heir."

Lili was aberrantly enraged. "To begin with Anastasio," she shouted, "I would never marry you unless I loved you! I have no concern how well-off you may leave me. I would only marry you for what I could do for you, not what you could do for me!"

"But, but Lili wait. I…."

"And furthermore, if God blesses me with a child it will be out of love, not because I am some kind of baby machine!"

With that, she spun Golden Belleza around and dug her heels deeply into the mare's flanks. Off they went like a shot from a catapult. Lili leaned over until her face touched Belleza's flowing silver mane as she raced between the trees and the fall foliage. Leaping over a downed log, she steered her mare on a full run to the road. Golden Belleza loved stretching out the distance for her master. Lili let the mare have full rein, running as fast as she could back to the hacienda stables.

Reining in the mare, she skidded to a stop at the stables, slinging mud and sod in the air. "Here," she said to Carlos, handing him the reins. "See that she gets a good rub down and some extra oats."

"Yes mum," said a bewildered Carlos. It was uncharacteristic of Lili to be bossy. Usually she would ask a question rather than give a direct order. "Would you mind? When you have time? Please, thank you, but not this evening. Something was amiss.

Later that evening Lili heard a light tapping on her door. "Hi Lucy."

Lucy was very nervous and wringing her hands. "Ah Miss Perez, mum, Don Velazquez would like to see you. He is waiting in the library," she said softly.

Well, he can just wait.

"Thank you, Lucy. I will be down in a few minutes."

"Ah yes, mum, I will wait for you."

"No Lucy, you may run along. I'll be a few minutes."

"No mum, I can't do that," Lucy said clasping her hands together. Her voice was breaking and she was nearly in tears.

Lili took both of Lucy's hands in hers. "Lucy, what is wrong? Why are you so frightened?"

Lucy looked both ways up and down the hall. "Miss Perez, mum, my whole family works for the Don. So does everyone in the valley. We are very poor and I cannot take a chance on losing my job. I was told to bring you."

"I see. Okay then, we will go now. But remember, I told you to call me Lili."

"Yes mum, but I cannot do that in front of anyone. The Don would not like it."

"Well, okay. But, when we are alone, I am Lili and you are Lucy," she said smiling and touching her finger to the tip of Lucy's nose."

Lucy broke into a big smile.

If I ever do marry him, there will be some changes around here…. Big time!

Lili found Don Velazquez in the library sipping a drink and puffing on his pipe.

"Please sit down Lili," he gestured with the pipe.

Lili curled her leg under her and plopped into the chair. No sooner had she sat, someone from the kitchen staff placed a glass of iced tea beside her, just as she liked it—a slice of lime, no sugar.

"Lili," he began, "we had a rather awkward start to a most serious conversation this evening. I hope you will allow us to continue in a much less bellicose attitude than a couple hours ago."

Lili pushed a strand hair behind her ear. Tilting her head, she gave him a half smile, which said, "I'm listening.

"As I tried to tell you earlier, Orlando is a different kind of…."

"Anastasio," she interrupted, I have been coming to the Corobici for over a year now and I don't recall ever seeing Orlando here."

"Ah yes, Lili. Orlando seems to enjoy spending his time, and my money, in your California city, San Francisco. He rarely comes home unless, of course, he needs something."

Lili still gave him a half smile that said, "I'm still listening."

So now that you know these details about Orlando's dubious, shall we say, alternate life style, it is highly doubtful that he will sire me any grandchildren and I cannot see how he would ever be able to run the Corobici. Therefore, I am faced with quite a dilemma as to how I shall leave the Corobici."

"Why didn't you say it this way this afternoon?" she asked.

"You will forgive my rather gauche approach. It was not my intent to offend you.

"Lili, I want you to come to the Corobici and be my wife."

"Anastasio, I am flattered and I am overwhelmed. I don't know what to say."

"Just say you will think about it Lili," he said.

"Oh, no worries there, I will definitely be thinking about it."

Lili got up and closed the library door.

"Anastasio, there are many things you don't know. Before this goes any further, there are some things I need to tell you. I know how important some things are in your culture. Before I came to your country, I...."

Velazquez held up both hands, indicating stop. "Lili, you are not going to tell me about your lawyer friend, Mister Barrett, are you?"

Lili was stunned. "Yes," she barely whispered. "How—how do you know about him?"

"How I know and what I know is not important," he said. "What is important is that all this happened in the past. Let's leave it there."

Memories of Ted flooded Lili's mind like a giant avalanche. Her eyes began to tear.

How could he know? Where is my Teddy Bare...?

"Anastasio, I don't know what to say," she hardly managed.

"When one does not know what to say, perhaps it is best to say nothing at all," he smiled. "Aren't you going to San Antonio next month for the Christmas Holidays?"

"Yes," she answered.

"Good." Please talk this over with your family."

He kissed her in the forehead and said, "I will wait for your answer." With that he was gone leaving Lili in the vast library staring at the book-filled walnut shelves.

He will be waiting.... She remembered the pilot's words. *"Mister Velazquez doesn't wait for anyone."*

In San Jose, Ambassador Thomas was in her office talking with FBI Agent Stockwell.

"So, Alex, did you have any luck finding this lawyer, Ted Barrett?"

"Sorry, ma'am, nothing. From what I could get, he seemed to be a pretty stand-up guy, member of the Federal Bar and the Texas Bar. Smart, good-looking, had a lot on the ball. Then one day he just disappeared. Nobody knows anything, just like he dropped off the face of the earth."

"What about Barrett and Lili?"

"From what I could find out, the two of them had quite a scorching thing going, then all of a sudden, nothing."

"I find that very, very strange, Alex."

"So do I, Ambassador. But if anyone knows anything, they aren't talking."

"Okay Alex, thanks. What do you say we let this little chat stay just between you and me?"

"Definitely ma'am."

CHAPTER TWENTY-EIGHT

The American Airlines, Boeing 737-800, Flight Twenty-one Twenty from San Jose gently touched down on San Antonio's northwest runway three zero. When Lili deplaned at the arrival gate, she was greeted by what seemed to be the entire Perez family. There were kisses and hugs. Everyone was talking at the same time through tears of joy. Tonight was to be a big celebration at her sister Gabriella's house. It was Christmas and it was nice to be home.

The evening overflowed with laughter and Christmas greetings. Lili began to realize how much she missed her family, but she knew telling them about Don Anastasio Velazquez and the Corobici was inevitable.

Lili spent the days following Christmas with her parents, Miguel and Rosie and with her sister Gabriella. She also stopped by to see her old family pediatrician, Doctor Ramon Gomez. Lili told them all about the Don and the grand Corobici. She showed pictures of the beautiful farms the ranch and especially her Golden Belleza.

Gabriella sat with Lili and the back porch of the Perez home. "Lili, are you insane? What an opportunity. To marry a man of such great wealth and live in such a lovely place."

"Gabbie, what do mama and papa think?"

"You know how they are. Mama kind of goes along, but papa? You know papa. He thinks you should marry someone from here and buy the house next door to him and mama," smiled Gabriella.

Lili laughed and shook her head yes.

"It's not their decision, Lili, it's up to you, but I know they would be all for it."

"But Gabbie," said Lili, "Costa Rica and the Corobici are so far away. Papa thought Dallas was too far away, remember—much less Costa Rica?"

"Lili a chance like this will never come to you again."

Lili poked a finger at an ice cube in her Doctor Pepper. She said, "Gabbie, I talked to you and to Doctor Gomez about this because you two are the only ones who know about Ted."

"Oh no, here we go again," exclaimed Gabriella, rolling her eyes at the ceiling.

"Hear me out Gabbie, please."

Gabriella nodded, Lili went on, "I love Ted, I have always loved him and I know he loves me. How can I allow another man to touch me? How could I ever give myself to another man the way I have with Ted? How could I ever love anyone as much as I love Ted?"

Gabriella sighed and looked at her handsome sister. "You won't. Lili, love is a gift. Ted was your first love and he always will be. This thing you had with him happens once in a lifetime. But it is O-V-E-R, over, Lili. It was just puppy love."

"It might have been just puppy love," said Lili. "But it's real to the puppy."

"I know I am younger than you, but I see things differently. Just like Doctor Gomez told you. You are fighting a war with no ammunition. Sweet Jesus, girl, it's been over two years!"

"But…."

"But, nothing sister. This Ted of yours is gone, gone, gone. You have been dumped. We all have been. Now get over it and get on with your life."

Gabriella asked. "Speaking of Doctor Gomez, did he mention whatever happened to that shrink you were seeing, Doctor Larson, ah, something Larson?"

"Nicole?"

"Yes, Nicole Larson, what happened to her?" asked Gabriella.

"Nobody seems to know, Gabbie. She just disappeared. Here one day, gone the next. Not a trace of anything. No forwarding addresses, no phone, nothing."

Odd—just like Ted…. Here one day and gone in an instant.

Lili slowly but surely began to absorb the advice given by her parents, her sister, and Doctor Gomez, all of whom she deeply respected.

Doctor Gomez' words lingered in her mind.

"Remember little one, everything that glitters, is not always gold."

Lili began to assess her situation with more gravity. The facts were: Ted was gone. She had never heard a word from him or about him. She did love Anastasio, but it wasn't the same. No one could ever be the same as Ted.

My Teddy Bare would never leave me—I know he wouldn't.... Never in a million years——I know he loves me—I will always love him....

Nicole's words echoed in Lili's ears. "The bastard dumped you. Simple as that, and didn't have the guts to face you."

"Yeah, I keep that picture around just to remind myself of how much I don't miss the sonofabitch."

Lili walked to her parent's telephone and dialed a lengthy number.

"Hello Anastasio," she said in Spanish. "I will be back in San Jose Sunday afternoon. Would you have the plane fetch me to the Corobici? I think we need to talk."

Lili listened for a moment. Then she said, "Yes, I have told them everything. I would consider it a great honor to become Mrs. Anastasio Velasquez."

She listened again and quietly said goodbye, then hesitatingly added, "I love you too." *I think....*

The room was deathly silent. Her brothers and sister sat gawking with their mouths open. Mister and Mrs. Perez stared. Suddenly the room broke out in clapping and cheers. Everyone was on their feet saying their congratulations. The Perez family was very happy.

Lili burst into tears.

CHAPTER TWENTY-NINE

"Go ahead Chobee-Who-Non-Wah, Ooki Nakni is listening on the UHF frequency," Ted said in Seminole, as the voice of Major Wildgoose crackled in his earphones.

"Ooki Nakni, it looks like from here the whole damn Commie Army is gathering and moving to where you are."

"You mean they are headed to…."

"Stop, Ooki Nakni, don't transmit the name of the town. Charlie will understand."

"Roger," said Ted. "You say they are building up?"

"Yeah, that's an understatement. We've been out here for a year or better and not much has been going on. Now, they are bringing in thousands of infantry, tanks, mortars and other light artillery too."

"Are they moving, Chobee-Who-Non-Wah?"

"Yeah, like I said looks like they are coming right at you. Something big is going down. They brought in a new general this morning."

"A general?" asked Ted.

"Yes sir, he got out of a staff car all duded up. He wore so many decorations that he looked like a damn pin-ball machine on tilt."

"Do you know who he is, Chobee-Who-Non-Wah?"

"Can't say I do," Wildgoose replied. "But I would appreciate it if you could check with the nice folks back in Washington and see if the same orders apply."

"Copy that, Chobee-Who-Non-Wah. Ooki Nakni, clear," said Ted.

"Chobee-Who-Non-Wah, clear."

Ted leaned back in his chair staring at the ceiling. He was thinking about his beloved Lili.

Lili darling, there is so much we have to catch up on. I know you are waiting for me.

His dreams of Lili were suddenly shattered by a commotion on the upper level of the embassy. Ted could hear people running and heard excited voices. Soon the "thump, thump, thump" of helicopter blades drowned out the other sounds.

Those helicopters are landing on the roof of the embassy!

Ted made a dash for the elevator when he met CIA Agent Clayton Grant coming toward him in a dead run or at least as fast as his portly frame could carry him.

"Grant, what the hell's going on?" he shouted.

"Can't talk," he panted. "The war is over. The president has ordered the immediate evacuation of all U.S. personnel. We have to destroy all the radio equipment and the codes."

Ted started to speak.

"Do it now, Commander!" Grant shouted. "The North Vietnamese Army is just outside the city."

Ted did as he was told.

Wildgoose was right!

"Let's get up on the roof. We are being flown out by helicopter," exclaimed the excited Agent Grant.

Both men scrambled up the narrow stairs forgetting the elevator.

On the roof, Grant yelled to Ted, "Commander, get in this chopper, I'm on the next one."

"Where are we going?" Ted shouted, trying to make himself heard over the roar of the helicopter blades.

"To one of our air bases Commander, then you are to be sent home," Grant shouted back.

Still yelling Ted said, "What about the Navy Seals?"

"Three of them have already left the other…."

"No! I'm not talking about the Marines. I'm talking about Wildgoose and his men," shouted Ted.

"I'm sorry, Commander. We…."

"Sorry about what, Grant?"

"Commander, we have no choice. We must evacuate now!"

Ted extended his arm pointing to the northeast and screamed at Grant. "You mean you are going to leave Wildgoose and his team in the jungle, in the middle of the whole damn Communist Army? Are you just going to let those boys die in that fucking sewer?"

"Commander," Grant yelled," we have direct orders from Washington."

"What about their orders, Grant? You know Wildgoose will never leave his post unless directly ordered to. He will die out there and so will the others. Are you out of your freaking mind?"

"Get in the chopper, Commander."

"Screw you Grant, and screw your orders."

Turning Ted said, "Culpepper, get in there."

"But sir," said Culpepper, "I…."

"Culpepper, just do it!" said Ted grabbing the Corporal by the shirt and shoving him in the waiting helicopter.

"Aye, aye sir," shouted Corporal Culpepper. He started to salute.

"Not now Culpepper, not now!"

Ted turned and ducking beneath the helicopter's swirling blades, he made for the stairs leading down to the embassy basement.

"Barrett you bastard!" he heard Grant shout. "You are on your own!"

I always have been—you gutless pile of horseshit!

Back in the embassy basement, Ted was frantically trying to find a working phone. Everything in the radio room had been smashed. He darted up the stairs taking three at a time when he burst into the main lobby of the embassy. He spotted the Army Sergeant Major.

"Sergeant Major, I need a phone."

The Sergeant Major struggling with a box, was rushing to the roof. "The ambassador is gone, try one of his," he yelled, jerking his head toward the ambassador's office.

Ted dashed into the office anxiously trying one phone after the other. Finally, he found one with a dial tone. "Thank you, God," he whispered. He quickly dialed a five digit number.

"Colonel Abernathy," said a strained voice in his receiver.

"Josh, I need your help. It's an emergency!" said Ted.

"Now?" gasped Abernathy.

"Yes, Josh, right now. I need to get across town to your Army post."

"Commander, do you have any idea what's going on?" asked Abernathy abruptly.

"Yes, of course I do, Josh. We haven't got time to talk, just get me over there."

"Alright, Ted. There will be a jeep out front in ten minutes."

"Roger that, and thanks, Josh"

Josh was true to word; a jeep pulled up in front of the embassy. Ted hopped in.

"Don't spare the horses, Private. I have got to get to Abernathy now!"

"Yes sir," said the private.

The jeep ride through Saigon was something Ted could not have imagined. People were running and screaming in every direction. They were carrying what few belongings they owned, mothers' clutching their babies, all charging out of the city. Everyone was in terror of the advancing Communist Army.

Ted thought: *This doesn't make any sense—we have been fighting this awful war for eight years—now are we simply pulling out. That's it…. What has Kissinger been doing in the Paris peace talks all this time?*

"Ted," exclaimed Abernathy, "I'm trying to move my Army out of here in half a day and you want what..?"

"Like I told you, Josh, I need a helicopter and somebody who can fly it. Just get me to the eastern edge of Grid Area Sixteen. That's all."

"Oh! That's all Ted? You want me to get you a private egg-beater and a pilot, and take you to the middle of a freaking war zone, when I am trying to move the whole damn United States Army, and that's all?"

"Josh, we have been over this," said Ted. "Wildgoose and his guys are trapped out there. We can't just leave them."

"Yeah, I got it. I'll try but you understand, this is volunteers only," said Abernathy.

Ted shook his head in agreement.

Colonel Abernathy pushed a button on his desk and spoke into the unicom. "Cunningham, I need a volunteer chopper pilot, and see if you can round up a code Whiskey-Bravo too."

"Roger that sir, where we going?" said a voice.

"Sixteen," answered Abernathy. "We need to try to pluck four Seals out of the jungle. I need a chopper big enough to carry five passengers."

"Five?" asked Ted.

"Yes, five. We are picking up four Navy Seals, and we have one Whiskey-Bravo on board," said Josh.

"What is a Whiskey-Bravo?" Ted asked.

"Guess that's something you Navy boys wouldn't know about. A Whisky-Bravo is a color-blind fellow—a spotter."

"Color-blind?"

"Yes, Ted, color blind. They can spot things in the jungle that people with normal vision can't see. They are not affected by camouflage. A color-blind guy can spot Charlie in a second. Here in the real world we call them spotters."

"Oh, good point," said Ted. "By the way, Josh, make that chopper a six passenger."

"Why?"

I'm going too."

"No way Commander. This is where I pull the plug out of this operation. I can't let you go in a…."

"Josh, let's cut through the bullshit. They are my people and I'm going!"

"Ted, we don't even know where Wildgoose is. There's a big jungle out there, not to mention the swamp."

"Just get us to a landing zone in Sixteen, Josh. Wildgoose will find us; we don't have to worry about finding him."

"How will he know?"

"He will just know," said Ted.

Abernathy thought for a moment and said, "Okay Commander, it's your ass."

"You sent for me, sir?" said a young Warrant Officer, saluting and stepping into Abernathy's office.

Abernathy returned the salute. "Yes, thank you for coming, Holly. Commander, meet Warrant Officer Horatio Hollingsworth. Holly, this is Commander Ted Barrett of the United States Navy."

"A pleasure sir," said Hollingsworth tilting his head toward Ted.

Ted nodded back.

"Holly," said Abernathy, "you do know this is strictly a volunteer mission?"

"Yes sir, absolutely, sir."

"Private First Class Jones is going to spot for us. He knows and he volunteered right away. Ah sirs, if you don't mind my opinion…."

"No, Holly, go ahead. What's on your mind?" asked Abernathy.

"Well sir, from what I hear the NVA is getting damn close. If we are going, we better move our asses, sir."

"Commander that's about it. Holly is ready when you are. I put out some fatigues. You can't be out there in Red Cross Whites."

"Look Josh, I owe you one and…," Ted started to say.

"Don't thank me," said Josh, grinding out his cigarette in a tin cup. "I might not be doing you any favors. There is a Huey outside, an HU-1A; it will lift damn near anything you put in it. They are waiting for you."

They embraced and slapped each other on the back and then Ted was gone.

Lieutenant Colonel Josh Abernathy walked over to the window. He shook a Winston from the rumpled pack and watched the Huey as it rose and departed to the northeast barely skimming over the tops of the trees.

He lit the Winston and blew a cloud of smoke toward the ceiling. *Barrett, you crazy bastard…. You are never going to find those boys in that quagmire.*

The Huey was giving them a smooth ride. But occasionally it was punctuated with a loud noise and rocking motion bumps.

Ted shouted over the roar of the Huey's engine, "What was that Private Jones?"

"Sir, you can just call me Jonesy, everybody does. That was ground fire, sir."

210

"Ground fire?"

"Yes sir, but not to worry though; we are low and fast. By the time they know we are here, we're gone. I've been out here lots of times, never taken a serious hit. Besides sir," he said smiling, "Charlie is a piss-poor marksman."

Ted took an instant liking to the cheerful young spotter. He had a warm smile and a charismatic personality. Apparently, he wasn't very concerned about the ground fire. He didn't seem to be.

Probably a veteran of a hundred missions like this.... Ted thought.

"Where you from Jonesy?"

"Oklahoma sir, little town called Ada. I got my Mom, two brothers and two sisters still there."

"What about you, sir?"

"Florida," Ted said.

"How old are you, Jonesy?"

"Nineteen sir," Jonesy began laughing. "Now you take Warrant Officer Hollingsworth up there," he said, throwing his index finger like a dart in the direction of the cockpit. "He's an old man."

"Like how old?" asked Ted.

"Ah twenty-two sir, he'll be twenty-three in May."

"I guess I must be Methuselah," said Ted.

Both laughed.

"Okay Commander, we are entering the eastern edge of Grid Area Sixteen sir," shouted the pilot, Horatio Hollingsworth. "What do you want me to do?"

"Good Holly. Find a spot that would make a good landing zone. We'll hover for a few seconds then retreat back towards the mountains."

"Sir?" said the confused pilot.

"In other words Holly, we are telling our Seals down there to go to the landing zone. We will disappear for awhile and give them time to get to it. Then we can come back and pick them up."

"Will they know how to find the L-Z, sir?" asked Hollingsworth.

"They will know," said Ted.

"Maybe I'll be able to spot them," said Jonesy.

"Jonesy, I respect your abilities," said Ted, "but these guys are Seminole Indians. I doubt if we could spot them if they were in this helicopter with us."

Warrant Officer Hollingsworth swung the Huey around facing the southwest corner of Grid Area Sixteen.

"There's a good spot Commander," he shouted.

Ted saw where his gaze was fixed.

"Looks pretty marshy doesn't it, Holly?"

"Yes sir," he answered, "but I can't get any closer, our blades will hit the trees. They will have to make it about two hundred yards from the jungle to that clearing there."

"Okay Holly, you're the boss. We have marked the spot. Let's get out of here."

The helicopter banked to the right and made a course to the northeast toward the mountains.

"I don't like it," said Jonesy.

Jonesy, what is the matter?" Ted asked.

"Too quiet sir, I just got a feeling that Charlie is up to something."

"I don't like it either Commander," said Hollingsworth through the headphones. "Everything's too quiet, no activity down there."

I thought quiet was a good thing, thought Ted.

Hollingsworth motioned for him to come forward to the cockpit. Ted leaned in the door.

"Sir," said Hollingsworth, "we are headed back to the L-Z, please understand I can only hover for a few moments. When I say go, we have to go. I am starting to be concerned about low fuel."

"I understand Holly," said Ted, still speaking through the headset.

"I won't be able to land this thing in there; it's too soupy. We will never be able to lift off, especially with that kind of load, sir."

"What are we going to do?"

"Well sir, I can get her down to just a couple feet off that mire, they will have to jump on board."

"No problem, Holly."

The helicopter turned around and made a course directly for the landing zone.

Warrant Officer Hollingsworth guided his ship no more than five feet above the smelly morass.

"That's the landing zone just ahead sir, I can hover and give them time to get to us from the trees," said Hollingsworth.

This kid is good, thought Ted. *Flies this thing like he was born in it....*

"Too quiet," said Jonesy.

Suddenly, the sky filled with explosions. Black smoke was all around them. The noise was deafening and rocking the Huey violently. Ted held on his shoulder straps with a death grip. He was almost blinded by the flashing flack bursting in the air.

Charlie may be piss poor marksmen, but they sure as hell got us in their crosshairs today!

"Abort, abort!" yelled Hollingsworth. "We gotta get outta here!"

"No!" shouted Ted, unbuckling his shoulder harness and bolting toward the door.

"Sit your ass down Commander," shouted Jonesy, ignoring his rank. "Hollingsworth is in command of this aircraft. Abort means abort!"

"Holly get me over those trees," yelled Ted, pointing to some dense jungle growth covered with heavy vines.

"Whatever you say sir," replied Hollingsworth.

Like Abernathy said, Commander, "It's your ass...."

The helicopter had risen to an altitude of thirty feet. Ted could see the tall marsh grass and reeds blowing sideways. The trees were shaking ferociously in the hurricane downwash from the chopper blades.

He stood at the door.

I have to do it now—if I think about it, I won't... I have to land butt first.... Less chance of breaking anything—I could stay aboard and go back to Saigon. Back to my precious Lili, I could hold her warm body against mine again—kiss her sweet soft lips—I could once again see that majestic smile. Those perfect teeth, her long black hair...her laugh...her voice...her smell, we could make love every day.

All I have to do is sit down.... But Wildgoose is down there—I have to get to him. Alright Goose, I'm betting it all on you...

Lili, I miss you... I love you so much.

Ted jumped.

CHAPTER THIRTY

Γ he downwash of the helicopter blades jetted Ted
down with startling speed. He felt the static
electricity from the blades making his hair tingle. He crashed
through vines, tree leaves and limbs like a wrecking ball.
They did precious little to cushion his fall.

Ted felt like every bone in his body was broken. He was
bruised everywhere, but he was alive. He felt his body for
protruding bones and looked for blood. There was none but
he was dizzy and nauseous. He felt a stabbing pain in his
lower back. Thankfully, he was well hidden in the foliage.

He could hear in the near distance the "whomp, whomp,
whomp," of the helicopter blades.

At least they got out of here unscathed.

Through the leaves of his jungle hideout Ted caught a
glimpse of the departing helicopter. It was spinning
viciously in a tight circle. Black smoke was pouring from its
engine. He lost sight of the Huey but heard the explosion.
The Huey was obliterated into a million pieces. Along with
it the young lives of Warrant Officer Horatio Hollingsworth
and Private First Class Jones.

"Oh no. No!" he cried aloud.

The dizziness and nausea overcame him. Ted tried to stand, but the world was reeling in all directions. He could feel the raw vomit in his throat. As he lay in the fetid water under the jungle trees, a black cloud descended over him. Ted fought the blackness. He stared up through the trees and vines.

I cannot pass out—I must stay awake—I must—I must....
Lili is calling me—Lili—Lili....

The darkness settled over him.

Unconscious, Ted lay in his jungle lair.

Ted became aware of voices all around him. A splash of the putrid water in his face brought him fully awake. He opened his eyes and was staring into the quizzical eyes of several North Vietnamese Soldiers. The air was full of a strange language, all of them excitingly talking at the same time.

They motioned for him to get up. He tried but could not stand. One of the soldiers, apparently the leader, jerked Ted to his feet and shouted to him what must have been instructions. Ted cried out in excruciating pain. All the soldiers were chattering and groping him as he towered above them. The language sounded like gibberish to Ted, but occasionally he could make out, "American."

The leader clasped Ted's arms behind his back and slid a bamboo pole between his two arms. After binding him tightly, cutting off the circulation, he gestured for Ted to follow. Ted was barely able to walk but trudged along the best he could. The rest of the group trailed behind still jabbering.

Thank God, Abernathy gave me these fatigues without any officer insignias.... If they find out, I am an officer it would be worse.... If they find out, I am a translator I am a dead man. I'm probably a dead man anyway.... Lili my love, I am so sorry.

After what seemed like miles to Ted, they came to a large Army bivouac area. Ted made quite an entrance with enemy soldiers forming a gauntlet. They were spitting on him and jeering when they came to two cabins at the edge of the camp.

The cabins were elevated to protect them from the monsoon floods. A small man dressed in a snappy North Vietnamese tan uniform started down the steps. He wore knee high brown boots and was carrying a riding crop in his right hand slapping it in his palm. Ted could see from his uniform brass that he was a colonel.

"Well, well. What have we here, an American?" said the colonel in broken English.

Ted said nothing.

"You are surprised I speak your language, yes?" he said. "I am Colonel Phong, but perhaps you know me by my better name, 'Colonel Death.'"

Ted stared straight ahead.

"Oh! So you choose to ignore me?" said the colonel. "You choose to disrespect your capturers?"

With that, the colonel lashed out with the riding crop striking Ted across the chest. His body reeled with the pain, which was like having his chest laid open with a dull hatchet.

Ted thought: *You insufferable little prick.... If this was one-on-one, and you didn't have all these half-witted midgets around, I would take that riding crop and give it to you for a suppository.*

Ted glared at him.

"Very well, Mister American, no need to talk now. The general will be here the day after tomorrow. We will all have a nice talk then. We have a special way of encouraging people to talk."

Ted continued to glower at the colonel.

The colonel said, "Then it shall be my pleasure to kill you—very slowly." Waving his riding crop he ordered, "Take him away."

They half shoved, half dragged, Ted to a location on the edge of the camp where there were many small cages. Some of the cages enclosed chickens leaving barely enough room for the hen to move. *The chickens provided eggs for the camp,* he thought. There was chicken droppings piling up on the ground along with peelings, bones, cans, papers and all kinds of other garbage. Ted could only surmise that this was the garbage dump for the camp.

Behind the chicken coops, abutting the jungle foliage, lay a stagnate ditch approximately six feet wide, holding a couple inches of contaminated water. Resting in the ditch was a larger bamboo cage.

One of the soldiers motioned for Ted to get in the cage.

Hey, I'm six-two…. I could never fit in there!

The soldiers forced Ted into the bamboo cage, which was so small he had to bend halfway over. He was too weak to put up much resistance. They bound his hands in front, and ran the bamboo pole behind his knees. His hands were then tied to the pole, forcing Ted to remain in a bent over position. He could not sit nor stand. Five inches of septic water covered the bottom of the cage.

The soldiers left as night began to engulf the camp.

So this is how it all ends...? Here I am in this cesspool; with chicken shit running ankle deep, the stench is unbearable.... Jungle Pythons are just a few feet away.... What kind of draconian torture awaits me...?

Lili, I didn't want it to end this way. I didn't want it to end at all—when I read Vladimir Mayakovski, I always thought of you—in his poem, "You," he wrote:

You came determined, because I was tall,

Because I was roaring,

But on close inspection,

You found a mere boy,

You seized, and snatched my heart away....

Ted righted himself as best he could. He said aloud, "How stupid. Here I am in this putrid sewer, in God knows where, Vietnam, thinking about Mayakovski. What the hell is wrong with me? The general will be here in a couple days. They will torture me to death, thinking I know something."

Lili, I am so, so sorry— I have always loved you....

CHAPTER THIRTY-ONE

The wedding celebration at the Corobici was like no other. Don Velazquez had the entire Perez family flown in from San Antonio and provided them accommodations in the hacienda. The Don had invited many of his local aristocratic friends along with political dignitaries. The President of Costa Rica was expected to attend; so security around the Corobici was tight.

An orchestra setting was in place on the carpet lawn behind the hacienda. A long narrow white carpet between a huge assembly of chairs led down the sloping lawn to a wedding arch on the edge of the river.

"Oh Anastasio, everything is so beautiful!" Lili exclaimed. They stood watching the workers make the final preparations for the big event. "Our wedding arch is made completely of flowers. I wonder how they did it?"

"I'm sure it took some time," he replied. "Tomorrow afternoon we will be standing under it taking our vows."

"Yes, I know," Lili quietly said.

That evening Lili was in her room. Gabriella, her Maid of Honor, said, "Lili, for Pete's sake, you haven't stopped crying since I have been here."

"Gabbie, I can't help it. I just can't help it," she sobbed.

"Sister, your tears have been flowing like high tide at Padre Island Beach. You can't get married with your eyes swollen and red like that."

Lili sat on the edge of her bed and put her face in her hands. "I know Gabbie, but I can't help it."

"Lili, you are not bawling because of that lawyer, Ted Barrett, are you?"

Lili said nothing but sobbed louder at the mention of his name.

Lili's thoughts drifted back to the previous week. Ambassador Thomas had come to her office. Leaning against the door jamb, she shoved a pencil behind her ear and said. "Lili are you sure you are doing the right thing marrying Don Velazquez?"

"I think so," she quietly whispered.

"Lili," said the ambassador, "thinking so and knowing so are two different things."

She met the ambassador's gaze but said nothing.

"Think about it," said Ambassador Thomas. She quietly retreated and returned to her own office.

It was late. Gabriella had returned to her room. Alone Lili lay in the still darkness staring at the ceiling. The ambassador's words stuck in her mind.

Thinking so and knowing so are two different things....

Lili closed her eyes hoping for a little sleep. Sleep deserted her. It always did unless she was beside Ted. After their lovemaking she would snuggle against him and drift into a deep, peaceful, refreshing sleep.

Oh Teddy Bare, come take me away from all this…. Take me back to our little apartment in North Dallas—we were so happy there. I will never stop loving you.

The following morning Gabriella burst into Lili's room. "Okay, big sister, today is the day. You are going to be an esposa."

Lili said, "Big sister, Ha! You are taller than I am Gabbie."

"Everybody is taller than you are Lili. Come on, let's get you dressed."

"It's good to see you in better spirits," said Gabriella.

Lili smiled.

It might appear to be good spirits on the outside, but you don't know what is on the inside….

Lili's choice of a wedding gown was nothing extravagant, although she had her choice of anything she wanted. Gabriella and her sisters-in-law were more prodigal in their spending habits and had selected several expensive dresses with delicate embroidery and long trains. Instead Lili chose a more simple dress with a modest train and a beautiful veil with a flowered headpiece.

A light rap sounded on her door. A sister-in-law answered the knock and opened it to Lucy.

"Oh Miss Perez, mum, I am so happy for you!" exclaimed an excited Lucy.

"Dear Lucy, please come in and remember my name is Lili."

"Oh Lili, I am so happy for you, mum," she squealed jumping on her tip toes. "You are so beautiful!"

"Thank you, Lucy," said Lili. "Someday a handsome prince will marry you and you will be even more beautiful."

"Oh mum, do you really think so? Really, really?" exclaimed Lucy.

"I know so, Lucy," she said, touching her finger on the tip of Lucy's nose, as she often did.

"Ah mum, I almost forgot; here are the white orchids for you to carry in your bridal bouquet."

"Thank you, Lucy."

"Yes mum," she said, and started to leave.

Ah mum," Lucy said shyly, shuffling her feet and looking at the floor.

"Yes, Lucy?"

"Mum, would it be okay if I gave you a hug?"

Lili knew what Lucy was asking. Lili was her friend. In a few moments she would be "Señora" Velazquez. From that time on any socializing or contact with hired help was unthinkable.

"Lucy," she said. "Nothing would give me any greater pleasure than getting a hug from you on my wedding day."

Lucy's smile was so wide Lili thought her face might split. They embraced and Lucy left. Both were crying.

When Lili stepped out in the sunlight the crowd gasped. Everyone's eyes were upon her. The orchestra struck up the traditional *Wedding March*. She slipped her hand through the arm of her father. Together they walked down the narrow carpet to Anastasio, waiting under the flowered arch by the river. He too was dressed in white. A tuxedo with a blood red cummerbund around his waist draped to his right side.

At the arch, Miguel slowly raised Lili's veil and kissed her cheek.

"With tears streaming down his face" he said, "Vaya Con Dios, mi pequeño, Angel. Go with God, my little Angel."

"I love you, Papa."

Lili joined hands with Anastasio.

Why can't you be Ted standing here beside me…? Why can't you be my Teddy Bare…?

Moments later Lili was Mrs. Anastasio Velazquez.

Orlando was loudly absent.

The events which followed were spectacular, there was much going on. The orchestra played lively tunes. People were dancing and everyone was having a wonderful time. All except one.

There were tables of potato salad, baked beans, tubs of yellow and white rice, salads and vegetables of all sorts. There was pork and chicken roasting on the open charcoal pits. The Don had ordered a steer butchered and brought up from the ranch so there was plenty of beef.

Don Velazquez and Lili stood in front of a long receiving line greeting the many guests and well-wishers. Everyone wanted to meet the new Mrs. Velazquez and to see if she was really as lovely as they had heard. She was.

Lili greeted the guests and captivated them with her special smile, speaking to them in Spanish and English.

Anastasio was extremely proud of his youthful prize.

A rather portly gentleman dressed in a dark brown suit approached the new couple. He was wearing a Stetson hat, cowboy boots and carrying a drink in his hand.

"Lili, I would like you to meet, Mister...."

"Hang on there, Anastasio," he interrupted. "Why she's even purdier then her picture."

The visitor took off his Stetson and said, "Howdy there little Miss. My name is Vernon Baxter, from the Great State of Texas. I hear you are too."

"Yes Mister Baxter, I'm from the San Antonio area," she said.

"It's pretty down there in the hill country. I used to spend quite a bit of time in that area. Well, I'd better go find my Missus before she runs off with one of them good looking Costa Rica boys," Baxter said, as he laughed and winked at Anastasio.

The Don forced a smile.

Baxter kissed Lili on the cheek, "Why I'da walked all the way from Lubbock to kiss a purdy gal like you." He waved and walked away re-donning the Stetson.

Ambassador Thomas was at the bar ordering a white wine when Baxter came up beside her.

"Hello Mister Baxter."

"Howdy ma'am," he said with a puzzled look, again taking off the Stetson.

Seeing that Baxter was at a disadvantage and did not remember her name, easing his confusion Ambassador Thomas said, "Mister Baxter, my name is Julie Thomas, I work in the American Embassy in San Jose."

"Oh yes ma'am, I remember you. Didn't we meet at Senator Powell's party in Washington a couple years back?"

"Yes."

"Work at the embassy, hell." Baxter exclaimed. "Ain't you the ambassador?"

"That's what they keep telling me," she smiled.

Ambassador Thomas continued. "As I recall you were meeting with the senator about some oil drilling leases here in Central America."

"Yes ma'am, I think I was."

"I remember, Mister Baxter. You said you were coming down here and make some things happen."

Vernon looked past the ambassador and stared directly at Lili. He said coolly, "Yes ma'am, I know how to make things happen."

CHAPTER THIRTY-TWO

As the afternoon passed to evening at the Corobici there was no indication of the celebration slowing down. Even though there was still some daylight left, the fireworks began. The sky was filled with splendid colors and displays from the exploding munitions. People were still dancing, eating and drinking. Tucked out of sight upstairs, Lucy and her cousin, Carlos, the stable boy, watched the festivity. She said to Carlos, "Lili is in love."

"Of course she is in love, she just married Don Velazquez."

"No, she is not in love with the Don. Lili is in love with someone else."

"Who?"

"I don't know."

"How do you know a thing like that?" asked Carlos curtly.

"Because Lili is my friend and I just know."

"Lili? Since when do you call the Don's wife by her Christian name?"

"Because she is my friend and she told me to."

"No way. She is not your friend! Now she is the matron of the whole hacienda. She is your jefe, your boss. You are just a demestico, like me."

"No," she flatly stated. "We are as good as anybody else."

"Who told you trash like that?"

"Lili did. Lili said so!"

"Someday I am going to meet a handsome prince and have a big wedding just like this, even bigger."

"Ha!"

"Ha yourself, Carlos and I will just as beautiful as Lili."

"Ha, ha!"

"Come my love," said Anastasio. "It is time to go."

"Where are we going?" Lili asked.

"It is a surprise," he said. "Quick now, let's change our clothes. Lucy has packed your bags and they have been brought down."

When she came downstairs from changing clothes, Lili found Anastasio and Carlos in the golf cart. Carlos drove around the circular fountain, down the long driveway to the Corobici's airstrip. The pilot, Ray Corbin was waiting beside the open door of the airplane.

"Anastasio, where are you taking me?"

"I cannot spoil the surprise my love. You will soon see."

The Beech was only in the air for a few minutes. It might have been longer, but everything was happening so fast. They touched down on a cleanly mowed grass strip and taxied to a covered Jeep.

"Please," said the Don, as he held out his hand and helped her settle in the passenger seat. Quickly he went around to the driver's side. She had never seen him drive before except the golf cart. The Don steered the Jeep up a winding mountain road. Lili could tell they had to be going very high up the mountain.

Soon they arrived at a lodge built of timber logs and large white stones. Lili noticed smoke coming from the chimney. The undeniable inviting fragrance of the burning piñon logs captured her nostrils. She loved the floor to ceiling glass windows and the large veranda which girdled the entire lodge.

"Anastasio, this is so, so beautiful. This must be the most beautiful place on earth."

"Thank you, my dear. This is our hunting lodge," he said. "Come look. We are on the very northwest corner of the Corobici. See the river and the valley far below. And if you look way over there," he pointed over the acres of coffee trees. "It is almost dark now, but on a clear day you can see the hacienda."

Inside was just as impressive. The floor and walls were done in a highly varnished tongue and groove knotty pine. They were greeted by a white-coated Costa Rican boy who was to fend for them. A cook was in the kitchen preparing their evening meal.

The lodge inside was built completely of wood. From the large living room one could look out over the mountains in any direction. Toward the back of the room was a staircase leading up to the sleeping quarters. Lili tried not to look in that direction.

Walking over to a mirrored wet bar, he said, "Would you like some Champagne?"

"Yes, thank you. I will try some."

The newlyweds sat and talked for awhile, sipping their champagne. The Don noticed the cook standing in the doorway of the lodge's dining area.

"I believe dinner is ready," he said. "Are you hungry?"

"Not really, but I should try to eat something."

The dinner was exquisite served with stewed venison and an assortment of steamed vegetables. Lili barely touched it and just poked at her food, dreading what was to come. When they had rested for awhile and after the Don had another drink, he said. "It has been a long exciting day; shall we retire for the evening?"

"Ah-hum," Lili answered, slightly shaking her head.

Upstairs Lili came out of the bathroom wearing a long powder blue night gown. She kept her panties on. She slipped between the satin sheets and pulled the covers up to her chin.

This is so different than when I was with Ted—we would chase each other around our apartment stark naked. I was never modest or ashamed with him—everything was so natural—the only man who has ever touched me is my Teddy Bare.

She listened as Velazquez came up the stairs. He went into the bathroom. It seemed to Lili he was in there a long time. He finally came out dressed in white silk pajamas. He climbed in the bed beside her and kissed her lips.

The Don reached over and snapped off the table lamp, blanketing the room into darkness.

Lili closed her eyes together as tightly as she could and bit her lip. She braced herself for the inevitable.

The Don's attempt at lovemaking was clumsy at best. She smelled the sweet, sickening odor of his mouthwash as he groped her. The Don was rough and uncaring as he pawed and fondled her. He didn't show much, if any, concern for Lili.

Once he was inside her, she could hear Don Velazquez's repugnant grunting and wheezing, vehemently in pursuit of his moment of pleasure. She felt the vomit in her throat and gritted her teeth.

Teddy Bare, I am so sorry….

Afterward, Don Velazquez was snoring beside her, Lili lay wide awake. She couldn't sleep. She could never sleep well without Ted.

Lili wasn't thinking of the Don. She was thinking of Doctor Gomez' words:

"Remember little one, everything that glitters is not always gold."

CHAPTER THIRTY-THREE

Ted was in excruciating pain. There was no way he could get any relief. Any kind of sleep was out of the question. His lower back felt as if was full of jagged glass. Shortly after dawn two North Vietnamese soldiers pulled Ted out of his bamboo dungeon. He had no feeling in his hands or lower legs. Walking was impossible so the soldiers grabbed Ted under each arm and began to drag him.

That is when he saw it. Carved in the side of a tree sitting back from the ditch was a perfect "2," with a horizontal line carved in its center. It was no bigger than a paper clip and completely unnoticeable to an untrained eye.

"Goose, you magnificent sonofabitch, you know I am here!"

Ted was dragged about a hundred yards to a rancid hole in the ground about ten feet long and three feet wide. Ted guessed it four feet deep. Across the ditch lay a board. His guards began gesturing and motioning to him trying to make him understand this was a latrine and where he was to relieve himself. The putrid stench was unbearable. There were thousands of flies and countless other insects buzzing around his head. The ditch was half filled with human waste. The smell was so horrible it could not have been imagined. Ted shook his head no to the guards.

"So, Mister American, you do not approve of our rest room facilities," said the approaching Colonel Phong, a/k/a, Colonel Death. He was as yesterday, all decked out in his brash khaki uniform, brown knee boots and riding crop.

Ted said nothing but held an odious glare into Colonel Death's eyes. He saw something he had never seen in any man before. He saw evil.

Most of us, both sides, are here because we have to be. You—you pugnacious little bastard, are here because you love it.

"Perhaps," said the colonel, "we should make reservations for you to stay in your American Holiday Inn. Oh so sorry, there is not one here." He broke out in a maniacal laugh that sounded like the soundtrack from a horror movie.

He walked behind Ted and brought the riding crop down hard across the back of his thighs. Ted let a raucous shout of agonizing pain. Down he went in the grime and sludge.

The colonel said to the two soldiers. "Take him away. We must save him for the general's entertainment in the morning."

They dragged Ted back to his polluted mew. One of the soldiers handed him a small clay bowl filled with rice. Crawling in the rice, Ted could see worms and maggots and other little forms of diminutive life he had never seen before. He shook his head no.

They forced him into the bamboo cage and as before, bound his hands to the bamboo pole behind his thighs. Ted could neither sit nor stand. His pain was becoming unbearable. His back felt like it was on fire.

I hope the general comes soon—then this will be over with. They are going to kill me—I hope they do it quickly—they won't.

Late that afternoon a small convoy rolled into the camp. From his disintegrating enclosure Ted could make out the general as he alit from a covered jeep. He too was bedecked in a khaki uniform, knee boots and all the trimmings. He wore so many metals on his chest it reminded Ted of a fruit salad.

Colonel Death greeted the general with a snappy salute and a big smile. He kept gesturing and pointing in Ted's direction. The general looked at Ted with great interest and gave a cruel smile.

An aide-de-camp showed the general to the cabin next to the colonels.

Night began to fall on the camp. Ted had given up on getting any sleep at all. Sleep was impossible in the position which he was bound. His back rested against the rear of the cage abutting the jungle. Ted was becoming delirious from the pain and the hunger.

The evening wore on and passed into deep night. Ted could only speculate it must be in the early morning hours, the camp was as quiet as a morgue. The only sounds breaking the stillness were from the jungle. Frogs were croaking, crickets were fiddling and a litany of other creatures joined the symphony. A deep heavy fog, as thick as chowder, settled over the camp.

Suddenly Ted felt something heavy. Something very strong was wrapping itself around his neck. It was crushing him.

Ted's mind flashed.

A python! I have come all this way... just to be crushed to death in this freaking septic tank.... Sorry General—sorry Colonel—I hate to spoil your torture party tomorrow. But at least you won't get me!

Ted struggled against the giant's powerful grasp as best he could. It was useless. He could not defend himself against the giant's massive strength. Because of the binding cords he could barely move. He struggled desperately for life-giving air. He couldn't breathe. He felt himself fade in and out of consciousness.

So, this is what it is like to die....

Ted's vision became blurred. He saw dimness all around him. Then the dimness turned to blackness. The last conscience thought he had was the beautiful face of Lili Perez.

CHAPTER THIRTY-FOUR

Ted was trying to stir. His vision was so contorted he could scarcely make out objects and colors. He thought the top of his head was going to explode because of the stabbing migraine headache. He felt his hands and legs. He was no longer tied to the bamboo.

"It's about damn time you woke up Commander and started earning that fat government salary of yours," he heard a familiar voice say.

Ted's vision was slowly coming into focus. He looked in the direction of the voice.

"Goose? Goose! I knew you would get me out of there!" he fairly shouted.

Major Gary Wildgoose, Ted's childhood friend was a full-blooded Seminole Native American. A handsome man with long black hair that he wore in a ponytail. He was tall for a Seminole, standing at six feet even. Wildgoose was trim and muscular, clearly an athlete. His olive skin matched a pair of piercing brown eyes.

"Shh, not too loud, Commander; we got Charlie all around us. They've been looking for you for hours."

"How long have I been out, Goose?"

"Oh yeah, sorry about that Commander, I had to choke you down. Couldn't risk you making any noise or we would have had the whole frigging Commie Army all over us."

"I understand, Goose. How long have I been out?" asked Ted again.

"Most of the day, sir, I decided to let you sleep awhile. I know you didn't get any while you were there. I managed to get some soup down you."

"Soup?"

"Heck yeah. We eat better than in the chow hall at Pendleton. Wild hogs out here, birds and plenty of vegetables."

"Vegetables?"

"Sure Commander, you just have to know where to look. Don't you remember anything from the Everglades? Only thing is the water. You have to watch what you drink."

Ted looked around. They were in a clearing completely encircled by a large thicket.

"Those two who were supposed to be guarding you," Wildgoose went on. "One is up there talking to Jesus right now," he said jerking his index finger toward the sky. The other one took off in the jungle— deserted. Can't say I blame him. The general is some kinda pissed-off over losing you, and Colonel Death is dodging him like a ricocheted bullet."

"Goose, I have a lot to tell you. The war is over. We've got to get out of here."

"Your war might be over Commander, but I still have an assignment," said Major Wildgoose, shoving a piece of straw between his lips.

"What do you mean Goose? What assignment?"

"Commander, all respect intended, Washington has not canceled my orders. I was instructed to eradicate the general, and now I might throw in a colonel as a little bonus."

"Goose, you didn't hear me. The freaking war is over."

"As I said Commander, I have specific orders from Washington and until I hear differently, I will carry them out."

Ted could see that trying to persuade the major any differently would be a waste of time. He sighed and shook his head in agreement with the major. He folded his hands and said, "Goose, you have called me Ted my whole life, now all of a sudden I am Commander?"

"You are the ranking officer, sir. When we were boys on the football field in Big Cypress, we played for points. You were Ted, I was Goose. Out here it's a war zone, we play for keeps. Now, you are the commander."

"In that case, Major Wildgoose, I'm giving you a direct order. You are to take command of this operation and get us the hell out of here."

"Aye, aye Commander, sir," replied Wildgoose, feigning a salute. "As soon as my assignment is carried out."

"Goose, we got Sergeant Osceola."

"Yeah, I know."

"Why didn't you just send a message in Seminole, instead of making me figure out all that crap about St. Joe and Jesse James and all?"

"Couldn't take the chance, Ted. Somebody in the embassy might have happened over the message once you de-coded it and spilled the beans. They would have sent a bunch of Army boys to get him and Charlie would be waiting for them on the high ground north of the road. That's the first place they would have looked. They would never have looked in the swamps. Charlie sets a trap and then you have a massacre; those boys would have all been killed."

"Why me?"

"Because I knew you would figure it out and I knew you were the only one who could find him."

"Goose, I got out here in an Army chopper, and I…."

Wildgoose interrupted. "I know, Ted. We found the wreckage. Charlie was everywhere around it. I know what you are asking. No one survived. Most likely they will be listed as MIAs."

Those two men, not men, boys, Holly and Jonesy are dead because of me.

"Alright Ted," Wildgoose said as he stood up. 'Here's a change of clothes for you and there is a little creek over behind that coppice. You can wash up there. From smelling you, I think you could use it. The water's not too clean but at least it is running water, not stagnant. I got the leeches and ticks off you, but you better check your privates. Don't pull off leeches. Just pour a little alcohol on them. And Ted."

"Yes?"

"Try to get some rest. We have a long night and a busy morning ahead of us."

Ted didn't have to be asked twice. He was dead tired and every bone ached. He felt like the nerves in his body were on fire. Nevertheless after he washed he did his best to ignore the crushing pain in his back and fell into a deep much needed sleep.

Someone was shaking him awake. Ted sat up.

"Commander, it's time," said a SEAL dressed in fatigues speaking in Seminole.

"Time for what?" Ted asked, replying in same.

"Please sir, join the major. He is over there by the trees."

"Right away, thank you." Ted said. "Hey, what time is it?"

"About midnight, sir."

Ted found Major Wildgoose talking to his assembled men in Seminole.

"Commander, did you police your area?"

Ted nodded yes. He knew what Wildgoose meant. Seminoles never left any trace that anyone had ever been there. No trash, no ashes, no waste materials, no nothing.

"Alright, everyone knows their assignment and the rendezvous point," the major was saying. "Commander, you come with me."

Ted shook his head yes.

"Israel," said Wildgoose addressing one of the Seminole Seals. "I have something for you."

Thought Ted: *Israel? A Seminole named Israel...? A Jewish Indian...? Oh well.*

Wildgoose reached in a small canvas sack. What he pulled out made Ted gasp in terror and take a step back.

Clutched between his thumb and index finger was an Asian Bungarus Krait—*Bungarus Fasciatus.*

"This is one of the deadliest snakes in the world," he said. The creature hissed and began wrapping its slithering trunk around Wildgoose's arm. Ted thought it about two feet long and it was black circled by light yellow stripes.

"Goose, you crazy bastard," exclaimed Ted.

"Don't worry Commander. These things are all over the place out here. The Asian Krait's bite is like a King Cobras except sixteen times more toxic. Her venom is a pre-synaptic neurotoxin. In other words, you die of paralysis. It collapses the nervous system, you can't breathe and you die in agonizing pain. It only takes five or six minutes. Some of the GI's call them a 'two step.' Once she bites you can go only about two steps."

He handed the reptile to Israel and said. "Okay guys, everyone knows his job and you all know what to do and where to meet up. If any one of us is not there by dark tomorrow the rest of us will leave. That's an order. We will assume you didn't make it. Good luck!"

Ted was looking at the canvas bag which had held the snake. He looked up and only Wildgoose was there. The others were gone. They faded into the jungle. Nothing moved. There was no sound. Ted had watched Seminoles do this since he was a boy. The Seminoles were opaque. One instant they were there. The next they were gone— vanished. They just melted into the swamp.

Ted made a mental note: *someday I need to learn how they do that.*

Wildgoose motioned for him to follow. It seemed like they walked for a long time. Wildgoose turned and placed his index finger on his lips, making the universal gesture to be quiet. Soon they came to a large tree.

"Let me show you something," Wildgoose quietly said. He scaled up the tree with Ted behind him.

Twenty feet above the ground was a huge crotch in the tree where two men could rest comfortably. Ted could see this vantage point gave them a panoramic view of the NVA camp. He could see both roads coming in and out of the camp, the fuel depots and the ammunition arsenal.

"This is where I used to sit and watch Charlie," he whispered. "Then I would call it in to you."

Ted nodded.

"It will be daylight soon," Wildgoose said. "We must remain very still. My boys are going to set off a few firecrackers, so be ready."

Ted shook his head that he understood.

Ted remained where he was in the tree as Wildgoose sighted in his crossbow. Taking account of the range, distance and what little wind there was.

"I need to do this while it is still dark," he said. "We can't risk any movement after it gets light."

Ted understood and tried to get comfortable, at least as comfortable as he could under the circumstances. It would be light soon as Ted could see the first peeks of dawn breaking in the eastern horizon.

Wildgoose had lifted the crossbow to his shoulder and was taking aim. He was as still as a stone. Another trait of the Seminole. They could remain frozen still for hours. He waited.

The first streaks of daylight raced across the sky and began chasing the darkness from the jungle. Soon the NVA camp was bathed in the early morning sunlight. From his vantage point Ted could see the entire camp, which was about fifty yards away and the two officer's cabins facing them.

Abruptly, a blood-curdling scream ripped through the silence of the morning. The door of Colonel Death's cabin flew open and the colonel ran out on the small porch shrieking like a banshee. He was dressed in a knee-long white night shirt and was flailing his arms in the air like he was on fire. He was screaming at the top of his lungs like a madman.

Ted watched the fray and like everyone else wondered what was going on. Colonel Death pulled up the nightshirt and grabbed what looked like a piece of rope from his genitals.

Wait a minute, thought Ted. *That's not a rope—that's a snake! That's the Krait Wildgoose gave to Israel—well, Colonel Death, if that viper bit you on your balls, you're sure going to find out who your real friends are!*

Colonel Death was wallowing and flopping all over the porch like a fish out of water, until the paralysis set in.

He lay on the porch, his mouth wide open. He couldn't breathe. The colonel was completely aware of the pain and his collapsing lungs, but he could not move. He awaited his perdition. He waited to die.

Ted was thinking. *Well, well, Colonel Death—I thought you were supposed to be Leviathan. One of the seven princes of hell—its gatekeeper—a prince of evil—you are mentioned six times in the Hebrew Bible. You are supposed to be indestructible. You don't look so indestructible now.*

The general came out on the porch of his cabin, dressed in an identical nightshirt as was the colonel. He looked sleepy and very annoyed.

Ted heard the almost silent "pssst" of the crossbow, as Wildgoose took careful aim and released the arrow.

The general was about to ask about the cause of the commotion when he noticed something that tasted like metal in his mouth.

Strange, he caught a pungent smell of iodine. A very strong odor. Something warm was seeping down his chest. The general touched his chest. The warm liquid was blood—his blood.

The general reached up frantically clawing at his throat. He felt the stainless steel projectile lodged in his neck, severing both his jugular vein and choroid artery.

The general's eyes bulged and blood spurted from his mouth and nose like an open fire hydrant. Gagging and choking in his own blood, he put out his hands to cushion the fall. A cushion was not necessary. The general was dead before he hit the ground.

At that same instant a series of explosions rocked the camp. Ted saw a large streak of fire race down the center of the compound as if someone had ignited a river of gasoline.

Explosions were triggering explosions. The sky flashed and was filled with smoke and debris.

It must have hit their fuel and ammo dump, thought Ted.

The just awakened NVA soldiers were frantically running in every direction. Everyone was screaming and shouting in a cacophony of confusion. Many fled hysterically into the jungle, still in their underwear. Others were looking for their weapons, which had somehow mysteriously disappeared during the night. Some of the soldiers were on fire as they began to roll and writhe on the ground. The camp was in panic and total chaos.

"Okay Ted," said Wildgoose. "Ease down the tree and head back exactly the way we came."

In a few minutes they were back in the jungle. Ted had a difficult time keeping up with Wildgoose, who knew exactly where he was going. Ted's right hip began to cause him severe pain.

"Goose," he said, "wait up."

"Sure Ted, are you all right?"

"I don't know what is wrong, Goose. My hip feels like someone stuck a knife in it. I must have hit it pretty hard when I bailed out of that chopper."

"No doubt, Ted. Being tied in that cage didn't do it much good either. We can take a few minutes."

They rested and Ted said, "Goose, aren't we running a risk just sitting here and not moving?"

"Nah man, I told you, those little piss-ants couldn't find their dicks with an anvil tied to it."

"How did you get all those explosives?"

Wildgoose chuckled. "We borrowed them."

"You borrowed them?"

"Yes sir, we borrowed them. We borrowed them from Charlie himself. Now, how's that for a class act?"

"From Charlie himself?" laughed Ted.

"Yessiree. We blew up Charlie with his own friggin gunpowder. We've been stealing it a little at a time for a year."

"How are you feeling, Ted? We need to get moving."

"I can make it, Goose, let's go."

They trudged on for what seemed like hours. Finally Ted plopped down in a jungle clearing exhausted.

"Goose, my hip is not going to let me make it, something in there is broken. You go on."

"This is not the time for jokes, Ted. We are in this together and we are going to stay together."

"Goose, you have to get to the others. Now, I am giving you a direct order. Go!"

"Sorry Commander, sir those explosions affected my hearing. Can't hear a word you are saying besides, you wouldn't make it a day in this jungle alone."

"What?" exclaimed Ted. "I was raised in the Glades just like you, Goose."

"Yeah, that's true enough Commander, but you are a white man and a white man would never make it in here on his own."

Ted knew that Goose was right. The Seminoles possessed an innate instinct of survival in swampy, jungle-like environments. No one on earth could match them.

Wildgoose cut a limb with a 'vee' in it.

"Here Ted, try this for a crutch. It might help."

The crutch did help. A few times Wildgoose had to use a fireman's carry to get Ted over water and rough ground. Eventually they came to a clearing on the banks of a huge river. Ted thought it was easily a mile wide.

"Where are we, Goose?"

"That my friend," he said, pointing to the river palm up, "is the mighty Mekong. It is well over a couple miles wide here."

Wildgoose went on. "She's one of the largest rivers in the world and the twelfth longest. Comes out of the Tibetan Plateau, through China's Yunnan Province, and on through Burma, Laos and Thailand."

"Is this our rendezvous location?" asked Ted.

"Sure is," said Wildgoose. "Look across the river. That's Cambodia on the other side. The Mekong is the border between Vietnam and Cambodia."

"Where are our guys? Please tell me they made it."

"Ted, I thought I raised you better than that," Goose smiled. "Look around."

Ted looked but he didn't see anything.

"Here," said Goose. He pointed to a small sapling. Hardly visible carved on the sapling's trunk was a "2,"no larger than a man's thumbnail, with three horizontal lines through the center.

"See three lines. All three are here."

Wildgoose cupped his hands around his mouth. He made a birdcall identical to a black, red-beaked bird indigenous to the Florida Everglades, the Common Moorhen, *Gallinula Chloropus*, known in the Glades by the locals as a "Coot."

The response was immediate and soon all were gathered on the bank of the Mekong.

"Listen up guys," said Wildgoose in English. "We need to cut some floating logs, and...."

"Already done, sir," spoke up Israel.

"Good show guys. We will leave here after it gets dark. Let's go one at a time in three hour intervals. This way if anyone is caught Charlie might think you are alone. I will go last with Commander Barrett."

"Where are we going?" Ted asked.

"The river flows southeast Commander, through the Delta and empties into the South China Sea. We have to drift through a lot of hostile territory, but once we get further south there will be friendlies. Just identify yourselves and get to the nearest military installation. Remember, before it gets daylight go ashore and bury yourself somewhere. No daylight travel."

Everyone understood Wildgoose's orders.

"Come on Commander," he said. "Let's go back in the jungle and get out of sight. We need to get some sleep.

"For the rest of you guys," said Wildgoose, "good luck. It has been a privilege serving with every one of you."

Yes sir, likewise," they echoed.

The three Seminoles faded out of sight. In an instant they were silently gone into the jungle like a mist.

Wildgoose shook Ted awake.

"Are you ready to take the plunge," he asked. "It is after midnight."

Ted wondered. *How do these Seminoles know the time? None of them wear watches.*

"Yeah, let's do it."

"How is your leg?"

"It's mostly my hip," said Ted. "Hurts like hell."

"Wildgoose frowned. "We have to go. Maybe the buoyancy from the water will help."

"Doesn't matter; we gotta go," Ted said.

They eased into the Mekong. The water was warmer than Ted had expected. Grasping the log they drifted southward.

After an hour, maybe more, Ted had lost track of time, Wildgoose warned him to be quiet. They quietly floated past an NVA camp. No one was astir but Ted could see a small fire burning.

Once past the camp, Wildgoose whispered, "That was a NVA patrol. There's bound to be more. It will be light soon. We better find a place to go ashore."

Ted signaled, making an "O," with his thumb and index finger. The pain in his hip running down his leg was becoming excruciating. The constant kicking in the water was taking its toll on his injury.

"Here, this is good," said Wildgoose steering the log with the current toward shore.

They hid the log and walked inland a few yards. Wildgoose found a small cemetery. "Here Ted, crawl in."

"In a grave?" Ted exclaimed in disbelief.

"It's perfect. Charlie would never think to look for you in there."

"What about you?" Ted asked.

"Don't worry about me. I'll stand watch."

"But…" Ted started to say.

"No buts, Commander. Just get in."

Ted obliged and climbed in on top of the corpse resting in the shallow sepulcher. Wildgoose covered him with leaves and plants.

"Okay Ted, I'll be in the jungle. If I'm not back here by dark, you go on. Stay close to shore. Around daybreak tomorrow you should be around friendlies. The Navy still patrols the river; they will spot you."

"How do you know?" Ted asked.

"Because my guys will tell them," with that he was gone.

Ted knew that he must get some sleep, but the pain in his hip and leg would not allow him any relief. Sleep was not to come. He lay still.

He heard them. Maybe a dozen NVA soldiers were in the little cemetery. They were all around him. One stood so close that his boots were only inches from Ted's face. Ted didn't breathe. The Cong soldiers stabbed in the brush with their bayonets, but there was nothing in the small cemetery of interest to them. He listened to their chatter and soon they were gone.

Wildgoose knew what he was talking about. The soldiers did not look in the graves.

Ted could see through the leaves covering him that it was beginning to turn dark. Slowly he rose from his burrow of death and silently made it back to the river. He was very cognizant not to leave any tracks.

Wildgoose was nowhere to be seen. Ted waited.

Goose would never leave without me. What if Charlie got him? No, that's not likely—he told me to go if he wasn't here.

Ted waited another hour. He slowly began to get the floating log from where it was hidden when he heard the distinctive cry of an Everglades Moorhen. Ted answered back. In a few moments Wildgoose appeared splashing out of the river.

"Man, you would never fool a Seminole with that Coot call," he laughed.

"Okay," Wildgoose said. "There are two more Commie patrols about ten miles downriver. We shouldn't have any problem getting by them, but we are going to have to wait awhile until they sack out."

Ted said nothing, but shook his head that he understood.

"How is your hip?"

"It is getting worse. Hurts like hell," Ted replied.

Around midnight Wildgoose said, "Let's go. I'm sure they are asleep by now."

The two men quietly entered the Mekong and drifted southeast. They passed the two camping NVA patrols without incident.

"I don't like it," said Wildgoose.

"Don't like what?" Ted slurred.

He was nauseous and starting to hallucinate. Major Wildgoose had to hold on to his collar to keep him from going under the strong current of the Mekong.

"It is going to be light soon," said Wildgoose. "We shouldn't have waited so long to leave. I'm not sure we are far enough south to meet up with friendlies. But we had no choice. There is no way you could survive another night in that jungle."

As dawn broke Wildgoose steered the log away from shore to get into the faster moving current. They were drifting at an amazing speed.

"Well Theodore, old pal, it's broad daylight. We are going for broke."

It was an hour after sunrise, maybe two, when both men heard the engine of a boat. Was it friend or foe?

A U.S. Navy fifty-foot, Swift Boat came into sight rounding a bend in the river. The Navy's code name for the Swift Boats was "Operation Market Time."

A young ensign was on the bow of the Swift Boat speaking through a bullhorn, "Ahoy, Major Wildgoose?"

"Over here!" shouted Wildgoose waving.

The boat pulled over to the waterlogged men and quickly hoisted them aboard.

"Sir, are you alright?" inquired the young ensign.

"Never mind me," snapped Wildgoose, still holding Ted's collar. "This man needs a doctor, like now!"

"Is that Commander Barrett, sir?"

"One and the same," answered Wildgoose.

"We'll come about and get him to a hospital," said the ensign.

"Make it so," ordered Major Wildgoose.

Most of the American equipment and facilities in Vietnam had either been shut down or abandoned. However, a ramshackle hospital was still there.

The hospital staff provided Ted with nutrition and found him terribly dehydrated. A nurse started an I.V. He recovered quickly, but the pain in his hip and leg was unbearable.

A young Asian doctor approached Ted. "Relax Commander, I am American. We are not equipped to treat you here, but there is an Air Force transport plane out of here this afternoon going to Clark Air Force Base in the Philippines. I have you on it."

Ted thanked him and that afternoon Ted was on his way to Clark, which is on the Island of Luzon, approximately forty miles northwest of Manila.

At Clark, Ted was well received and well treated. An Air Force physician visited him.

"Commander," he said. "We can treat you here or I can get you on a transport leaving tonight going to Andrews, just outside Washington, D.C. Perhaps you might like to go to Bethesda, the Naval Hospital in Maryland."

"Doctor, I would like nothing more than to get to Bethesda, but I could never make it with this pain."

"No problem there Commander," the doctor smiled. "I can give you a shot and a couple prescriptions and you will want to do the Charleston all the way to Andrews."

"Make it so," said Ted.

CHAPTER THIRTY-FIVE

L ili adapted fairly well to life on the Corobici, but there were many concessions she had to make.

She missed not working, an endeavor strictly forbidden by the Don. She missed her friends at the embassy and the bustle of the office. Lili offered to help Don Velazquez with the Corobici's accounting and bookkeeping. The Don would have none of it.

She did not like being waited on hand and foot. Lili would often go in the vast kitchen to prepare her own drink or make a snack. At first the staff was appalled that the "Lady of the Hacienda," would fix her own lunch and pour her own drinks. They soon became used to Lili darting in and out of the kitchen. She was down to earth and never looked upon them as factotums. They all liked her very much.

Often she would eat with the staff at the large table in the kitchen talking and joking with everyone. Much to his chagrin when Don Velazquez heard of Lili's conduct and her socializing with the staff he reprimanded her sternly.

"Lili," he said. "We have demesticos and their job is to serve you. Whatever you need, all you have to do is press a button. Anything you might require will be brought to you."

Lili began. "But, Anastasio, I…."

"Lili," he broke in, holding up his hand, "a lady does not prepare her own meals."

Lili shook her head. She remembered reading about Abraham Lincoln. When a cabinet member came upon the martyred president shining his boots, he remarked: "Mister President, a gentleman doesn't black his own boots." To which Lincoln replied: "If a gentleman doesn't black his own boots, who does?"

Lili could never understand the class differences. To her, people were just people.

Pursuant to the Don's wishes, and much to Lili's surprise and delight, the Don stayed in his large master bedroom, downstairs and on the opposite side of the hacienda. Lili resided in the same suite where she had always stayed when she visited the Corobici. The Don had never invited her to his bedroom. She thought it strange a married couple would co-exist in such an arrangement, but she said nothing. She liked it this way.

He made an occasional visit to her room and she performed her martial duties, but he never stayed the night with her. It was the same every time. The Don sought his own "joie de vivre," and paid little, if any, to Lili's needs.

Lovemaking with my Teddy Bare was wonderful… I could never get enough of him. The Don leaves me cold—sex with him is nauseating…. Oh Teddy Bare, I miss you so, so much.

His visits became less and less frequent, which suited Lili just fine. She often thought that perhaps the Don had one of his doxies visit his bedroom late in the night. She had heard rumors about his philandering, but never gave it much gravity. Lili just plain didn't care.

Lili filled her days galloping her palomino around the Corobici, inhaling the fresh mountain air and enjoying the beautiful countryside. Don Velazquez had shouted at Carlos, the stable boy, for allowing Lili to saddle her own horse. He forbade Carlos to allow her to brush the mare after her morning rides. Lili brushed her anyway. She usually called Carlos to let him know when she wanted to ride so he could saddle the mare for her. She did not want to cause Carlos to get on the bad side of the Don again.

She often rode her mare into the mountains to enjoy the fields of flowers and the sweet aromas of the forest. Under the huge trees, she would curl her knee around the saddle horn and sit drinking in the sight of the river and the valley below. Sometimes she would lie under the trees and let Golden Belleza graze nearby.

She always thought of Ted. The words of Isak Dinesen, who was in fact, a nom-de-plume for Danish author, Baroness Karen Von Blixen-Fineche, lingered in her mind.

Meeting you was fate,
Becoming your friend was a choice,
But falling in love with you,
I had no control…

Lili often rode Golden Belleza to the huge packing plant, on the Corobici, where the workers were sealing the coffee beans and boxing them to be shipped, mostly to the United

States. Many of the workers were pretty, young Costa Rican girls in their late teens and early twenties. The Don did not like her to be in the area.

I wonder why…?

One day late in January Lili rose early. She felt dizzy and quickly grabbed the bedpost to keep her balance. Her stomach felt queasy. She rang for Lucy.

Lucy found her in the bathroom leaning over the toilet.

"Miss Lili, what is the matter?" Lucy exclaimed.

"I don't know Lucy, I have never been sick, but this hit me all of a sudden."

"Oh, querido," said Lucy. "Miss Lili maybe you have the flu."

"Please Lucy, help me back to my bed. I need to lie down."

Lucy got Lili back in her bed and said. "I am going down to the kitchen and ask my mama to make you something hot that will ease your stomach."

Soon Lucy was back with Carmella, her mother.

"Señora Velazquez," said Carmella, "pardon me for asking mum, but when was your last time?"

"I don't know," groaned Lili. "I never keep up with it. I'm very regular though. It has been a while. I should have had it by now."

"Tell me, mum," said Carmella, "are your breasts sensitive and tender?"

"Why yes, Carmella. I noticed it yesterday while riding my horse."

"Oh Señora, perhaps you are encinta?"

"Encinta?" asked Lucy.

"You think I'm pregnant?" Lili cried in English.

"I think you should see a doctor, mum."

Two weeks later Lili was sitting across from the Don at the dining room's long table, which could easily seat twenty. As was their custom they were dining alone. The dining room was adjacent to the library where Don Velazquez relaxed with a drink after dinner. He rarely invited Lili to join him anymore. The distance between them was becoming more and more apparent. The Don knew she still loved Ted Barrett. A fact he seemed to ignore.

Lili was his. She was his trophy.

"Anastasio," she said, piddling at her plate with her fork.

"Yes?"

"I had the airplane fly me to San Jose last week."

"Oh? Did you go shopping?"

"No, I went to see a doctor, an Obstetrician."

"An Obstétrico?" asked a startled Don Velazquez.

She didn't look up. "Yes, Anastasio, you are going to be a father again. I just found out this morning."

"Lili, that is wonderful news!" the Don exclaimed. He always called her "Lili." No longer did he use the pet pseudonyms as he so often did a year earlier.

"Do you suppose it is a male child?" he asked eagerly.

"That is God's decision," she disgustedly replied.

Lili thought. *Anastasio, you indecorous windbag.... Don't you know that it is the male who determines the sex of a child? Henry the Eighth, House of Tudor, desperately tried to produce a male heir…. Henry thought, mostly out of vanity and also because of the fragile peace that existed following the War of the Roses, England needed to be led by a male monarch. So, he went through six wives and had two beheaded because they did not produce a son. Finally Queen Jane, Jane Seymour, gave birth to Prince Edward, the future Edward the Sixth.*

Contrary to most couples who grow closer together during a pregnancy, the Don grew more distant. After finding out Lili was expecting, he never touched her again. He knew his pregnant wife was in love with another man; a fact he lived with but never seemed to concern him.

The summer passed and Lili had never felt better. She ate healthy and exercised regularly. Maintaining herself as the beautiful Lili she had always been.

Accepting an invitation from Ambassador Thomas, she was flown to San Jose and stayed with the Ambassador in the American Embassy to await the birth of her baby.

On a pretty, sunny day in late September Lili felt the first pangs of labor. She was driven to the hospital and Don Velazquez was notified.

The Don arrived at the hospital four hours later, but refused to go into either the labor or the delivery room. He chose instead to sit in the waiting room enjoying a cigar. Later that day, Augustino Perez Velazquez was born.

Don Anastasio Velazquez had a male heir.

CHAPTER THIRTY-SIX

Ted's stay at Bethesda Naval Hospital lasted from an anticipated month or so to much longer. The medical care he received at Bethesda was among the finest in the world but his hip and leg still bothered him.

The doctors had told him the problem was not in his hip or leg. The injury was in his lower back. Ted had suffered a herniated disc, *Prolapsus Disci Intertebralis,* or in layman's language, a "pinched nerve."

"Commander," the doctor had said. "There is not much we can do to fix your problem unless we operate. Back surgery like this is risky, but if you ever expect to regain full use of your hip and leg again, it will have to be done."

"When?" asked Ted.

"Can't say for sure, Commander. It's going to take a few months to get you healthy and up to speed. You were hurt pretty bad."

"What do you expect me to do until then? Hobble around like a ninety year old?"

"No sir, we have an excellent Physical Therapy unit here and I feel they can help you. We have to get you healthy and mobile before we can do any surgery."

"Doctor, then when are you going to cut me loose?" Ted asked.

"Hard to say, Commander. It is not so much the surgery, it's the physical therapy and rehab afterwards. All in all Commander, I would…."

"All in all, my butt," Ted blurted. "When can I get out of here? I need to find someone and you people are burning my daylight."

The doctor put his hand on Ted's shoulder. "Ted, we can probably get your surgery done in three to four months, but you are looking at least a year of rehabilitation, maybe more."

Ted couldn't believe his ears. *I have got to find Lili.*

Ted looked into the hazel eyes of the doctor. "Okay, Doc. Let's get started."

CHAPTER THIRTY-SEVEN

Ted began a rigid exercise program at Bethesda. His back surgery had gone well and in a few months his back and leg did feel better. He was able to leave the hospital on occasion with the aid of a cane.

He had tried for months to find Lili. Nobody knew anything about her. He could not reach anyone in her family who would talk to him. Besides, finding someone named Perez in San Antonio was like trying to find a Smith in New York City; the old needle in a haystack syndrome.

"Where shall I drop you, sir?" said the young petty officer driving the Navy van.

"FBI. The Hoover Building, 925 Pennsylvania Avenue, please," said Ted.

Ted walked up to the reception desk and a very businesslike woman spoke. "May I help you, sir?"

"Yes ma'am, I would like to see Director Macaphee, please."

"Oh sir, I'm afraid that is not possible. You just can't walk in here to the FBI and demand to speak to the director."

"Ms. Walker," said Ted, reading the name plate on the horseshoe desk. "I wasn't demanding anything. Please tell him or someone up there, Commander Barrett, Theodore Barrett, would like to see the director."

"Well sir, this is highly unusual, but I will try."

In a matter of minutes an agent of about thirty, Ted guessed, walked out of the elevator. He was in the standard FBI uniform; coat, tie, and looking as if he had just stepped out of a fashion magazine.

"Commander Barrett?"

"That's me."

"Please come with me sir. The director will see you right away." Ted gave Ms. Walker a half smile and a wink.

"They took the elevator to the top floor and Ted was ushered into a large office. Everything was neat and in its place. His eyes captured many photographs of Macaphee shaking hands with various political leaders. One of a smiling Macaphee with the president and a family portrait. Crayon drawings were taped along the wall behind the Director's desk chair. Ted assumed the artwork of his children.

"Commander Barrett, well, well, well." said Macaphee, walking across the room extending his hand.

Taking the Director's hand Ted snapped, "Macaphee, this is not a social call. I need something from you."

"Commander, you sound annoyed. Sit down, please."

"Annoyed? Annoyed Macaphee? You and your cohorts left four Navy Seals in that freaking jungle to die. I wound up with them, that makes five. I just spent over a year in Bethesda and will have to live with this pain in my back for the rest of my life. Annoyed? Yes, you could say that I am a little annoyed, Mister Director."

"Commander Barrett, I assure you it wasn't the FBI."

"I know," said Ted, calming a bit. "But it was the whole damn bunch of you. My career was taken from me, my home, and most of all my girl."

"Commander, what can I do to help you?" Macaphee asked.

"You know what I want. Where is she?"

"She?"

"Come on, Mister Director, don't play dumb with me. You know exactly who she is," said an agitated Ted. "All you have to do is get on that phone and her file will be up here in a matter of seconds."

"No need, Commander, I have it here," he said. He walked over to a large filing cabinet toward the rear of his office.

"You know I can't let you see this" he said opening outer doors of the stand-up filing cabinet with his back toward Ted. "It's still classified."

"Bullshit," said Ted. "I spent a year and a half of my life translating top secret codes in Vietnam and you're worried about me seeing my girlfriend's file?"

"Commander, it's been well over three years since you have seen Miss Perez, a lot of things can change over that amount of time. I can't let you see the contents of the file. But, I'll tell you what I will do…."

Ted raised his eyebrows.

Macaphee unlocked the second drawer of the filing cabinet which was marked in red letters, "TOP SECRET" he began thumbing through the file under 'P.'

Um, let's see, Parker, Penolli,———, Phipps... Perez? No Perez—where the hell is the Perez file?

Macaphee checked the drawer again. There was no Perez file to be found.

"You were saying?" said Ted.

"Yes, as I was saying Commander," turning to face him, "I will have the file sanitized and get back to you," Macaphee lied.

"And when will that be?" asked an impatient Ted Barrett.

"Right away, Ted."

"Okay Dan, much obliged," he said, starting to rise.

"Hang on a minute, Ted. I'll get you a car and a driver. Where would you like to go?"

"I need to get my things. I know my car was left in Texas and I would like to stop by my old JAG Office over at Quantico."

"Done," said Director Macaphee. "Your car and things have been stored in one of the hangars over at Langley. I will call Payton and have them shipped wherever you want."

"To my mother's place for now," said Ted. "But I want my car. I think I'm going to drive to West Palm Beach. It might be a nice ride."

"You okay to drive, Ted?"

"Well between us, it's against the doctor's orders, but I won't tell if you don't."

Both men chuckled.

"Ted, it was nice seeing you again. My office is always available to you whenever you…."

Ted interrupted, "Dan aren't you forgetting something?"

The director furrowed his forehead.

"The box," said Ted. "Remember? The box in my apartment in Dallas?"

"Oh the box, of course, I remember. It has been stored in our vault down in the basement," exclaimed the Director. "I will have it sent up right up."

"Dan if you don't mind, I would rather for us to fetch it personally. You understand?"

"Sure Ted, I can't let you in the vault but you can go with me down to the basement."

The two men took the director's private elevator to the basement. Soon Ted was holding the beautiful mahogany box inlaid with the mother-of-pearl. He retreated a few steps away from Director Macaphee. He cracked the seal and slightly opened the box. He peeked inside and smiled. Everything is there—just like he left it.

"Man, whatever you have in there must damn sure be important," said Machaphee."

Ted just smiled at him.

"May I ask what's in the box?"

"Yes, you certainly may ask," smiled Ted, as he began to walk away.

Director Machaphee stood in silence with a blank look on his face as it became abundantly obvious that Ted Barrett was not about to reveal the secret of the box. Ted turned back to Macaphee. The two men shook hands.

Ted left.

CHAPTER THIRTY-EIGHT

Back in his office, FBI Director Daniel Macaphee watched Ted exit the building on the closed circuit TV cameras. Once Ted disappeared he was instantly at his office door. "Michelle, get in here!" he barked to his secretary, who was sitting in her adjoining office. "And find Sunny Stewart. Isn't she still head of security around here?"

"Yes, yesss sir," an astounded Michelle stuttered. She had never heard the director raise his voice before. "Miss—Miss Stewart is our chief of security."

"Tell her I said to get her butt up here right now!" said Macaphee.

"Yes sir."

"Hello Miss Stewart," said Michelle, cupping her hand over the phone's mouthpiece. "The director wants to see you in his office right away. Uh-huh," obviously answering a question. "I would get up here right away if I were you. He's really in a tizzy."

In a matter of minutes both women were standing in the director's office. Macaphee was pacing and half shouting. "Can either of you explain to me how a top-secret file in that locked cabinet," he exclaimed, slinging a hand toward the filing cabinet as if he had just burned it on a hot stove, "in my locked office can disappear from one of the most secure and closely guarded buildings in the world?"

Michelle Goeble, an attractive, petite, dark-haired woman in her 40s appeared to be close to tears. Sunny Stewart, an agent, seemed to be a bit more calm and in control but still apprehensive of the director's wrath.

"Mister Director," Sunny began, "no one, literally no one, would have access into this building and especially to this office. The security codes are changed every day."

"Well, somebody damn sure did," exclaimed Macaphee. "What about the custodial personnel, maintenance and people like that?"

"Mister Director," spoke up Sunny Stewart, "only a handful of people have the blue clearance code ID tags to be in the building after hours."

Looking at the nervous Michelle he said, "Mrs. Goeble, you can go."

Michelle was out the door almost before he stopped talking.

"What handful? Like who?" demanded the director to Agent Stewart.

"Well sir, the round the clock shifts, like the computer people, janitorial services, security, some Secret Service from Treasury, the CIA; people like that."

"But what about my office?"

"Mister Director, nobody, not even the president would have access to your office."

"What do you mean CIA? What the hell would the CIA be doing here at the FBI?"

"Sir sometimes they use our tech labs and firing range over at Quantico."

"Do they come here to this building?"

"Yes sir."

"Why?"

"I really don't know sir. I am not privy to that information. I know they all have blue security clearances on their ID tags and I know they use our computers on occasion for domestic info and backgrounds."

Macaphee walked around his desk and sat down in his brown leather chair. He interlocked his fingers behind his neck and stared at the ceiling taking a long and thoughtful pause.

"Okay Agent Stewart, you may go. I want you to keep this between us. No leaks."

"Yes sir," and with that Agent Stewart briskly hastened out the door of the director's office blowing a sigh of relief.

FBI Director Daniel Macaphee was silent for a long time. "Of course. Yes, of course!" he said aloud and slapped his hand on the desk. He buzzed Michelle Goeble.

"Yes Mister Macaphee?" she quietly said as she appeared in his office doorway.

"Mrs. Goeble, please get this number for me," he said, handing her an index card. "And, Ms. Goeble, make sure it's on the scrambler phone and make sure it's coded."

"Yes sir, right away."

Macaphee picked up his phone and heard the familiar series of beeps and clicks.

Someone on the other end picked up the scrambler phone.

Macaphee cried, "Hello Payton. You son-of-a-bitch!"

CHAPTER THIRTY-NINE

"What?" said Payton coldly.

"Payton, just who the hell do you think you are? And what self-appointed right do you think you have to break into my office and steal my files? I'll…."

"Hey, slow down there, Danny boy, don't get your panties in a twist or you'll end up with a wedgie."

"Payton just who the hell do you think you are breaking into my office and taking my files?" shouted Macaphee.

"Hold on there, Danny boy," Payton said. "To begin with, it's not your office and it's not your file either. They belong to the United States' government. I have as much right to that file as you do. And we didn't break into anything. You weren't there so I just had one of our boys kinda borrow it for awhile."

"Payton you bastard, you can't get away with this. And how do you plan on handling Ted Barrett? And stop calling me Danny boy!"

"Mister Director," said Payton, "we will handle Mister Barrett when the time comes."

"Well Payton, you better get to handling, because he just left here and he is none too happy."

"You saw him today?"

"Yeah, within the hour. Are you surprised?" said Macaphee.

"I thought he was laid up over at Bethesda."

"Think again, Mister CIA Director. I thought you Sneaky-Pete spy guys were on top of everything. I want that file back today!"

"Okay Dan, okay. I will dispatch the Perez file back to you. But it is still classified, so it will have to go out with a secured courier."

"I don't care if you have to get it here by horseback, just have it back in my office today!" shouted Macaphee, slamming down the phone.

Curtis Payton rang off the speaker phone and leaned back in his office chair. He gazed out at the vast CIA complex and the Virginia countryside four stories below. Taking out his handkerchief he moistened it with his tongue and began to scrub a bit of salad dressing from his necktie. "Well," did you get all that Vernon?" He said to a rather portly, balding man sitting on the office sofa.

"Yeah, I got it Curtis, but I don't like it. There's just something about this Barrett fellow. He's smart and he ain't no quitter, and if he makes up his mind to find the Perez girl, he'll do just that."

"So what if he does Vern? She's married to one of the richest men in Costa Rica. What threat could Barrett be? Besides, she has probably forgotten all about him by now."

"I don't think so," said Baxter. "Remember Curtis, there ain't no dollar signs in the word love. No stop signs either. I don't want him anywhere around Costa Rica."

"Okay Vernon, if it'll make you feel any better I can put a tail on him. At least we'll know where he is and what he's up to. We'll keep him busy."

"That sounds good," Baxter said. "Curtis, I don't want to play hardball with you Washington folks, but this thing with Barrett is going to have to be done my way."

"Your way, Vernon?"

"Yes my way, Curtis. I don't want him finding the Perez gal. Don't make me remind you of the president's re-election coming up and who controls the purse strings of the petroleum industry and a dozen other lobbies. If he is not re-elected, you fellers will be out of here on your asses, and none of you ever earned an honest buck in your lives 'cept off the public till. Yeah, damn right. I want things my way."

Payton was getting more and more annoyed with Baxter's authoritative ways and how he propped his cowboy boots on the coffee table. This is Washington, for Pete's sake, we don't go around in boots and ten gallon Stetsons. Baxter's cigar smoke was driving him crazy, but he knew he was right. Baxter could swing a presidential election, or at the very least, have an enormous impact on who won and who lost. His only option was to play ball with Baxter.

"Say Vernon, how about some dinner before you head home?"

"I'd love to Curtis, but my plane is waiting for me at Dulles right now. I promised Liz'beth, I'd be home this eve'ning."

The two men shook hands and were saying their goodbyes. Vernon Baxter spoke up. "Remember, Curtis, I want that boy back in Texas and nowhere near Costa Rica."

"Why Texas?" asked Payton.

Baxter took in a deep breath and let it out slowly. He put his arm around Payton's shoulder. "Well Curtis, that's som'thin you Yankees will just never understand. You see, there's Texas… and then, there's everywhere else."

CHAPTER FORTY

L ate the next afternoon Ted walked into the JAG Offices at Quantico. He did not recognize the Chief Petty Officer at the reception desk.

"May I see Admiral Burnside, please?"

"I'm sorry Commander," said the Chief, noticing Ted's rank. "Admiral Burnside retired almost a year ago. Admiral Kidwell is the skipper now."

A pretty face peeked around the corner. "Does that voice belong to *Loo-tenant Commanda,* Ted Barrett?"

"It's Commander," said Ted looking in the direction of Elaine Baxter.

"Ted, what a nice surprise," she crooned.

"Good to see you again Elaine" he said embracing her.

Tell ya what, Ted, I'm about outta here. What say we get a cup of coffee or a stiff drink?"

"Sounds good Elaine. I could use one about now."

"You hungry?" she asked. "We could get something to eat."

"That sounds good to me Elaine, I'm pretty hungry, so let's do all three."

They exited the base and found Ma & Pa's Bar-B-Que Diner off State Road 284. The food was delicious. Compared to the hospital food Ted had been subjected to Ma and Pa put on a banquet.

"Say fella, you must be hungry," remarked Elaine.

"Yeah, guess I was. In the hospital I think the diet rule is if it tastes good spit it out."

Both laughed.

"Elaine, I see you made lieutenant commander. Congratulations."

"Why thank you, Ted."

"How has a pretty girl like you stayed single, Elaine?"

"To tell you the truth Ted, I didn't. I got married a couple years ago, but things didn't work out and stuff. Things never work out the way you think they will. You know?"

Ted rubbed his temples. *Tell me about it…* "Yeah, I sure do," he said profoundly.

He watched her tear off the top of a Sweet'n Low and dump it in her coffee. She was wearing a dazzling white-gold bracelet with studded diamonds and rubies among other valuable gemstones.

"Elaine," he said. "That is quite a bracelet you have there. Is it regulation?"

"Goodness no Ted, I could never get away with wearing this around the JAG Office. You know how persnickety the Navy can be and stuff; so I keep it in my purse."

Ted could not help being amused at how cute she was. The way she was talking with her hands, emphasizing and being so emphatic was adorable. She was peppy and lively.

Ted held her wrist and gave the bracelet a careful look.

"Gift?"

"Well no, and yes." she exclaimed.

Ted raised his eyebrows as if saying, "what?"

"It was a gift to myself," she said. "My daddy gave me fifty thousand dollars and he told me I could spend it any way I wanted. So, I bought this lil ol' bracelet. See, that's my birthstone," she said holding up the bracelet, "and these di'monds are my mama's birthstones and these rubies are my daddy's."

"It's very nice to have something like that."

"You would think so now, wouldn't you? But my daddy got all mad, all the way down there in Texas. My daddy said that was the last fifty thousand dollars he was gonna give me till I learned not to waste money and stuff."

"Well, I can certainly see how that could be a deal-breaker," smiled Ted.

"Oh not to worry," she said. "If I want sumthin', I just whine until my daddy gives it to me."

Ted smiled.

"Say Ted, where are you staying tonight?"

"Over at Quantico in the Bachelor Officer Quarters."

"Why don't you stay with me?" she asked eagerly. "We could watch a movie and have a few drinks. It's Friday, we don't have to get up early."

Ted was tempted. Elaine had everything a man would want, but she wasn't Lili.

He thought of the lonely rooms in the BOQ. They were nice enough, but Elaine offered good company and down deep he wanted the warm company of a woman.

"Elaine," he said, "I am out of here first thing in the morning."

"Oh shoot, Ted, we haven't seen each other in ages and I…"

Ted made a decision, he interrupted. "I haven't checked in at the BOQ yet. Are you in the same place?"

"Yep and it's close to the Interstate."

"Let's go."

The evening with Lieutenant Commander Baxter was enchanting. Ted liked the pretty Texan. She was warm, full of personality and witty. As normal and ordinary as she seemed to be it was hard for him to surmise that she came from such enormous wealth. Ted sipped a Chivas and Elaine poured herself a Chardonnay.

"What would you like to watch?" she asked walking over to a very nice TV console.

"We have a choice?"

"Yes Ted, you silly. My daddy bought me one of those new video tape machines, like they have on Johnny Carson and stuff."

Did she say, "You silly…?" Oh, no…, he groaned.

"How about a John Wayne movie, he's got to be a Texas boy," she said.

"Actually, I think he was born in Iowa," said Ted.

"Well, that's north Texas, isn't it?" She laughed, "How about *North to Alaska?* "

"Sounds good to me," he replied. "I haven't seen a movie in years."

They settled on the sofa, Elaine snuggled on his shoulder and they waited for "The Duke," to shoot everybody, get in a few brawls and once again come out the victor. As always, he gets the girl.

Country Music legend Johnny Horton was singing *North to Alaska's* soundtrack. Ted heard Johnny's words.

"A man needs a woman to love him all the time, remember Sam a true love is so hard to find...."

With all Ted's past philandering he had experienced true love only once.

Lili was his one and only true love. *I guess the old saying is true,* he thought.

First love, always love.

Ted tried to concentrate on the movie, but the late hour found them both dozing off. Elaine got up and went into her bathroom and emerged soon wearing nothing but a sheer nightie.

From where he was sitting Ted watched Elaine. The bathroom light was behind her and he could see her perfect shape through the thin gown. Her pert breasts were pointing at him.

"Come on, Ted, let's lie down."

Ted wanted nothing more. It had been a long since he had been with a woman. Suddenly a circuit-breaker flicked in his memory—a memory of Lili.

Lili, I have never been untrue to you. I'm not going to start now.

"Elaine," he mumbled. "If it is all the same to you, I'm going to sleep in your guestroom."

"You're going to sleep where?" she said in disbelief.

"In your guestroom; please try to understand."

Ted expected her to be angry. Elaine mustered patience she didn't know she possessed. She walked over and kissed him, brushing her breasts against his chest.

"Goodnight Ted, if you get cold, you can come in here. I will keep you warm."

Ted smiled and said goodnight to her.

Ted opened his eyes. It was daylight. He looked at the clock on the night stand. *Nine already...?"*

He felt something warm beside him. Elaine was sleeping peacefully on his shoulder. She opened her eyes.

"Good morning, Rip Van Winkle," she said referring to the well-known story by Washington Irving. "Hope you don't mind the company."

"Good morning, yourself," he replied. "When did you sneak in here?"

"Couple hours ago," Elaine smiled. "Let's go in the kitchen. I have something for you."

In the kitchen, Elaine served him a plate of ham, scrambled eggs, toast and hot coffee.

"Elaine, did you fix all of this?" Ted exclaimed.

"Nope. My daddy said he didn't send me to law school to learn how to cook. So, I called the café down the street."

"They deliver?"

"Not usually. But if you give them a big enough tip they will," she laughed. "If they didn't, I'd just tell my daddy to buy the place and fire everybody." she laughed again.

Ted took a quick shower and got into some casuals. He embraced Elaine in a big hug and gave her an affectionate kiss.

Her body tingled at the touch of him.

"So long Tex, thanks for everything. It was really great to see you again," he said truthfully.

"Tex?" she said. "Ted, is that going to be your sweet name for me?"

"If you want it to be. Sure beats having to say lieutenant commander all the time and it's shorter," he teased.

"When will I see you again?"

"I have a few things to take care of in Florida. We'll be in touch soon."

"Ted, I want to see you again."

Ted leaned against the door jam and slowly looked into her aqua-eyes, he said, "another time, another place. Bye, Tex."

"Bye, Ted," she said under her breath.

I think I love you....

Ted drove to I-95 and headed south.

"Another time, another place," Ted had no way of knowing how profound his statement was.

The telephone rang in a north Dallas mansion.

"Hello."

"Mister Baxter, this is Herb Pendergast, your man in Washington."

"Yes Herb, how ya doin?"

"Everything is okay here, Mister Baxter. Just wanted you to know that Commander Barrett left Elaine's this morning about ten o'clock, he's headed south on I-95."

"Thanks Herb. Did they spend a lot of time together?"

"No sir, not really, just the night. I don't know what went on inside. So, I can't tell you what happened."

"Don't you worry none about that Herb," said Baxter. "I know how to make things happen."

CHAPTER FORTY-ONE

Ted arrived at his mother's condo in West Palm Beach late Tuesday evening. He spent the week visiting with his mother and tending to personal business. His two younger sisters, both married with their own homes and families, stopped by almost every day.

It was Ted's intention to resume practicing law, but he had no inclination to enter government employment again. Coincidentally, through a friend, Ted began a rather promising practice in aviation law. He represented various airlines regarding their issues with the Federal Aviation Administration. Although he was not admitted to the Florida Bar, he was a member of the Federal Bar. Thus, his practice was limited to the federal courts where all FAA cases are heard.

Time seemed to have a way of slipping by. Seasons came and went. Although Ted didn't stay all that busy he wasn't idle either. But he could not concentrate on law. His mind was always focused on Lili and how to find her. Ted had even hired a private investigator in San Antonio. The only good that came of it was he found out where her sister, Gabriella, lived and the address of her parents.

Ted immediately flew to San Antonio and easily found Gabriella's house in Uvalde. Getting out of his rental car he observed a dark green sedan parked fifty yards away. He noticed two men were sitting in the sedan.

I wonder if that is the same green sedan I saw at the airport?

Ted knocked on Gabriella's door. Gabriella answered the knock, but did not invite him inside.

"So, you are the infamous Ted Barrett?" she said. "Lili, was right about one thing. You certainly are a good looking sort, but I have nothing to say to you."

Ted started to explain about his exhaustive search for Lili.

"You broke her heart, Mister Barrett. She's happy now. Why don't you leave her alone?"

"But…" Ted started to say.

"Haven't you hurt her enough? Leave her be!"

The door closed and Ted could hear the deadbolt click.

He walked back to the rental car and noted that the dark green sedan was no longer there.

I've got to stop imagining things…. I've often thought I am being followed. That's ridiculous—who would be following me…?

Two hours later, Ted pulled up to a neat little house on the west side of Uvalde. He found the reception at the Perez home a bit cooler than at Gabriella's. Papa Perez had answered the door and when Ted identified himself the door slammed with an ear shattering bang.

Back in his rental car a frustrated Ted headed toward San Antonio's airport. Two blocks ahead his eyes caught a glimpse of a dark green sedan. Ted accelerated to catch up to the sedan, but it made a right turn and disappeared.

I'm imagining things again…. I need to see Macaphee— I have a case in D.C., next month at the FAA Tribunal. I'm calling Macaphee.

The following month, Ted was sitting in FBI Director Macaphee's office. After exchanging the polite pleasantries and inquiries, Ted said, "Dan, I'm though messing with you and Payton over this Lili thing. Someone, somewhere, knows where she is, and damnit I'm through playing your sophomoric games."

"I can understand, Ted, we've…."

"No, you don't understand, Mister Director," Ted blurted. "I have been searching for her for almost four years. I have run out of money and most definitely out of patience."

"Ted," Macaphee began.

"Hear me out, Dan." Ted interrupted again. "See this briefcase, Dan? In here I have every piece of information that I could gather on this whole stinking operation and a lot of it isn't too pretty. Something very crooked is going on."

The Director said nothing. He stared at Ted's briefcase.

"If I don't get some answers this moment… this day, then I am going, with this briefcase, to every committee and every sub-committee in the House and the Senate. I will go to the attorney general. I will go to the president if I have to."

"Ted," said Macaphee, "what I was trying to tell you earlier, we have Miss Perez' file right here and…."

"That's what you told me the last time," Ted interrupted yet again.

"No, it's right here Ted," said Macaphee, reaching in a drawer and placing a manila file on the desk. Ted could see that it was clearly marked, 'PEREZ.'

"It hasn't been completely declassified yet so I really can't share it with you, but…."

"But what?" asked Ted, disgustingly.

Macaphee continued, "I am going to put you in touch with our resident agent in the embassy in San Jose. The name is Alex Stockwell and…."

"San Jose? San Jose what? California?"

"San Jose, Costa Rica," said Macaphee.

"We have the FBI in Costa Rica?" asked Ted.

"We do at the embassy. It's pretty standard. We keep agents in almost every embassy in the world."

"Why Costa Rica?" Ted wondered.

"I can't tell you where she is because I don't know. But, I think Agent Stockwell can help you."

Ted put his index fingers together and placed them under his chin.

"Okay Dan, thanks." Ted's anger had diminished. He could see the Director was truly trying to help him without breaching the confidentially of the file.

"That's all I know, Ted. San Jose has a better finger on this than I do. I think Agent Stockwell might be just the person."

The FBI Director and Ted said their goodbyes. Ted started for the door. He stopped and turned. "Oh Mister

Director, tell Payton that he can call off his wolf-pack now. And he really shouldn't send rookies out to tail somebody like me. And oh yeah, tell them sedans come in more colors than green."

CHAPTER FORTY-TWO

Early Monday morning, a week later, Ted boarded American Airlines, Flight 1712, from Miami direct to San Jose, Costa Rica.

Slightly over three and a half hours later Ted was through customs in San Jose and driving a compact rental car. He parked at the U.S. Embassy and was greeted at the door by Marine Sergeant Taylor.

"I am here to see Special Agent Stockwell please," he said to Taylor.

"Yes sir, if you will follow me," replied the Sergeant. He led to an office in the back of the embassy.

An attractive woman in her late thirties sat behind a cluttered desk. She rose when Ted entered the office. She was tall woman, maybe five eight, Ted thought. Her hair was golden blond and she greeted him with a pair of twilight gray eyes. She was clad in a deep yellow business suit, which complimented her flaxen hair.

"May I help you?" she asked.

"Thank you, no," said Ted. "I am waiting to see the resident agent, a Mister Alex Stockwell. Is he here?"

"Well no, 'he' isn't here but I am," she said, smiling broadly and tapping the name plate on the desk, which read: SAC Alexandria Stockwell.

"SAC?" he said.

"Yep, Special Agent in Charge."

"You are Special Agent Alex Stockwell?"

"Live and in color," she smiled. "You must be Commander Barrett."

"How did you know?" said Ted asking a rhetorical question.

"The director, himself called me about you. He told me to help you any way I could."

"I have been with the FBI for fifteen years and that is the first call I have ever gotten from the Ivory Tower," she said, jabbing a finger north toward Washington D.C. "You must be important."

"No, not really," he said. "I'm just trying to clear up a few personal matters."

"Yes, I know," said Stockwell. "Commander, I...."

Ted interjected, "You can drop the commander; I went inactive a couple years ago."

"Okay then, Mister Barrett...."

"You can drop the Mister too. My first name is Ted."

"Good," she said. "That will make things easier. I am Alex."

"Good."

"Ted, I cannot share what's in here," she said resting her elbows on a file trimmed in red tape. He could see the name "Perez," printed on the cover.

"I think the best way is to show you."

"Show me?"

288

"Yes," she said. "Isn't that what the Chinese say? One picture is worth a thousand words."

"So I hear."

"I can tell you this much, Lili is a close friend of the ambassador. She lives up on the Corobici, that's common knowledge around here. The rest you will have to see for yourself."

"What is a Corobici?" Ted asked.

"The Corobici is a river and large valley. But for your purposes, the Corobici is the name of a huge plantation. It farms coffee, other things, and cattle, but mostly coffee."

"Does Lili work there as an accountant?"

"No, Ted, not exactly."

"Well, let's go," he said.

"Whoa hang on, cowboy. We will leave first thing in the morning. It's only about 150 miles or so, but the roads here aren't exactly like our interstates," she said. "So we need to get started early. Besides, I'm going to need a couple hours to get word to my contact up there."

"Okay Alex, I am ready when you are."

"One more thing Ted, Ambassador Thomas, would like to meet you and she has invited you to stay as a guest here in the embassy."

"Perfect. Thank you."

The next morning shortly after daylight Ted and Alex were driving northwest on CR Highway 1. It was a perfect day and they had the windows down. Both were enjoying the cool fresh air. Ted was drinking in the mountain scenery. Special Agent Stockwell was right. The Costa Rican road was no interstate. What would have been a three hour drive in the States took them over half a day.

Ted watched the agent's golden hair blowing in the wind and wondered whether such lovely hair was natural or perhaps she used a pigment enhancement. A cliché he had learned from his sister.

Never use the word "dyed," she had said. Always say, "pigmently enhanced."

They arrived at a small village, which seemed to Ted like a century out of the past. There a few small shops where the locals were selling their wares to anyone who would, or could, buy them. A small boy walked past leading a donkey loaded with local produce.

Alex turned onto a rough dirt road. It seemed to Ted that they had driven for miles when Alex pulled off the road into a small clump of trees and turned off the engine.

"What are we doing?" he inquired.

"We wait."

In a short while a Costa Rican boy appeared out of the brush.

"Hi Carlos. How are you?" Alex said in Spanish, handing the boy a handful of American chocolates.

"Hello Señorita Alex. Gracias."

"Carlos," said Alex, "this is Ted, the gentleman I told you about. He would like to ask you a few questions."

"Si, he can ask me in English. I speak English good now."

"Carlos when did you learn English?" Alex asked.

"Señora Velazquez, Missa Lili, she teach me and my cousin Lucy English good."

"Where is Miss Lili now?" Ted asked.

"Come with me, I show you," said Carlos.

The three crept through the brush and came upon a small hill overlooking the Corobici's stables. Concealing themselves under the branches of a large tree, they had a bird's eye view of the stables.

"Missa Lili, she come here every day, this time," said Carlos.

They waited for at least a half hour. Ted was about to give up the surveillance when he saw the black hair and a distinctive walk. She was holding the hand of a very active little boy. Ted guessed the lad about two years old. There was no doubt. It was Lili.

He watched her take a golden mare out of the stall and feed her some sugar lumps. She then began to brush the horse.

"Carlos," Ted whispered, "what does Miss Lili do on the Corobici?"

Carlos looked at him dumb-founded. "Señor Ted, Missa Lili, is the wife of Don Velazquez, the owner of all the Corobici."

The wife?

"And the boy?"

"The boy, Señor Ted, is her son, Augustino."

Her son?

Ted had seen enough. He didn't want to know anymore.

They all withdrew from their observation post and slowly walked back to the embassy staff car.

"Carlos," he said, "is Miss Lili happy?"

"Oh si, si, Señor Ted. Missa Lili very happy. She ride her horse all over the Corobici. She have mucho dinero. Sometimes though, my cousin Lucy say, Missa Lili sad."

"What does Lucy do?" Ted asked.

"Lucy, she Missa Lili demestico."

"What is a demestico?"

"A servant," said Alex.

A servant—that doesn't sound like Lili—

"Carlos, does Lucy work for Velazquez too?"

"Si, Señor Ted. Everybody work for Don Velazquez."

"Thank you, Carlos" Ted said and handed him a twenty dollar bill.

"Wow! Twenty dollar American. Mucho gracias, Señor Ted."

The ride back to San Jose was silent. Ted's grief was deep. Sensing that, Alex said little.

It was late when they arrived back at the embassy. Alex said, "Ted, why don't we go down to the cafeteria. It's closed by now, but we could whip up some soup and a couple sandwiches?"

Ted really didn't feel like eating, but he agreed to go with the blond agent.

After having a quick dinner of soup and sandwiches, Alex said, "let's go to my quarters and have a stiff drink. I keep some liquor and it looks like you could use one."

"Alex, I think that is a good idea."

Alex's embassy apartment was spacious and comfortable. They listened to music and enjoyed a few drinks.

Feeling the effects from the vodka and tonic, Alex grasped Ted by the hand and pulling him up, she said. "Let's dance."

"I have a bad hip, but I'll try."

She snuggled against his neck and hummed with the music. Ted could feel her breasts against him and he smelled the golden hair as it pressed against his cheek. He felt a boiling sensation in his belly. His blood was flowing faster.

Ted tilted his head down. She met his lips with hers. Ted felt her warm lips press against his. The tip of her tongue was teasing him. He was becoming more and more aroused, as was Alex.

They fell back on the bed, exchanging passionate kisses. Hands were touching each other everywhere. Ted was ready.

Alex sat up in the bed and slipped off her blouse and bra. Standing beside him she slid out of her slacks and panties. Ted followed her and stripped off his clothes. His arousal was obvious.

Lili, I love you—I will always love you—but you are another man's wife now.

"I'll get the lights," said Alex.

CHAPTER FORTY-THREE

The next morning Ted looked out the window of the Boeing 727-200, as it smoked through the sky on its way to Texas. He had decided to go back to Dallas and see about his old job with the District Attorney's Office and to look around.

Alex thanks for everything. I bet I am one of the few who can give expert testimony that you definitely do not use a pigment enhancement.

Ted drove his rental car to the DA's Office only to find that it had moved to a new multi-level office building. Once at the new building Ted recognized no one. Everything had changed. Wayne Hendry had retired and there was a new District Attorney. Even his old secretary, Susan, had re-located.

Ted found out his aide, Ray Scott, had been admitted to the bar and was employed as a lead prosecuting attorney, but was on vacation. Ted was disappointed. He had always liked Scottie and was anxious to see him.

He drove by the apartment he had shared with Lili. It appeared vacant and drab. Nothing was the same. He found the manager-handyman, Pete Crozier, who opened the lock for him. The apartment had never been re-leased. As Crozier had explained, someone in a business suit showed up every year and paid for a year's rent in cash.

Looking about he knew at once that he could never stay here again. Everything was a memory. The walls echoed her footsteps, he could hear her voice. In his mind he saw her grinning and bouncing across the room to greet him. He glanced quickly toward the bedroom. An avalanche of memories popped in his mind like a thousand flashbulbs.

He missed her teasing, he missed her touching, he missed her giggle and the way she wrinkled her nose when she laughed. He missed her big brown eyes. Ted missed everything about Lili. He never stopped missing her and he never stopped loving her.

Ted finally acquiesced to the idea that Lili was gone for good and married to another man. He couldn't stay in Dallas. There were too many painful memories. He flew back to Florida and sat for the state bar exam, but he was not very productive other than drinking and staring at the ocean for hours.

It was his mother who stepped in. "Teddy, you are a big boy now, you are my only son, and I love you, but I am kicking you out of my house. Whatever it is that's crushed your heart so terribly you must put it behind you and get on with your life. Time has a way of healing all wounds."

Like all mothers, Mrs. Barrett was right. Right except for one thing. Time did not have a way of healing all of Ted's wounds. The memories of Lili were with him day and night. He thought of a quote by Isak Dinesen:

"The cure for anything is salt water. Tears, sweat, the sea...."

Ted thought: *"Isak, ol' boy, you are probably right for the most part. I certainly have sweated, I have shed enough tears to fill a reservoir and I live on the ocean so there is plenty of salt water, but there is no cure for my love for Lili...."*

Ted did manage to put a lot of the ache out of his mind, at least for some of the daytime, but at night the same hauntings visited him. He got over the war and most everything else; but he never got over Lili. He remembered reading Sir Walter Scott's words in his 1819 classic, *Ivanhoe.* Isaac of York spoke:

"My heart broke long ago, but serves me still...."

He would love her until the day he died.

CHAPTER FORTY-FOUR

Life on the Corobici was pleasant enough. Lili played with Augustino and home-schooled him, teaching him both English and Spanish. He followed her daily on his little pony as Lili rode Golden Belleza about the farms of the Corobici. Life was good. Lili had everything anyone could ever want, except she was lonely and needed to be loved. She didn't have Ted.

Every night was the same. The sleeplessness haunted her. She would lie in bed for hours thinking of Ted, the cherished love they had shared, and the unbridled lust they had for each other. Their love was intense and complete.

Lili thought of the writing of Pedro Caldren de la Barca.

"When love is not madness, it is not love...."

"That is what Teddy Bare and I had," she whispered aloud. "Our passion for each other was madness."

Don Anastasio Velazquez did not have the slightest thought or concern about Lili's comings and goings, or in any interests she might have had. They rarely dined together anymore and sometimes she would not see him for days. He never discussed his business or activities.

Lili didn't ask.

The Don liked to show her off at the rare social events they attended but she knew he wasn't thinking of her. He was thinking only of himself. He would introduce her among the others. She would smile and curtsy, being the good wife; the Don's trophy.

"Thinking so, and knowing so are two different things...."

As her unhappiness continued to grow, Lili began to envisage, in the back of her mind, leaving the Don. She knew that if she remained in Costa Rica, her chances of keeping custody of Augustino were slim to none due to the Don's great wealth and power. She was trapped. And just as Lili had feared in the beginning, she was a bebé factoria.

In her trap, Lili resigned herself to what the Don had determined was her sole responsibility—to raise Augustino and nothing else. She could not leave the Don or the Corobici. To do so without Augustino was unthinkable.

"Remember little one, everything that glitters is not always gold...."

Lili continued to visit her therapist, Doctor Mildred Shuenberger, once a week. The Corobici airplane would fly them to San Jose and Lili would leave Augustino in the embassy nursery, his only time to socialize with other children, since Don Velazquez had forbade him playing with the employee's children.

Visits with Doctor Shuenberger were the times when Lili could vent and explain her exasperating lifestyle, lavish as it might be, confinement on the Corobici. The doctor was slowly, but surely, helping her to understand that Ted was gone and out of her life and how she could best manage her circumstances. Still, Lili hung on to a tiny sliver of hope that maybe someday….

Through Doctor Shuenberger, Lili began to realize her feelings for Anastasio had turned to indifference. Hate is not the opposite of love. Hate is still an emotion, explained the doctor. Indifference is the opposite of love; when you simply don't care anymore. Lili's feeling for Anastasio was indifference.

She had only experienced true love once.

Late that summer Lili's prayers were answered. She heard a light tap on her door.

"Yes Lucy?"

"Miss Lili mum, Don Valazquez would like to see you in the library."

"Thank you, Lucy."

Lili was getting a belly full of the Don's stoic summoning her as if she was a paid demestico, which in his mind she was. The Don was born into the aristocracy, she wasn't. A reality in which he seemed to take great pleasure in reminding her.

Entering the library she said. "You wanted to see me, Anastasio?"

"Yes Lili, sit down please."

She curled both legs under her and sat facing him.

"Lili," he began. "Augustino will be starting school in a couple of months and I feel he is at the age, which he should begin his education with more intensity than we have here in Costa Rica."

She shook her head but said nothing.

"Therefore, I have made arrangements for him to attend one of the finer private schools in the United States."

"The States?" she asked, doing her best to remain calm.

"Yes, in America," he said. "Private schools in the United States are much superior to ours here in Costa Rica. I also feel going to school in America will enhance his language skills."

"Augustino is speaking English very well," she quipped.

"Yes, I know. But when the time comes for him to take over management of the Corobici it will be imperative that he have command of the English language. Most all of our business is with English-speaking countries."

Lili still looked at him, but said nothing. She thought:

What if he chooses not to be a farmer? What if he doesn't want anything to do with the Corobici? Maybe he wants to teach, or become an artist, or a thousand of other things?

Lili was sure the thought had never entered the Don's mind.

"Anastasio," she said slightly raising her voice. "Were you planning on sending our son to school in the United States and not even consult me?"

"Let me finish Lili," he said. "No, of course not, I am sending you to stay with him in the States. I am also sending Lucy for whatever reasons you may need her."

The Don continued. "You are not to work. You and Lucy are to see that Augustino has the proper care. I have already made arrangements for your living accommodations and local transportation."

Lili's mind was turning like a drum major spinning a baton.

You were going to do all this and not once did you consult me about anything? But I am going to the States—I don't care where—just get me to the States!

She looked intently at the Don, and said, "Is that all?"

"Yes," he replied, waving his hand dismissing her as if he were excusing a waiter.

The next morning Lili was dialing the telephone to Ambassador Thomas' private number.

"Hello Lili, how nice to hear from you," said the voice of the ambassador.

"You too, Julie," Lili said. "I am going to be in San Jose next week and I need to pick up some information from you."

"Certainly. What can I do to help you, Lili?"

"I need an application form for U.S. citizenship for a juvenile and the name of a good divorce lawyer."

"Oh?"

"I will tell you all about it when I see you, Julie. And Julie…."

"Yes?"

"I cannot emphasize how confidential this is. It must remain just between the two of us."

"Okay, Lili. I understand. We never had this conversation."

"Thanks, Julie. See you next week."

Lili started packing.

Deep in the basement of the embassy Antonio Casares re-played a tape. He picked up a coded telephone.

"Hello Mister Payton…."

CHAPTER FORTY-FIVE

Ted knew he faced a future without Lili. She was gone. She was a mother and married to one of the wealthiest men in Central America. She had everything. How could she not be happy?

In his heart he knew that he would always love Lili, but he also knew that he had to get on with his life. He could not stay shackled to a memory forever.

Ted picked up his phone and punched the 202 area code and the number he had committed to memory long ago. He was put through immediately to the extension he requested.

"Loo-tenant Commanda Baxter," answered a familiar Texas accent.

"Hello Elaine," he began to say.

"Oh Ted, is that you?" she said excitedly, recognizing his voice.

"Yes listen, Elaine, I…."

"Ted, where are you?" Are you here in town?" she blurted.

"I'm in Florida."

After exchanging a few pleasantries and the usual polite inquiries, Ted asked: "Elaine are you seeing anyone these days?"

"That depends, Ted, are you asking me out?"

"Well, if it's possible I thought we could spend some time together," he replied.

"In that case, no. I'm not seeing anyone."

Ted said, "Monday after next is Independence Day, so it will be a three day weekend. I thought maybe you would like to spend it here in Palm Beach. That is, if you don't have other plans."

"No Ted, I don't have any plans," she said, as she quickly scribbled a memo on her notepad.

"Call Harry, cancel July third and fourth."

"Do you live in Palm Beach?" she asked.

"Not exactly. I'm in West Palm Beach. That's where us poor people live," he joked.

"Oh goodness, yes, Theodore, I would love to!"

"Great then—it's a date," he said. "I will make reservations for you on Continental or U.S. Air. They both have direct flights from National Airport, or Dulles to PBI."

"Ted, there you go being silly again."

"What?"

"I'll just call my daddy and he will send one of his airplanes for me. Why he would get all mad and stuff if he knew I was flying on the airlines."

"Yes of course," he said. "I sure wouldn't want to disappoint your daddy."

Excuse me…. I must have blanked out there for a moment—heaven forbid you would have to fly on a commercial airline.

304

"I will leave right after I get off work Friday eve'nin'," Elaine said.

"Sounds great. I look forward to seeing you. Goodbye, Tex."

"Goodbye, Theodore."

On Friday "eve'nin'," July third, Ted was standing in the arrival gate lounge of Jet Aviation at Palm Beach International Airport, most commonly known to the locals as PBI.

A silver Saber-Liner taxied to the gate, its jet engines screaming. Ted saw the Texas Flag of the Lone Star State, prominently painted on the tail of the airplane, standing out like a mermaid tattoo on a sailor's chest. Underneath the flag, clearly printed in bold letters was BDI.

The airplane's engines were barely whining to an idle when the stairs folded down and out bounced Elaine Baxter. She wore a pair of white short shorts, a light purple pullover top and no bra. On her feet were heavy white socks and a pair of jogging shoes. Spotting Ted she ran to him like a sprinter and flung her arms around him.

They didn't say a word of greeting. As they kissed Ted felt Elaine's tongue go past his lips and deep into his mouth. The clutch of her body and her loose breasts against his chest immediately started to arouse him. It had been a long time since he had felt the warmth of a woman's body so close. Elaine Baxter, was indeed, a very sexy woman.

One of the pilots appeared beside them and said, "Miss Baxter, where would you like your bag delivered?"

Ted spoke up. "Put them in the white station wagon over there please," he said pointing to his car.

"Them?" asked the pilot.

"Oh Theodore darlin, I only brought the one bag," Elaine said.

"One bag?"

"This is Florida isn't it? What do I need clothes for?" she said, giving Ted a sly grin.

Arriving at Ted's house, he asked, "What can I get you to drink, Tex?"

"I'm good right now, darlin," she replied. "But, I'll tell you what you can do."

"Sure," he said.

She draped her arms around his neck. Looking down the hall, she nodded and said, "You can take me in that bedroom of yours and give me the screwing of my life, you big Texas stud."

"But, I'm from Florida," he mumbled.

"Nah," she smiled. "You must be a Texan. Everything's big in Texas!"

"Everything? How do you know?"

"Cuz, I felt you against me at the airport."

Ted took her by the hand and led her to the bedroom, where he fulfilled her request.

The July Fourth weekend passed quickly for them both. Their days were filled with exciting Florida things. They went to the beach every day. They had picnics, went water-skiing, rode on Ted's jet-ski, and made love every morning and every night. They snuggled together in a lounge chair on the upstairs deck of Ted's house and watched the holiday fireworks explode over the Inter-Coastal Waterway.

No woman had captured Ted's emotions since his, "Lili days," back in Dallas like Elaine did and she did it by just being herself. Elaine was like a breath of fresh air. She was charming and witty, and just plain fun to be around. She had not succumbed herself or sold her soul to the mammon of her father's massive wealth. A stranger would never have the slightest clue that she was the daughter of a billionaire.

Monday night they were saying a clinging goodbye at the Jet Aviation Gate. The sleek Saber-Liner with the kitschy "tattoo," was outside, its engines whining.

"When will I see you again?" she asked.

"How about next weekend?" he replied. "Can you pick me up at National?"

"Does a Raggedy Ann doll have cotton tits?" laughed Elaine. "Absolutely, I will be there."

She slipped her arm down between them and grasped his member. "May I take this with me?" she asked smiling.

"Fraid not. I'm going to need it."

"Need it for what?" she demanded, feigning look of astonishment.

"It does have other functions you know," he laughed. "Besides, it needs a rest."

They both laughed and she climbed aboard the aircraft.

"Bye, bye Theodore," she said blowing him a kiss. "See you in a couple days."

"Bye, Tex."

With that, she was gone. Ted watched the Saber-Liner lift off and rocket through the clouds. He was excited about seeing Elaine again.

Ted flew to Washington the following Friday afternoon, which set a precedent. He and Elaine were together almost every weekend. Either he would fly to her or she would be flown to West Palm Beach. Ted found himself becoming more and more intrigued with "Tex," as he called her. She always referred to him with a sweet name or "Theodore," a rarely spoken noun except often used by his mother when he was a misbehaving child.

Their time together was cherished. Ted began to be careful of what he wished for around her. Every time he mentioned something like a book he wanted to read or an item he needed to pick up at the store it suddenly appeared. Ted had mentioned to her on several occasions that he could tend to his own things himself. Elaine would have none of it.

One lazy Sunday afternoon they spread a blanket on the soft grass of the National Mall, just under the shadow of the Washington Monument. Ted said, "Tex, honey, look at how pretty everything is with the leaves changing."

"I know darlin, it's like this every season. Fall is my favorite time of the year."

"Mine too," he said. "I wish we could go up to New England and see the foliage. Folks up there call the tourists, Leaf Peepers."

"Wish, smisch," said Elaine. I'll just call my daddy, and…."

"Never mind your daddy," Ted exclaimed. "Today is October second and you are off on Columbus Day, the eleventh; let's hop on Delta and fly up to Boston. We could rent a car."

"Let's do it!" she squealed, as she threw her arms around him and forcing him back on the blanket. Her tongue was warm against his and Ted began arising to the occasion.

"Not here," he whispered.

"Where then?" she murmured teasingly.

"Your place."

They departed the mall.

Ted and Elaine drove out of the rental car agency leaving Boston's Logan Airport with the top down in a shiny new convertible. The New England air was brisk, but the day was bright and sunny. He turned south on Highway 2 and soon found Interstate 90 and headed west toward Springfield.

At Springfield, the couple turned north on Interstate 91, and soon found themselves over the Vermont State Line at Brattlesboro. From Brattlesboro they drove north along the rushing Connecticut River and through the Green Mountain National Forest.

"Oh my, Theodore, have you ever seen anything so beautiful and so many colors?" exclaimed Elaine, waving her hands above the windshield at the polychromatic scenery.

Ted was admiring the beautiful Green Mountains covered in a blanket of multitudinous colors.

Certainly some of the Lord's finest architecture, he thought.

"Check out all those colors, Tex."

"Oh yes, yes darlin," she exclaimed. "Just look! There is every color imaginable: oranges, reds, browns, greens, and yellows, everything."

Ted sighed. *No paintbrush in the hands of the most skilled artist nor could any camera capture splendor like this—only the Almighty could create such magnificence!*

"See Theodore, I knew being Leaf-Peepers up here in north Texas would be beautiful this time of year."

"North Texas?" he asked. "I thought you said Iowa was north Texas."

She replied. "Iowa is north, north Texas. Here in New England is northeast, northeast Texas!"

They were both laughing when Ted drove the convertible under a rustic covered bridge and into Montpelier, Vermont's Capital, the nation's smallest capital city.

"Did you know the Coolidges were from Vermont?" he said.

"You mean Tom and Rachel Coolidge over on 59th Street?" Elaine was laughing.

"No, you know who I mean. Calvin Coolidge, the thirtieth President of the United States."

"So was, Chester A. Arthur, the twenty-first President," said Elaine.

"Really?"

"Yep that's right," she continued. "Both were Vice Presidents and took office after the death of the incumbent president."

Ted was surprised. Elaine often astonished him with things she knew.

"Theodore, darlin', I'm getting hungry."

"Ditto," he said and eased the car into a parking space of a cozy Bob Evans restaurant.

After placing their order Elaine was thumbing through a local magazine. "Theodore, sweet," she cooed.

Ted arched an eyebrow but said nothing.

"Did you know," she said, giving him a pious look and placing the magazine in her lap, "that people can get married in here in Vermont without a waiting period?"

This time he cocked both eyebrows, but still said nothing.

"Says so right here," she said, putting the open publication in front of him.

"Married, Tex?"

"Think about it darlin'. We have known each other for years and we have been an item since July. We've practically live together and stuff. You know you love me, and I know I love you."

Ted's mind was racing like a movie on fast forward.

Marriage? That is a huge life-changing decision—I really do love Elaine. She is everything any man would want—she has looks, personality, brains, and she sincerely cares, and I know she loves me… with all that, coupled with her insatiable libido, she would be a great catch for anybody. On the other hand there is Lili.

It has always been Lili.

The full moon was shining brightly that crisp October evening in Vermont. The entire valley was bathed in bright moonlight casting an enchanting hue over the forest of colorful Maple trees. That night, at eight thirty eight p.m., Mr. and Mrs. Theodore F. Barrett registered in the bridal suite of the Best Western Motel, at 41 Blush Hill Road, just outside Montpelier, Vermont.

Ted had read the writing of the Roman Philosopher Cicero.

"The first look of love is the last look of reason...."

Somehow the wisdom of Cicero had escaped him.

In north Dallas, Elizabeth Baxter answered the ringing telephone.

"Lanie, what a nice surprise," she said. "You are where?"

"You did what?"

After listening for a moment, Elizabeth stood with her mouth agape and slowly hung up the telephone.

"Liz'beth, what is it?" asked her husband.

"Vernon, it was Lanie, she says she just got married."

"Lanie did what?" Baxter demanded.

Elizabeth's words were barely audible. "She just got married, Vernon. To that lawyer she met in the Navy. They took off to Vermont and got married."

"At least she eloped," he said under his breath. "Last time she got married cost me a half million dollars."

"Still in a state of shock Elizabeth said, "Married? I don't know how that could have happened."

Vernon Baxter leaned back in his easy chair. He swiveled the bourbon in his glass and held it up to the light from the lamp. He squinted through the amber liquid.

I know how to make things happen....

CHAPTER FORTY-SIX

Lucy was beside herself with joy. America was everything she dreamed it would be and more. America was a long way from the Corobici and the iron-fisted rule of Don Valezquez. It was free here and so busy, quite different from the mundane life she knew as a demestico in Costa Rica. Moreover, here in America she had a future.

Lili had given her complete freedom to do as she pleased, but did insist Lucy attend school. Due to Lili's tutoring she became very proficient in English. Lucy applied, along with Augustino, for U.S. citizenship and thanks to pressure applied by Ambassador Thomas her application cut through the government labyrinth of red tape in amazing speed.

Once Lili had secured a dual citizenship for Augustino and Lucy, she allowed him to spend summers and some holidays at the Corobici, accompanied by Lucy.

Lucy had developed into a shapely ebony-haired beauty. She had a bubbling personality, large dark eyes and was often mistaken for Lili's younger sister. She was also quite in demand by the handsome suitors who called on her.

Lili, on the other hand, chose not to enter the social spotlight. Although she was definitely noticed by the gentlemen, she had no desire to become involved. Lili was again working as an accountant, contrary to the Don's orders, and she loved it. Her feelings for Ted still burned in her heart, but the lesson she learned had scarred her memories forever.

You dumped me once, Teddy Bare; I have never gotten over you—I could never go through that kind of hurt again. We could never be the same—wherever you are I wish you love and happiness.

It was late when the last of the guests left. The two women were clearing the paper cups and plates from Lucy's 28th birthday party. Lucy was very popular and had many friends from the university and, of course, many young gentlemen all vying for her attentions.

Lili lifted what was left of the large birthday cake and placed it on the kitchen counter. "How about another slice of cake, Lucy?"

Lucy turned and patted her behind. "No! Muy gordo!" she laughed.

"Ah, ah, ah Lucy. Remember? You and Augustino must speak English only."

"And?" asked Lucy.

"And me too," said Lili. Both women laughed.

Lili was bent over a large brown garbage bag discarding some of the paper plates and cups. "Miss Lili, mum," said Lucy.

Lili stood bolt upright and gave Lucy a quizzical look. "Lucy, you haven't called me Miss or Mum since we left the Corobici. What's wrong?"

"Nothing's wrong, mum; don't you think it's time to tell me?"

Lili furrowed her thick eyebrows. "Tell you? Tell you what, Lucy?"

"Whatever it is that hurts you so much. The secret that you carry around inside you," said Lucy. "Is it that Dallas lawyer?"

Lili was stunned. Her breath was coming in short gasps. "You, you know about him? You know about Ted?" she finally managed.

"Only by watching your reaction to certain things," Lucy replied. "And I heard the Don talking to a private investigator he sent to the States about him, but that was years ago."

Lucy leaned over and braced herself on the back of a kitchen chair. Lili explained, "It's about a trap Lucy, a snare. It is about love, Lucy, pure, true love. Once it's true, you are caught in it forever; there is no escape. It stays with you for life. No matter where you go or what you do, it is always there. And, Lucy, I always assumed that you were too young, and…"

"Miss Lili, mum," Lucy interjected, she thrust her breasts toward Lili. "In case you haven't noticed, I am fully grown."

"Lucy, stop that!" she said firmly.

"Stop what?"

"Stop calling me mum, and stop doing that with your chest."

Lucy didn't respond. She looked at Lili with the same curious expression. "You still love him don't you, mum?"

Lili pushed the garbage bag she had been holding to the side of the sink. She stared out the kitchen window through the darkness toward the drifting Potomac. She did not respond or turn around.

I have never told the whole story. Never. I have shared with my sister Gabriella and Doctor Gomez. I have told Nicole and Doctor Shuenberger many things, but never the whole truth to anyone....

Lili stared out the window for a long time. Finally, she walked over to the sink and took down two glasses. She scooped ice into both of them and poured in birthday punch. She slowly walked to the kitchen table and sat down.

Lili interlocked her fingers and with her toe pushed back the chair beside her. Very softly she said, "Sit down, Lucy."

CHAPTER FORTY-SEVEN

Elaine and Ted had been back in Washington for only a couple weeks, when Elaine said, "Theodore, darlin', my daddy wants us to come down to Dallas for supper Saturday night."

"Oh," he said. "Just skip on down to Dallas. Sure. It's only 1500 miles or so," said Ted.

"There you go being silly again, Theodore. My daddy said for us to use the Saber."

"Is he going to send it for us?"

"Nope," she replied. "It's already here."

Ted was dreading the day when he would again be face to face with Vernon Baxter. He said, "Well, I guess we are going to have supper in Dallas Saturday. I sure wouldn't want to disappoint your daddy."

The reduction of power on the Saber-Liner's engines alerted Ted they were about to land. Soon the jet touched down to the southeast, on runway one-five at Addison Airport, on the north side of Dallas. A long black limousine was waiting.

After a short ride Ted could see an enormous opulent house on what appeared to be about fifty acres of pristine Texas real estate. Riding up the long winding driveway, he said to himself.

This place is Tara, the O'Hara Plantation, right out of Margret Mitchell's novel, "Gone with the Wind."

An elderly black man rose from a rocking chair and greeted them at the door. He was dressed in a white coat, and had a shock of white hair.

Ted thought: *This old gentleman adds even more flavor to this place….*

"Mister Copper, it is so nice to see you," exclaimed Elaine. She embraced the old man and kissed his cheek.

"You too, Miss Lanie. You jest don come home to see us old folks often enough."

Elaine grabbed Ted's hand. "Mister Copper, this is my husband, Ted Barrett."

"Pleased," said Mister Copper.

"Mister Copper," Ted said, looking deep into the old man's eyes. He saw sadness, and decades of wisdom.

"Yo husband?" asked an approaching voice.

"Oh Miss Annie, come meet my new husband," Elaine exclaimed to a smiling black woman.

Miss Annie was also elderly. She was wearing a white uniform draped by a yellow kitchen apron and was about as round as she was tall. Ted could immediately see the love and the bond between them.

"Mista Ted, I got lots to tell you bout this here child, I raised her from the day she was born. Me and Mista Copper there; we wiped her nose and changed her diapers, and she used to come to my room and sleep, and…."

"Now, Miss Annie, don't start all that in front of my new husband."

"Now, child," said Miss Annie, "don you start sassin' me. You ain't too big for me to take a hairbrush to yo backside, jest like I used to do with yo daddy when he was little."

"I'll never get that big, Miss Annie," she laughed. They embraced.

"Where is my mama and daddy?"

"They's waitin' in the den. Yawl go on in there. I'll bring you somthin' to drink."

"Thank you, Miss Annie."

They were walking down a long marble hall, well adorned with photos, plaques and other mementos. Elaine said, "Mister Copper and Miss Annie have been here long before I was born."

"And they are still working?"

"Goodness, no. My daddy retired them years ago, but they kept on coming to work and stuff. Miss Annie still won't allow anyone in her kitchen."

"Do they live here?"

"Sure they do. They have their own place right here on the property."

Ted was becoming more and more impressed with his new wife. She was warm and compassionate toward others. He noticed she always preserved their dignity and addressed them by "Mister," or "Miss."

Elaine was not my first choice. But circumstances changed everything—Elaine is my wife now, and I do love her. I am a lucky man. I don't have the same fire in my belly with Elaine like I did for Lili—a scorching blaze like that only burns once in a lifetime.

It has always been Lili.

After an extravagant dinner, served by a white-coated staff, Vernon spoke. "Come on, Ted, let's me and you have a drink." He led him into a large room with a fireplace. Above the mantle was a set of horns from a Longhorn Steer.

Ted thought, *The animal must have been enormous. Those horns have to span at least six feet.*

The room was completely set in white tile and the floor to ceiling plate glass windows allowed a magnificent view of the Baxter estate, cloaked in pecan trees and lazy looking weeping willows.

The opposite wall was adorned with the stuffed heads of various animals; the murderous results of some of Baxter's hunting trips, Ted guessed.

He thought, *Why not leave these beautiful animals alone? If you must hunt, and pull a trigger, do it with a camera.*

Baxter motioned Ted to a large black easy chair.

"What'll you have, Ted?" said Baxter stepping into to a sunken, well-stocked bar encompassed in mirrors. "Scotch isn't it?"

How do you know?

"Yes thanks."

"Tomorrow," Baxter continued, "me and you will run down to Houston. I need to start introducing you around to the folks at BDI."

Houston? That's 250 miles from here. BDI...?

"Mister Baxter...."

"Call me, Vernon," Baxter interrupted. "We're family now."

"Okay, Vernon. What is BDI?"

"I'm sorry, Ted, I thought you knew. BDI is Baxter Diversified Industries. We got more irons in the fire than just awl."

"Yes, I remember Elaine telling me some things," said Ted.

"Yeah, we got banks, shipping, refineries, and companies like-at. You need to jump in and get your feet wet if you're going to be the ramrod around here."

"Ramrod, sir?"

"Yeah, you know Ted, run things. I'm getting older and who better could I hand over the reins of BDI to than Lanie's husband? My son-in-law."

"Mister Baxter, I mean Vernon, I am overwhelmed and appreciate your generosity, but I don't know. I'm a trial lawyer. I don't know a thing about big business."

"Then we better get started, hadn't we?" exclaimed Baxter. "You name your salary. You'll have a car, use of the airplanes, and of course, an expense account."

"And Elaine?"

"Lanie? Why she can move back here to Texas and you all can have all the babies you want."

"Babies?"

"Tell you what Ted, sumthin' else too. I know a congressional seat that's ripe for the pickin'. The guy in it is a real pussy. I think you could beat him."

"Congress?" Ted exclaimed becoming overwhelmed.

"Hell yes, Congress!" Baxter almost shouted. "After you do a couple terms in the House, I think Powell is going to retire. That leaves his Senate seat wide open for us."

"Us?"

He was beginning to decipher Baxter's real bottom line.

Looks like Baxter has my whole future all mapped out!

Ted said, "Vernon, all this sounds wonderful and great, but I am just a country lawyer. I don't know a thing about Congress. I have been handling some cases for the airlines and some involved with the Federal Aviation Administration, lately and I like it. I...."

"You like what?" broke in Baxter.

"It's mostly contracts and regulations and there is a fair amount of trial work. It is all in the federal courts and I'm comfortable there," said Ted.

"But, Ted, you are perfect for politics," said Baxter. You have the looks, the education, I damn sure have the money, and you are a war hero for Pete's sake."

War hero? How do you know? That file is supposed to be sealed.

The Saber-Liner was blazing through the sky that night on its way back to Washington. Ted was deep in thought and stared out the window toward the static lightning flashing behind the distant clouds. Elaine's head rested in his lap as she peacefully slept.

Vernon's offer was certainly generous and definitely tempting. He could raise a family in north Dallas and have more money than he had ever dreamed about. His wife, Elaine, was a good woman and he knew she would be there for him. A career in national politics was promising and there was no limit as to what the future might bring.

Ted thought about a book he had read as a boy, *Doktor Faustus,* by the German author, Thomas Mann. A forceful tale of a man who makes a deal with the devil. The devil agrees to the terms in exchange for his soul. The man lives twenty-four years of supernatural power and sinful pleasures, but in the end his doom is sealed.

Am I willing to spend my career, or what's left of it, under Baxter's thumb? To be his political gofer? I don't think so—it would not be my life, it would be his. I like my work and I like where I live.

But, what about Elaine? She is used to so much more than I could ever provide—hell, Baxter tips more than I earn.

Ted did not have to perpend Vernon's offer for very long.

The answer was no.

CHAPTER FORTY-EIGHT

Two years slipped by and Ted and Elaine were satisfied enough with their marriage, but something was missing. Ted divided his time between Palm Beach and the FAA trial courts in Washington D.C. Elaine had resigned her commission in the Navy and worked in Texas for her father as an executive with BDI. They often spent weekends and most holidays together in Florida or Texas, thanks to the use of BDI's fleet of jet airplanes. Their lack of time together and distance apart, which would normally be an inconvenience to most contemporary marriages, seemed to work for them.

Ted was on his porch staring at the Inland Waterway, swishing the untouched scotch in his glass.

"Theodore, honey, can you come inside for a minute?" asked Elaine.

"Sure."

"Theodore, we need to talk," she said, sitting down in a chair beside the table.

"Sure." He repeated.

"We" need to talk really means, as he had learned; *"you" need to listen.*

Elaine said, "I'm sure you know as well as I do, there has been some ambivalence between us for quite a while."

Ted gave her a curious look.

"It seems like when our sex life kinda petered out, no pun intended," she smiled. "We started drifting more and more apart. Maybe that's all we had?"

"I still love you, Tex."

"Yes, Theodore, and I love you too, but sometimes love is not enough."

"I know," he stammered.

"My daddy had big plans for us, and…."

"Elaine, we've talked about this a thousand times. I didn't marry your daddy; I married you."

"I know, Theodore, but there has always been something else—always, always," she sighed, tightening her grip on the armrest of the chair. "Something I can't fight. A battle that I could never win."

"What are you talking about, Tex?"

"If I must tell you, Ted. I could never compete with Lili Perez—no woman could."

Ted was staggered. "You know about Lili?" he said astounded.

"Of course, I know about Lili. I knew about her before we ever got married. You have always been in love with her. I knew that from the beginning. It has always been Lili."

"But how? Why?" he stuttered.

"It's not important now, Ted. I have decided to move back to Texas, for good and take over my daddy's businesses. I'm trying to make this as easy as possible."

Ted knew what was coming. "Make what easy?"

"Here," she continued. "My daddy had these divorce papers drawn up by his lawyers. Ted, you and I both know this is for the best."

Ted gave her an ignominious stare, but in his heart he knew it was the end of what he had been anticipating.

"Kind of cut and dry, isn't it?"

"It's easier this way, Ted. You have to sign right here," she said, X-ing the signature line.

Ted reached for a pen. "Thy will be done."

Ted scribbled his name on the bottom of the document. "I sure wouldn't want to disappoint your daddy," he said exhaling.

"Did you read the bottom line?" she asked. "My daddy said to cut you a check for a million dollars."

"Yes, I saw it," he said. "I scratched it out."

"You what?"

"You heard me, I scratched it out."

Ted reached under the stereo cabinet and retrieved an old LP phonograph record. "Here," he said, "give this to your daddy."

He watched her walk down the driveway for the last time, the phonograph record tucked under her arm. From where Ted was standing he could read the cover title.

The Beatles. *"Can't Buy Me Love."*

CHAPTER FORTY-NINE

As the seasons came and went, Ted built a good reputation as an aviation attorney. His practice was national and international, but mostly he headquartered in Palm Beach and Washington D.C.

Ted knew his marriage to Elaine would have never worked out and he knew it wasn't really fair to her. Nobody could measure up to Lili. Ted had resigned himself to living single the rest of his life.

Why hurt someone else again? It wasn't anyone's fault, but quite simply Lili was the only one.

Ted never had any children and had content himself to a non-committed life. Not so much out of design it just seemed to work out that way. He enjoyed many friends and certainly the company of women, but when it came down to committing to a relationship; he couldn't do it. Nobody could come close to the memory of Lili.

Ted's Washington office was on the tenth floor of the Plaza Bank Building, overlooking Capital Plaza. He had a nice view of the federal city and employed eighteen attorneys and a support staff. The work was steady and busy; life was good, but lonely.

Ted was working at his desk when his secretary, Jenny, tapped on his door.

"Mister Barrett, there is a Congressman-elect Scott here to see you and he doesn't have an appointment."

"I don't know a thing about it, Jenny and I sure as hell don't know any Congressman-elect Scott," said Ted curtly. "Tell him I'm busy."

"What if she said Congressman-elect Ray Scott from the great State of Texas?" came a familiar voice from the door.

"Scottie? Scottie my boy!" Ted boomed as he rushed to the door. "Come in, come in, this is great! Jenny, this is my protégé from way back when. I raised this boy! We worked together in the D.A.'s office in Dallas. Scottie did you say Congressman? Congressman-elect?" Ted gave the Congressman-elect a bear hug.

"Yep, that's what I said, boss," said a grinning, Ray Scott.

"Thank you," Ted said nodding to Jenny, excusing her.

"Scottie, tell me everything. Congressman-elect, huh? I see that South Beach Diet is working out real well for you. And by the way, you're not dressed quite as noisy as you used to."

"Yeah, boss, I've had to tone down the wardrobe being a homeowner with a station wagon and all. And, yep, I've added a pound here and a pound there and I see your belt's let out a notch or two yourself," laughed Scottie.

"Yeah, prosperity and clean living," laughed Ted, patting his mid-section. "What brings you to Washington this time of year, Scottie?"

"We'll get to that, Mister Barrett, but whatever happened to you back there in Texas?"

Ted told him the whole story about how he was taken from Austin, his time in Vietnam and how he had built his legal practice. He never mentioned Lili and the nagging grief of losing her.

"I knew it had to be something big," said the Congressman-elect. "Man, we had federal agents running all over the place. Nobody seemed to know anything."

"Anyway, Scottie, what are you doing up here? The congressional session doesn't start until next month."

"What happened, Mister Barrett," Ray Scott began, "I followed your advice and got vested in the DA's office and moved to Houston. I was always pretty active in the party and they tapped me to run for a district, just north of Harris County, the Conroe area, and I won. I learned a lot from you. So, here I sit."

"Scottie, for Pete's sake, drop the Mister. We're not in that DA's office anymore. Congressman-elect? I should be calling you Mister." Both men laughed.

Asked Ted, "Family?"

"Yep, I married a gal from Abilene and we have two daughters and a boy. Here, I just happen to have a picture."

Ted admired the picture of Congressman-elect Ray Scott's family. Admittedly, they were beautiful children.

"So, why are you here in Washington?" Ted asked again.

"Oh yeah, I was telling you about that. I didn't know anything about what happened to you or that you had an office up here until I read an article about you in the Bar Journal; some aviation thing.

330

"Anyway, I'm here for the Republican Caucus and I hear they're going to appoint office locations, staff, and a few committee assignments. I don't have much of a chance getting any good committee appointment yet, being a freshman and all, but it looks like we're going to have a good Congress. The new Speaker is a good man, so maybe we can do some things that will help a lot of folks."

"By the way Mister Barrett, ah, Ted," mumbled Congressman-elect Ray Scott, "do you ever see or talk with Lili Perez?"

Ted felt like he was just hit in the chest with a jack-hammer.

"Who?" he almost shouted.

"Lili Perez you know, 'Mizz' Perez, the accountant. Dallas? I thought you two had quite a hot fling back in the old days."

"Oh Scottie, if you only knew," he sighed. "I completely lost my freaking mind over that gal. It was just like the devil himself took a white-hot rake and tore my living heart and guts out. It took me over two years just to get back to work after the war. If the truth is spoken, I never got over her."

Congressman-elect Scott nodded his head.

Ted went on. "Back there in Dallas, my life was in perfect order. Everything made sense. I had the world by the ass. Then along comes this gorgeous little accountant from south Texas and turned my whole life upside-down, then nothing made sense. She put my life into cartwheels and somersaults. I didn't know if it was morning or night, if it was winter or summer. I had searched my entire life for her. The girl of my dreams and all the while she was right in front of me. I wanted so many things in my life Scottie, and discovered none of them were important. Lili was all I ever wanted. Lili was my everything. She was the one. I wanted to spend the rest of my life with her."

"I thought things might have cooled off a bit by now Ted."

"Sure. Of course they have Scottie, it's been what— seems like a life time. But, when we were together, the fire burned like an inferno, I didn't have anything left, but ashes. I guess that's why I was such a disaster at marriage. My ex was a decent person, but after Lili I simply didn't have anything left to offer."

"Yeah," responded Congressman-elect Scott. "Something like that is like stopping a volcano with a wine cork."

"Scottie, getting over her was like trying to put out a prairie fire with a garden hose. Our love was just like a prairie fire; with a love like that you don't know if the fire going to warm you or burn the barn down."

"That's the funny thing about love, Ted. It's a game two people can play and both win."

"Yeah, or both lose. No telling where she is now, Scottie. I know she moved to Costa Rica and married a planter. Then I got wind she divorced and moved back to the States. I have tried to find her several times. Her last name could be anything and only God would know where she is."

"You don't have to ask God for that," said Congressman-elect Ray Scott. "She's right here in Washington."

"What?" Ted exploded, sitting bolt upright almost snapping his executive chair in pieces. "Here in D.C.?"

"Yeah boss, uh, Ted. I just walked by her a couple hours ago." said Congressman-elect Ray Scott, gesturing.

"Where Scottie? When?" said an excited Ted Barrett. "What did she look like?"

"Geez Ted, take it easy; I saw her coming out of the Government Accounting Office about noon, or a little after maybe. She was pulling one of those little carts, you know, like the pilots at the airports have. So, she must have been working."

"Tell me Scottie, what did she look like?" insisted Ted.

"Well, like all of us after a couple decades; her caboose is a little wider, but she's still the same 'Mizz' Perez."

"Are you sure it was her, Scottie?"

"Positive. No mistaking that woman, Ted," said the Congressman-elect. "She still stops traffic and could make a dead man's pecker whistle Dixie."

"Tell you what, Scottie, let me buy you a steak tonight. What say we meet at the Plaza Steak House about seven-ish. Okay?"

"It's a date, Ted, but only if you let me to buy my own steak. I can't afford to get in some gratuity accusation my first week in Washington."

"Deal." said Ted.

Ted watched Congressman-elect Ray Scott disappear down the hall. He smiled.

That boy just might make a fine Secretary of State....

Ted was immediately on the phone.

"Hello Kevin, who is the best private investigator in Washington?"

CHAPTER FIFTY

The first thing the next morning Ted was standing at the door of MacMillen Investigations, Inc., which was located in the not too nice, but not too seedy either, part of town. He imagined an overweight, rude, cigar-chewing, middle aged PI with dirty fingernails and a couple days growth of beard on his face.

He was greeted instead by a slender, nice looking young man, with dark hair, green eyes and very neat and clean.

Probably in his mid, maybe late thirties, Ted thought.

"Good morning, my name is MacMillen, Neal MacMillen," the young man said, extending his hand. "Are you the gentleman who called yesterday?"

"Yes, Ted Barrett, but if it's all the same to you, I'm John Smith." replied Ted, taking the young man's hand.

"What can I do for you, Mister Smith?"

"I need to find this lady," replied Ted, handing Neal MacMillen a small notebook. "I've put everything I can think of in here to help you. She's likely here in the greater Washington area, but where is anybody's guess."

"Fine," said MacMillen, "give me a couple weeks and I'll be in touch."

"Ah, Mister MacMillen," Ted began.

"Call me Mac, Mister Smith, everybody does. I like it better that way."

"Okay Mac," said Ted. "I was hoping you could get an earlier start on this."

"Sure, Mister Smith, if it means that much to you I'll get right on it. Some of my other cases are not all that pressing."

Ted mumbled his thanks. "Don't you want to get paid?" Ted asked.

"Yes, of course. Money is always good. I get two hundred and fifty bucks an hour plus expenses. I'll furnish you an accounting sheet. Just leave a deposit with the girl out front. Her name is Carolyn."

"Deposit?" Ted questioned. "How do you know I'll pay the balance?"

Mac replied. "Because I ran a background check on you last night and I know you are an honorable man."

Ted liked that. This kid was sharp.

Ted reached inside his coat and pulled out a thick envelope. "Never mind Carolyn, here's two grand. When can you get started?"

"Right away," said a surprised Neal MacMillen.

Ted rose and turned to leave.

Mac said, "Wait, aren't you going to watch me count this?"

"No," was Ted's reply.

"Why not?"

"Because I ran a background check on you last night and I know you are an honorable man. Goodbye Mister MacMillen."

"Goodbye Mister Smith."

Two days passed and Ted was thinking of spending a long weekend in Palm Beach.

Wonder if I should go home over the weekend? What if Neal MacMillen turns up something? Nah, no way, it's only been a couple days—I'm going home.

Ted was in the conference room negotiating a contract between Boeing Representatives and Overseas Airline executives, who were with their lawyers, regarding the lease of aircraft to OA.

"Gentlemen, would you like to break for some coffee? I believe Jenny picked up some pastries this morning. That might go pretty good about now," Ted offered. "Let me check."

Everyone nodded their agreement and Ted was off down the hall to the office kitchen. Jenny was there making sure the coffee was fresh.

"How's it going, Mister Barrett?"

"We've got to iron out a few wrinkles, but I think everyone will be happy," he said.

Ted was about to leave to invite the others down when Jenny said, "Mister Barrett, there is a gentleman waiting to see you."

Ted's reply was sharp. "Jenny, you know I can't see anyone now. We're talking millions of dollars in there.

Most of these guys came all the way from Europe and Asia. Who is it?"

Jenny, a little taken back by his rather austere question, said, "Says his name is MacMillen, um, Neal MacMillen. Here's his card."

"Holy Moses," breathed Ted. "I'll take him into my office. Get down there and stall for me."

"Do what? How do I stall them?"

"Jenny, you'll think of something. I don't care if you do a boom-boom dance on the window sill just get in there and buy me a couple of minutes. Take Steve or one of the other lawyers with you. Just do it."

Ted greeted Neal MacMillen with enthusiasm. "Mac, it's good to see you," he said shaking the investigators hand. "I didn't expect to hear anything so soon. Come in please," he said leading the way into his office.

"Whatcha got, Mac?"

"Well, Mister Smith…."

"Mac, we can cut through the crap. We both know that my name is not Smith," interrupted Ted.

"Mister Smith, your name is whatever you say it is. I work for you, remember?"

"Okay Mac, Okay. I'm John Smith, whatcha got?"

"Here it is," said Mac, handing Ted a large manila envelope. "Pretty simple case really. It's all there. Copies of everything. She's been with the Government Accounting Office for quite a few years here in D.C. She's an Auditor, lives across the bridge in Virginia, lives alone and still goes by Perez. Divorced, one kid, a boy who lives in Costa Rica and, Mister Smith, if you don't mind me saying so, she is a fine-looking lady."

"No, I don't mind you saying so," replied Ted softly. "Mac, how did you get all this so quickly?"

"Mister Smith haven't you ever heard of the computer age?"

Ted smiled. "You did a good job on this Mac, thanks a lot."

"Glad to Mister Smith, it appears like your Miss Perez can be a very focused lady," added Neal MacMillen.

"That's okay Mac, John Smith can be a very focused man."

"Oh Mister Smith, one more thing," he said, tossing an envelope on Ted's desk. "I didn't use all of your retainer. My fees and expenses totaled a thousand sixty-seven bucks and change. The rest is here."

"Tell you what, Mac, you keep this," Ted said, stuffing the envelope into Mac's pocket. "And Mac, if you ever need a job, give me a call."

"Right, thanks Mister Smith," said Mac, pointing his finger and thumb at Ted like a pistol, "but right now I like me, working for me."

"So long Mister Smith."

"So long Mister MacMillen."

Ted was ecstatic, overjoyed. He was overwhelmed. The love of his life was in Washington and she was single. He could not believe his good fortune. A maelstrom of thoughts raced in his mind. How could he contact her? What should he do? What if she didn't want to see him? What if she was seeing someone else? He quickly put it out of his mind. He could not bear the thought of Lili with someone else.

He thumbed through the file Neal MacMillen had provided.

She lives in Parksdale, that's close to the Beltway, not far, not far at all. She walks her dog at a small doggie park near her house every night around six, six-thirty.

The next evening, Ted waited at the doggie park. It was almost dark when he stepped into the shadows of the elm trees. It was cold and he pulled his overcoat tighter about him.

It's only late fall. It looks like a frigid winter is coming this year, all the more reason to be in Palm Beach.

He waited. No Lili.

Just as Ted was leaving he noticed a familiar, very distinctive walk from long ago. Chills shot up his spine like electricity. No mistake. It was Lili.

Ted watched as she walked her little dog around the doggie circle, which was placed with several mini fire hydrants. They would stop at one then another. The dog would sniff, do his business and then trot off to the next.

Ted positioned himself so Lili would have to pass by him, if she went back the same way she had come.

He was still in the shadows when Lili passed by him. He stepped out on the sidewalk behind her.

"Lili," he quietly breathed.

She stopped instantly, but did not turn around.

"Hello Teddy," she managed.

"I've been waiting. I was hoping we could talk," he said.

"I know. I saw you a half hour ago," said Lili still not turning to face him.

That pained him.

A half hour ago...?

"Lili, please turn around, can we talk for a just a few minutes?"

"No Ted, I don't have anything to say to you. We don't have anything to talk about," said Lili softly.

"Lili please," said Ted, as he walked around in front of her and gazed into her face. She was the same beautiful Lili. She was crying. The little bit of mascara she wore was streaking down her cheeks.

"Lili, I was hoping we could talk about some things."

Lili exploded at him, but kept her voice under control. "I can't talk to you. I can't go back! You killed me, Teddy. When whatever happened to us back in Texas, part of me died that day. Part of me is still dead because of you. You were my life, my whole life... my everything. I planned my forever with you, I would have followed you to the North Pole, and then....

"You killed me Teddy, you killed me. I spent years in therapy, just so I could function because of you. I never got over us. You were my first everything. I still can't hear the word Ted, or Barrett, or lawyer, or a hundred other words without being reminded of you. I can't go back, it's too painful. I could never make it through that kind of hurt again. I have a life now, Ted, and you're not in it. I haven't cried in years and now you show up. You killed me Teddy, you killed me!"

Ted took a step backward. He was startled at her harangue and softly said, "Lili, I have looked all over for you. I just found out that you were here in Washington. I have an office here and….”

“I know,” she said.

“You know?”

“Yes. You have the tenth floor of the Plaza Bank Building. I have seen you at the Plaza a few times and I have read about you occasionally.”

“You have seen me and you have known I was here and you have never said hello or tried to contact me?”

Lili didn’t answer. She stared.

All his hopes and dreams of Lili had been dashed at that moment. It was emotional napalm. Ted lowered his head and slightly nodded. His questions had been answered.

Lili turned and slowly walked away. Ted watched as she disappeared into the darkness of the damp evening. She was sobbing.

Ted had prepared himself for the anguish ahead. Losing Lili all over again was going to hurt. Surprisingly, he was calm and resigned himself to the fact that he would never have her again. After all these years, it was finally over. Ted accepted it and made a decision to start putting his emotional life together.

Ted Barrett was on the telephone to Palm Beach.

“Terry,” he said to his sister. “Go to my house and look in the foot locker, I have stored in the spare room; my housekeeper knows where it is. You will find an old briefcase and inside it a fine mahogany box in bubble-wrap. Please overnight it up here on Fed-X, UPS or whatever.

Maybe even U.S. Postal. Whoever can get it here the quickest."

Ted listened.

"Yes, yes I know it's strange. I will explain later. Just get it up here right away please. Thanks, Terry."

The next noon, Ted had the old briefcase and the precious box. He planned to return its contents to Lili. After all, it belonged to her. In the box he placed a single yellow rose.

He enclosed a note:

Dear Lili:

I know that you have been hurt. We both have. I never got over you either, but I know that you have a life now and all I would do is interfere. I still love you, Lili, I always will. I love you enough to step aside, to finally let you go after all these years. I love you enough to stop thinking of myself and give you the one gift I'm capable of giving. I'm giving you your life back. I'm getting out of it.

Ted

Ted picked up Neal MacMillen and together they drove to Parksdale. Ted parked the car and said to Neal MacMillen, "Okay Mac, like we talked about. I want this box delivered to this address, 3323 Meadow Lane; it's up there, second one on the right."

Ted got out of the car to wait. Neal MacMillen asked no questions. Soon, he disappeared around the corner to 3323 Meadow Lane.

He was back in ten minutes. Ted hopped back in the car.

"Everything go okay, Mac?"

"Oh yeah, sure Mister Smith, but her eyes were red and swollen. Looks like she was rubbing them with onion juice."

Ted felt a pang deep in his chest.

Oh Lord, I hope not.

The days passed, both Lili and Ted stayed busy. They tried not to think of each other. It was impossible. Jenny entered his office.

"Congressman-elect Scott on line two," she said.

Ted nodded his thanks. "Hey Scottie," he bellowed into the phone.

"Hey Mister Barrett, I mean Ted, dern-it, I can't get used to that yet."

"That's okay Scottie, what's up?"

"I only have a few days left in Washington until the session starts, I was wondering if you have time for lunch?"

"Tell you what Scottie, how about dropping by my office. I need to talk to you anyway. We can order in."

"Sounds like a plan. How does one o'clock suit you?"

"One is fine Scottie, see you then."

Ted and Congressman-elect Scott both had tuna salad, chips, and iced-tea. It was a good lunch with good company and with someone, Ted trusted.

"Scottie, I can't keep this inside any longer. I've got to tell someone." Ted told Congressman-elect Scott the entire story of his recent meeting with Lili.

"You know Scottie, I need her and I don't need anybody."

"Well Ted, maybe I can help get your mind off things. The Cowboys are playing the Redskins Sunday. It's Christmas Eve and I rounded up a couple box tickets."

"Scottie, how did you manage that?" exclaimed Ted. "Those things are impossible to get."

"Well Ted, let's just say being a congressman does have a few perks; even if you are a freshman."

"I'd love to Scottie, but I'm out of here for Palm Beach Sunday. Monday is Christmas Day and all. A client of mine has his private jet up here and they are going home empty, so he asked me if I needed a ride," said Ted.

"What time are you going?"

"Oh I don't know Scottie, we're out of Reagan, seven, or eight, somewhere in there. Why?"

"What's the 'N' number of the airplane?" asked the Congressman-elect, ignoring Ted's question.

"Heck Scottie, I don't know," Ted said. He rummaged through the mountain of paper on his desk. "Oh, here it is, it's a Gulfstream IV, N1861FJ, why do you ask?"

"I just wondered. Okay, here's your ticket. Kick-off is at one o'clock. You have plenty of time to see the game and make your flight. They won't leave without you anyway. I'll meet you around kick-off time."

"Okay Scottie, you convinced me, I'll see you there."

"Roger that boss man, roger that," replied the departing Congressman-elect and he was off down the hall toward the elevators.

Sunday was a bright and pretty day for this time of the year in the nation's capital. Ted was enjoying a box seat on the fifty yard line.

Scottie sure knows how to take care of his friends; that boy just might make a fine Attorney General.

"Are you, Mister Ted Barrett?" asked a stunning redhead with enormous breasts.

"Ah yes," Ted stuttered, guessing her to be around twenty-five, maybe twenty-six.

"My name is Brandee," she said, leaning over allowing Ted a charitable view of her abundant bosom, "I'm from Congressman-elect Scott's Office. He asked me to tell you that he won't be able to make it. He is tied up with some urgent business, but he will be outside gate seven after the game to take you to the airport."

"Oh thanks so much, Brandee," he managed, as he watched her bounce, bump and grind as she swayed into the crowd. Leaving no doubt in Ted's mind as to who did the hiring in Congressman-elect Scott's Office.

Brandee, you must be from Texas too!

It was a good day for the Cowboys.

"Good game," Ted exclaimed as he jumped into Congressman-elect Scott's limo.

"Glad you enjoyed it, Ted."

"What happened to you?" asked Ted.

"Oh, it's just some of the perils most of us influence peddlers here in Washington must bear. I was doing a favor for a friend and got tied up."

They rode in silence for a while. The limo pulled into the general aviation side of Reagan Airport beside a spotless silver Gulfstream Jet.

The engines were spooling up and the crew was already on board when Ted and Congressman-elect Scott said their goodbyes. Ted ran up the stairs and buckled himself in.

Kind of nice to have my own personal forty million dollar jet to zip around in all alone. I could get real used to this.

As the Gulfstream quietly left mother earth and climbed into the heavens, Ted's eyes were fixed on the Capitol Complex and searched for where he thought Parksdale might be.

The jet smoothly leveled off at altitude. A pretty young flight attendant approached him. "Can I get you a drink, Mister Barrett?"

"Yes, please. A scotch would be great."

Soon she returned and handed Ted a drink, and said, "Here, Mister Barrett, I made you a double."

"Thank you, Miss, but I didn't order a double."

"That's okay," she said, "you're going to need it."

Ted looked puzzled, but he thanked her and took the drink. He slid off his shoes and tilted the seat as far back as it would go.

It was a beautiful night and he could see the moon shining on the cloud deck below the Gulfstream. He was just about to doze when over the whine of the jet's engines came an unmistakable voice.

"Oh, Teddy Bare."

"What?" A stunned Ted Barrett shouted.

Lili? Can't be! Ted thought his heart had stopped.

"Yes, Teddy Bare, of course it's me, who else? You silly," she said, as she stood behind him, dressed in tan slacks and the omni-present Cowboy Jersey, her broad smile glowing.

Ted was numb. He had difficulty getting one foot in front of the other. She met him in the aisle and flung her arms around him.

"Te amo mucho," she exclaimed. After all these years Ted still didn't have a clue what she was saying.

"My most bravest, dashingest and most handsomest, lawyer-man in the whole wide world. Give me a smooch!"

It was hardly a smooch. Their mouths crushed together devouring each other. The crew discreetly closed the cockpit door.

"Why Lili, why are you here?" mumbled Ted. "How did you know? Where are you going?" he said hugging her tightly.

"I'm going to West Palm Beach," she curtly replied.

"Why?" he pleaded.

"Well, my Papasito, I am going to West Palm Beach, to spend the rest of my life with the only true love I've ever known. I'm so happy, Teddy Bare!"

"All I ever wanted is for you to be happy," he said, putting his chin on the top of her head. It was still a perfect fit.

"Teddy Bare, how could I ever be happy without you?"

It was if they had never been apart. It seemed to them not a single minute, not a single hour had passed since their days together in Dallas.

"How did you know? What happened?" he said, still stammering.

Ted snapped his fingers, "Scottie! That little snake."

Lili nodded her head, "Scottie, he told me everything about why you had to leave and the war."

She ran her fingers through his hair.

"Now I understand Teddy Bare. You were trying to protect me. And all that time I thought you had left me.

"Teddy Bare, I am so sorry for the time we have lost," she said.

"We can't change that," he said. "Let's be thankful for the time we have together in front of us."

They stayed in each other's arms until the jet landed in West Palm Beach.

Ted thought, *Scottie—that boy just might make a fine President!*

CHAPTER FIFTY-ONE

"Well folks, now you have heard it, that's my love story of the Amarillo Rose," Ted said, looking around the den. Nobody had stirred, nobody said a word. Everyone was transfixed on Ted.

"See, sometimes fairy tales do come true. Sometimes we are given a second chance; another chance to have that one great true love. Sometimes, if you are lucky, you find it right away. Sometimes you can throw it away. And, sometimes you have it and lose it. I almost did. Sometimes, we do indeed get to spend our lives with our true soul-mate. I am pained by the years we lost, but am so very thankful for the ones we've had and the ones ahead.

Laurel, never one to mince words, whispered to her husband Jack, "That perfidious ass, telling us all that about some woman named Lili in front of Analilia."

Jack motioned for her to be still.

"Hey Ted, what's in the mahogany box?" someone asked.

"Oh yes, the box. Every Christmas Eve we get it out," said Ted, handing the box to his wife, who took it into another room.

Just as he began to speak again, Analilia re-emerged wearing a Dallas Cowboy Jersey. Ted put his arm around her. A yellow rose was in her hair.

"My friends, every year she wears this old jersey just to remind us. You see, you all know her as Mrs. Analilia Barrett. I've always known her as Lili Perez."

It still hung down to her knees.

"Think not, you can direct the course of true love, for true love, if it finds you, will direct itself…."

Kahlil Gibran, *The Prophet.*

EPILOGUE

AUGUSTINO returned to Costa Rica where he learned the family business on the Corobici. He visits his mother and Ted often. Lili never returned to Costa Rica or the Corobici. She never saw or spoke to Don Velazquez again.

LUCY married a banker and they live in North Carolina with their two children. She was a beautiful bride, just as Lili had predicted.

GARY WILDGOOSE finished law school after Vietnam, and is a full partner with Theodore F. Barrett & Associates, P.A.

JESSE OSCEOLA recovered fully and is the Director of Native American Affairs for the State of Florida.

JOSH ABERNATHY retired from the Army as a full colonel. He lives in Livingston, Montana and leads hunting trips in the Yellowstone, where his clients shoot animals—*with cameras.*

ELAINE BAXTER, "Lanie" returned to Texas and became CEO of BDI. Two years later, she was elected to the U.S. House of Representatives, where she currently serves.

AMBASSADOR THOMAS retired from the State Department and raises prize thoroughbred horses with her husband in Kentucky.

RAY SCOTT, "Scottie" retired, after serving three terms in the U.S. House of Representatives and one term in the United States Senate. He lives on the shores of Montgomery Lake, in Texas and spends his days teaching at the local community college and playing with his grandchildren.

VERNON BAXTER was taken to Tri-County Hospital's Emergency Room with severe chest pains. His eyes fixed blankly on the glaring lights above him with their vibrato of finality. As Vernon sank deeper into the abyss of infinity, he realized at last, the only thing on earth that had any value was not his money, but time. All his billions, and all his power, could not buy him a single millisecond. He could no longer make things happen.

GOLDEN BELLEZA was retired and was put out to pasture in a life of leisure to frolic and graze on the rich grasslands of the Corobici.

To Lili:

A special thanks, for without you none of this would have been written.

Maybe someday together we will find the truth. Or better yet, perhaps truth will find us....

JT

ACKNOWLEDGEMENTS

Many people have contributed one way or another to this writing. I am in your debt and offer my sincere thanks to Bob Tischenkel, Maria and Michael Mahoney, Jack Galvan, Susan Kidwell, D.L. Phipps, and Stephen Steinberg.

A special thank you and appreciation to my editor and dear friend, Laurel Galvan, whose infinite patience with me, superb graphic and editorial skills made this possible.

ABOUT THE AUTHOR

Joss Tallman is an unheard of fifth generation native born Floridian and graduated from Florida State University and from law school in Washington State.

Tallman began his career as a law enforcement pilot with a Florida State Police Agency. After serving as a prosecutor with the State Attorney's Office he returned to his first love of flying both commercially and as an FAA Designated Pilot Examiner.

Although retired, Joss remains active as a legal aviation consultant and is often a guest speaker at various events. He still holds an FAA Airline Transport Rating and flight instructor certificates. He has been an adjunct professor at Palm Beach State College for over 18 years.

Tallman makes his home in south Florida with his little dog, Toby. He enjoys fishing, flying his airplane, and, of course, writing.

~Laurel Galvan

AUTHOR'S NOTE

I am always pleased, and flattered, to hear from my readers. Thank you.

However, if you visit my website at: www.josstallman.com, I will receive your correspondence much faster than writing my publisher, Author's Bridge, or via snail mail. So far I have been able to keep up with all the mail and answer you accordingly and I will try to continue to do so.

Please do not forward me attachments. I will not download them for obvious reasons. Please do not place me on your mailing lists for jokes, prayers, political causes, charities, etc. I simply do not have the time to download and peruse them; but thanks anyway.

I appreciate your kind offers and suggestions for upcoming novels but it is my policy to write only what is generated in my own mind, from my own experiences and from my own imagination, but thanks. If you have a good idea for a book; write it yourself.

I am grateful for those of you who catch typos and other errors but please take heart: I am well aware of them by now and must assume 100% fault for each and every one.

For those of you who wish to schedule book-signings, events, guest speaker or appearances, etc., please contact my website or LAUREL GALVAN at:laurel@cyberdiamond.net; or 320 Mamie Cook Road, Boone, NC 28607-7844.

For those of you who may be interested in buying literary rights such as films, television, copyrights, or any other related legal matters please contact my attorney: STEPHEN STEINBERG, Esq. At: stesteinberg@comcast.net or Steinberg Law Offices, 48 Brant Avenue, Clark, NJ 07066-1534.

I appreciate your patronage and wish you well. *KEEP READING!*

Blue Skies,

JT